ARIADNE'S WAR
SORCERER'S DILEMMA

ARIADNE'S WAR
SORCERER'S DILEMMA

John Sinisi

JOHN SINISI

Copyright © 2017 by John Sinisi.

All rights reserved. No part of this publication may be reproduced, distributed, or transmitted in any form or by any means, including photocopying, recording, or other electronic or mechanical methods, without the prior written permission of the publisher, except in the case of brief quotations embodied in critical reviews and certain other noncommercial uses permitted by copyright law. For permission requests, write to the publisher, addressed "Attention: Permissions Coordinator," at the address below.

BookVenture Publishing LLC
1000 Country Lane Ste 300
Ishpeming MI 49849
www.bookventure.com
Hotline: 1(877) 276-9751
Fax: 1(877) 864-1686

Ordering Information:
Quantity sales. Special discounts are available on quantity purchases by corporations, associations, and others. For details, contact the publisher at the address above.

Printed in the United States of America.

Library of Congress Control Number: 2017933691

ISBN-13: Paperback   978-1-946492-74-6
               Hardback   978-1-946492-75-3
               Pdf   978-1-946492-76-0
               ePub   978-1-946492-77-7
               Kindle   978-1-946492-78-4

Rev. date: 01/25/2017

Ariadne's War is dedicated to my dear friends David and Vicky Norris, who are still in love after forty-one years of marriage.

David was my colleague in the business school at Penn State Schuylkill. I have never known a teacher so willing to go the extra mile to help his students master the materials taught or obtain useful internships or get good jobs when they graduate.

Vicky manages two small businesses. Several years ago she saved my life by recognizing the early symptoms of a stroke in my face and behavior and ignoring her busy schedule, driving me to the emergency room.

CHAPTER

Bezriel is a tight-knit ethnic community with a deeply rooted religious tradition steeped in mysticism and sorcery. For most of its long history Bezriel was oppressed and exploited by more powerful neighbors and periodically suffered religious persecution at the hands of those who saw its practices of sorcery as enthrallment to demonic forces. The historic saga that ended with Ariadne's War began when three Bezrielites were charged with the capital crime of using witchcraft to harm others. The charges were brought by Baron Frederick a religious fanatic who wanted to eradicate witchcraft. He was the feudal lord of the province of Zandor in which Bezriel is located. At that time, Zandor was an autonomous region of Menkara, a large feudal kingdom whose provinces had long ago de facto become independent mini-states.

The three accused witches were William, a blacksmith, Sarah, a traditional healer, and Abigail, a midwife. In the official charges, William was accused of practicing necromancy, the forbidden and sacrilegious practice of working with demons to summon dead spirits from the underworld for ungodly rites and practices. Sarah and Abigail were accused of using discredited traditional and unsanitary methods of ministering to the sick and delivering babies. It was also charged that the potions they gave to their patients enabled demonic spirits to possess their souls and bodies. Few in Bezriel believed the charges against Sarah and Abigail of being in league with demons. Both were widely regarded as good women and skilled adepts of traditional medicine.

While the witchcraft trial was still in progress, Baron Frederick was toppled from power and the accused witches liberated by the invading army of Lord Soren of the neighboring province of Thorheim. The overthrow of Frederick was just one step in Soren's long campaign to become king of a reunited Menkara, a kingdom he hoped to restore to its former power and glory. Soren's deposing of the tyrant Frederick and freeing the accused witches was seen by Bezrielites as deliverance from oppression, but viewed with apprehension by most of the feudal lords of Menkara who feared Soren's growing power and ambition.

The feudal lords had good reason to worry. For Lord Soren, deposing the tyrant and freeing the witches was a mere public relations sideshow to his real goal, expanding his regional political and military dominance. After the invasion, he became intrigued by the military potential of the rumored power of William to command the dead and control nature. Once he was satisfied that William's powers were real and had military usefulness, a fateful deal was struck. William would use his sorcery to help Soren gain the throne in return for Soren funding and supporting William's experiments to expand the limits of sorcery.

At that time, after two decades of military campaigns and diplomatic intrigue, Soren was the most powerful lord in the kingdom, but opposed by more than a dozen quarrelsome regional lords, whose combined military strength would have far exceeded the might of Soren if they ever became truly unified. But that was before the entrance into the war of William, a sorcerer of unrivaled power. Within two years of recruiting William, Soren became king of a reunited Menkara, albeit with pockets of resistance.

It is now known that all of the accused were indeed powerful sorcerers, but I reject the claim that they were aligned with satanic forces. Every history book has a bias. Thus I, the author of this history, must introduce myself. My name is Bartholomew. I am a Bezrielite. I was a mere child of twelve when the three were arrested seventy long years ago when an agonizing period of turmoil for Bezriel began. At that time, I was emotionally swept up by events that sometimes scared me and sometimes inspired me. But as a child I saw only surfaces, not the strong underground currents shaping events. Needing to understand, I have spent a lifetime researching and thinking about that dark period that ended with Ariadne's War; reading through historical records and memoirs, gaining access to the personal papers and journals of many of the key figures, including the letters and papers of Ariadne, and talking with many of the men and women who played key roles. I have lost count of how many times I delayed publication of my book in the vain hope that decisive insight was just around the corner. At last I have decided to publish the results of my incomplete research.

The central figure in the history I recount was the young sorceress, Ariadne, daughter of the accused witch Sarah and her husband Daniel, a tailor. Ariadne struggled to come to terms with the prophetic dream of her pregnant mother that the child in her womb was destined to be a powerful sorceress who would lead Bezriel to either freedom or destruction. Ariadne was not told of the prophecy until the eruption at puberty of her great but as yet undisciplined powers to move objects and start fires with her mind. The emergence of those powers persuaded her parents to tell Ariadne of her mother's prophetic dream. They soon regretted that decision. Ariadne, already frightened by the discovery of her powers, was terrified by the prophecy that she would lead her people to either freedom or destruction. The unbidden eruption of her destructive powers of sorcery made the prophecy of her destiny seem all too plausible.

After her initial panic upon discovering her powers and hearing the prophecy of her destiny, the troubled teen outwardly scoffed to her parents about the prophecy. But inwardly she trembled. Since her foretold powers were real, she feared that the prophecy of her fate might also be true. She did not exult in the possibility that she would lead her people to freedom. She did not exult because she knew in her heart that she was not worthy to be the savior of Bezriel. She believed that if the prophecy were true, she was fated to be the doom of Bezriel.

To protect their daughter, Sarah and Daniel decided before her birth not to reveal the prophecy to the world. After Ariadne's powers emerged, they tried to keep her powers secret from the world as long as possible. If her powers became known she would be taken from her family and forced to work for Soren as a sorceress under the control and influence of William.

Such a fate for their daughter was anathema to William and Sarah, pacifists who had come to fear and distrust both Soren and William. Hence Ariadne spent her teenage years, living in relative isolation because of the need to guard against unwitting public revelation of her great powers through explosions and other mayhem that resulted when she lost her temper.

In the midst of this adolescent loneliness, Ariadne vowed to try to purify her soul so that she might use her powers to help push Bezriel towards freedom rather than destruction. Purifying her soul meant to this isolated and idealistic teen that she must never marry, never have children, never have a normal life. The only non-family member told of Ariadne's emerging powers and of the prophecy was the midwife Abigail, Sarah's codefendant and closest friend. Over time, Abigail became Ariadne's friend and confidante.

Despite her pacifist beliefs and upbringing, Ariadne, when not yet twenty, decided to join Free Bezriel, the guerrilla army fighting against King Soren for the liberation of Bezriel. In the eyes of the guerrillas, Soren had gone from being the savior who had freed

Bezriel from the tyranny of Baron Frederick to the cruel overlord whose taxes, oppressive governance, and conscription of its most powerful sorcerers for military deployment in the Menkaran army had become worse than the evils suffered under Baron Frederick.

Ariadne's reason for this drastic step was her belief that Bezriel's sorcery was being perverted into a military tool by the ambitious power-mad Lord Soren and his Bezrielite henchman William, thereby corrupting the Bezrielite tradition of sorcery as a source of mystical unity and healing. The ironic contradiction of becoming a soldier to try to reverse the militarization of Bezriel was not lost on Ariadne.

Shortly after joining the guerrillas, Ariadne revealed and demonstrated her considerable powers of sorcery to the charismatic Free Bezriel leader, Kaitlin. After the demonstration, Kaitlin saw the great powers of Ariadne as the answer to her prayers. Long weeks of rigorous training by Gwydian, her appointed mentor in military sorcery, elapsed before Ariadne was allowed to use her powers in battle. During this training period, Gwydian, a vigorous man in his sixties, became almost a second father to Ariadne.

While being trained, even her vow of sexual self-denial could not prevent the young sorceress' heart from being thrilled when two very different comrades fell in love with her. One was her impulsive childhood friend, Peter, who had worked with her in the campaign to build public support for her mother after her arrest for sorcery by Baron Frederick. The other was Marcus, a calm, idealistic sorcerer. After rejecting their advances she told them of her vow of chastity, but she did not tell them of the prophecy and hence did not reveal the reason for her austere commitment. Over time Ariadne's bond with Marcus grew stronger and her emotional ties with Peter grew weaker.

Soren and William were allies, but they neither liked nor trusted each other. Each saw the other as no more than a useful tool. Soren used the military sorcery of William to defeat his enemies on the battlefield, thereby clearing the way for him to reunite Menkara and become king. William needed the wealth of Soren to finance his experiments in sorcery and the political/military power of Soren to shield him from repercussions of popular hostility to his sorcery. For William's project was nothing less than testing and expanding the limits of the power of sorcery over all creation. Eventually mutual mistrust would turn their alliance into enmity.

Soren became king, but his reunification of Menkara and his coronation as king did not end civil warfare in Menkara. Guerrilla resistance remained in several regions of the kingdom. Free Bezriel was not the strongest of these opposition groups, but because it fought for the independence of Bezriel, the supply source of sorcerers for King Soren, it was the most important. Free Bezriel was a ragtag guerrilla army led, as I said, by the charismatic orator and tactician, Kaitlin, and her military adjutant, Joshua. Soren was stung by a humiliating defeat inflicted on Cerberus, his elite anti-guerrilla unit by an unidentified but very powerful Free Bezriel wizard. That wizard was Ariadne. To avenge the slaying of Gwydian, her friend and mentor, Ariadne had cast a confusion spell which caused the troops of Cerberus to fight and slaughter each other.

Ariadne, who had been taught reverence for all life by her parents, felt deep remorse for causing friend to slaughter friend. She wanted to resign from Free Bezriel and never use sorcery again. Her comrades in Free Bezriel tried to talk her out of this drastic step, but failed. However, a deeply emotional meeting with her mother, father, and Abigail, ironically all pacifists, led Ariadne to decide to stay with the guerrillas. Her family taught her to realize that while the confusion spell by which she had devastated Cerberus was evil, it was not sorcery but anger caused by grief that had led to her evil deed. The proper atonement for her sin was to renounce hatred and anger, not abandon sorcery and the causes she believed in. That realization combined with the pleas of Kaitlin and Marcus that she not abandon her comrades in Free Bezriel led to Ariadne's decision to remain with the guerrillas. She stayed, but with a caveat. The caveat was that she would henceforth use her powers for defensive purposes only. Desperate pleas from her comrades that she rejoin offensive maneuvers could not sway the heart-sore young sorceress.

The humiliation and decimation of Cerberus, his elite anti-guerrilla unit by Free Bezriel led Soren at long last to use William to hunt down and destroy Free Bezriel. Soren had delayed adopting this obvious measure because William was a Bezrielite and the king was uncertain of the sorcerer's loyalty in a battle against his own people. The devastation of an elite military unit by the unknown Free Bezriel sorcerer pushed Soren into taking that risk. He won that gamble. William no longer felt any loyalty to Bezriel and saw the assignment as final proof that he was invaluable to the king.

The night after William joined the hunt to destroy Free Bezriel, Ariadne had a dream in which the spirit of Esther, one of the Seekers, appeared to her. The Seekers were the powerful women who had founded the tradition of Bezrielite mysticism and sorcery. They were unhappy with wizards such as William for whom sorcery meant power, power over nature and power over people. For the Seekers sorcery meant unity with nature, not power over it, unity with other men and women, not power over them.

The Seekers had inspired Sarah's prophetic dream nineteen years earlier. Now they came to give Ariadne, their spiritual daughter, help in the fight against Soren and William. With help from the Seekers Ariadne erected an invisibility shield around the guerilla base camp that not even William could penetrate. That created a stalemate. As the stalemate dragged on month after month, king and necromancer were increasingly frustrated. But Free Bezriel was also frustrated, for if the shield kept Soren and William locked out, it also kept Free Bezriel locked in. The rebellion was dying.

That was when Sarah, ending two decades of silence, revealed her prophetic dream to the world. Not only did many Bezrielites believe the prophecy, but most of those who believed assumed that Ariadne was the prophesized savior not the prophesized destroyer of Bezriel. The reasons for both the belief and the optimism were the same. The first reason was that the dreamer, the mother of the prophesized savior, was the universally respected healer, Sarah. The second reason was that Ariadne had created the invisibility shield that was frustrating the most powerful army and sorcerer in modern times. Only a very powerful sorceress, could work such unprecedented magic. To do it at age nineteen with virtually no training in sorcery, she must be protected and aided by the founding mages of Bezriel. The belief in the prophecy reignited hope and patriotic fervor not only among the guerrillas, but throughout Bezriel.

Desperate to end the reenergized rebellion, Soren issued a challenge for a sorcerer's duel between William and Ariadne. If Ariadne won, Bezriel would be granted independence. If William won, the guerrilla insurrection would end and Bezriel would remain part of Menkara. Given Soren's overwhelming military superiority, the challenge was greeted with great acclaim and approval throughout Menkara and especially within Bezriel. Because of this diplomatic initiative Soren was hailed as brilliant, generous and humane. His popularity, which had been falling due to prolonged civil wars and high taxes to pay for the wars, soared to new heights.

On the appointed day, under a solemn pledge of safety from the king, Ariadne accompanied by an armed escort that included Joshua, Free Bezriel's second in command, emerged from under the invisibility shield to fight the sorcerer's duel. But within minutes, Ariadne was betrayed by Peter, one of her armed guards, whose treachery was motivated by a seething hatred for Ariadne and Free Bezriel that had been triggered by Ariadne's preference for Marcus. The hatred had led Peter to contact one of the king's agents. Soren promised Peter a big monetary reward and a lifetime sinecure.

Ariadne and her escorts were surrounded by troops from Cerberus and arrested for treason. Without Ariadne, the invisibility shield collapsed early the next morning, and the Free Bezriel guerrillas fled for their lives. The rebellion was at long last ended, defeated by betrayal from within and the treachery of Soren.

Soren's justification was that rebels against the crown were not worthy to fight an honorable duel that would legitimize their absurd claims. They were outlaws and must be treated as such. The immediate result for Soren were not only the devastation of Free Bezriel and the arrest of the powerful rebel sorceress who had humiliated him, but bitter protests both from Mentaxes his most trusted advisor on all matters political and from William, his most potent military weapon. Neither had been informed of the planned arrests. After the arrests, Mentaxes offered to resign since his opinions were now so worthless, that his advice was not even sought. Soren refused to accept the resignation and told Mentaxes to think more clearly about the proper relationship between the king and his advisors. If Mentaxes was grieved by Soren's treachery, William was furious. He saw the arrest of his dueling opponent as a demeaning insult to himself. The night after the arrests, he burst into the royal receiving room and before dozen of high ranking court officials denounced Soren as a deceitful coward. Despite this insult, William was not arrested, because Soren still needed his sorcery to consolidate his rule and realize his new dream, hegemony of Menkara over the entire continent. But the relationship between king and necromancer was strained to the breaking point.

Two weeks after the aborted duel, King Soren, in an effort to mollify Mentaxes, his invaluable aide, appointed him chancellor of the re-united kingdom of Menkara. No such peace offering was made to William.

Those struggling for freedom for Bezriel tried to come to grips with the bleak prospects created by Soren's treachery and their own stupidity in agreeing to the duel. Some in despair gave up fighting against what more and more seemed an irresistible force. Others, including Kaitlin, a condemned outlaw on the run for her life, and Ariadne, alone in her dungeon awaiting trial for treason, remained defiant and vowed to continue the struggle, even though it now seemed hopeless.

CHAPTER

Chancellor Mentaxes knew better than to tell King Soren "I told you so". Soren had always been a proud man, but there is pride and then there is pride. Once Soren's pride had been in the skill and valor with which he fought for the reunification of his homeland. Now his pride was that he was the most feared and powerful lord, not only in Menkara, but on the continent. Once he had valued good advice more than respect for his rank. Now the reverse was true. Pride remained, but it was no longer pride infused with virtue and wisdom.

Mentaxes had repeatedly warned that military reunification of Menkara would intensify cultural antagonisms. The defeated would split into hostile factions, a split between those who adapted to the new order by kowtowing to the victors and adopting their customs and values and those who rejected the new order and preserved their pride and self-identity by clinging to whatever was unique in their religion, culture and tradition. Mentaxes wanted to extend an open hand to the traditionalists. But Soren, who was fixated on a unified Menkara, saw no value in preserving the old differences that divided Menkara, differences that led most of his subjects to identify themselves by their religion or ethnicity rather than as Menkaran. He did not persecute those who clung to the old ways, but all positions of authority and opportunity were given to those that embraced the new order. As a result there was traditionalist discontent with the new regime in all parts of Menkara.

The problem was most intense in Bezriel. Most Bezrielites had always been very concerned to preserve their self-identity and unity as a people. Very few Bezrielites had ever blended into and become part of the culture and life of their more powerful neighbors. The current crisis was how to deal with Bezriel now that the Free Bezriel insurrection had been crushed. There were two aspects to the crisis. The immediate problem was what to do with the captured members of Free Bezriel, especially the sorceress Ariadne. The long-term problem was how to integrate Bezriel into the reunified Menkara. Since Soren's military superiority was rooted in military sorcery and Bezriel was the acknowledged center of sorcery in Menkara, solving what came to be known as the Bezriel problem was extremely important to King Soren and Chancellor Mentaxes.

Effective governance is very difficult when power rests solely on military might with no real consent of the governed. That was now the case in Bezriel. True there was a minority in Bezriel that supported King Soren, but a big majority saw him not as their legitimate ruler, but simply as their military overlord. Mentaxes wanted to again raise the issue of the usefulness of smoothing over religious, cultural and ethnic antagonisms, but without reminding Soren that he had previously rejected similar advice.

What should be done with the young sorceress and other Free Bezriel guerrillas captured at the site of the aborted duel? That was the most pressing question. Four days after the arrests, Soren summoned his chief advisers, Chancellor Mentaxes and General Danton, to discuss this issue. During those four days, Soren had been preoccupied organizing the hunt for the dispersed guerrillas. He especially wanted to capture Kaitlin, the rabble-rousing orator who was the leader of Free Bezriel. The hunt was severely hampered by the refusal of William to participate.

At the meeting with Mentaxes and Danton, Soren revealed his plan for dealing with the Free Bezriel prisoners. Ariadne and all the other captured guerrillas would be tried for treason, but only after weeks of a non-stop royal propaganda offensive about the grave damage that Free Bezriel had done to Menkara. This, he believed would create public support for their conviction and execution. General Danton, recently promoted from leader of the elite anti-guerrilla brigade, Cerberus, to head of all military operations, voiced strong support for the king's plan.

That left Mentaxes with the sad duty to inform the king that his plan would backfire. Ariadne was already being glorified by balladeers as a patriotic heroine, stabbed in the back by her false friend, the turncoat Peter. And, although, few had the courage to criticize Soren in public, disenchantment with the king was widespread because he had lured the guerrillas out from behind their invisibility shield and into an ambush by a solemn royal pledge on which he had reneged. Mentaxes argued that a show trial would backfire and lead to further glorification of Ariadne and opprobrium for Soren. Execution would transform Ariadne into the most dangerous of all enemies, a martyr.

Mentaxes was pleased when Soren thought long before replying. But he was not pleased with what the king said. "The popularity of Ariadne will sooner or later pass. But I must make it clear that armed insurrection against the throne is unforgiveable and can only end in the death of the traitors and dishonor for their families, including seizure of all that they own. If I show mercy to Ariadne because she is young or popular or well-intentioned, I would be issuing an invitation to future rabble rousers to organize the people against me. Preparations for the trial must begin immediately."

Mentaxes wanted to argue the point, but realized that this was not the time. Soren had called armed insurrection unforgiveable. Mentaxes believed that armed insurrection was treason, hence in a class by itself as an offense. But calling it unforgiveable went too far. There were times, he believed, when common sense dictated that governments should negotiate with rebels and compromise.

To refuse might be principled. But it was also stupid. Mentaxes was convinced that the current situation in Bezriel could only be resolved through compromise. He was unsure if he could ever convince Soren of that, but he knew there would be far better times than now to try.

But what of Kaitlin and the many Free Bezriel guerrillas who had avoided being captured? The invisibility shield protecting the guerrillas had held for almost a full day after the arrest of Ariadne. That had had given the guerrillas under the shield time to flee. They were further aided by the fact that because of his anger over Soren aborting his duel with Ariadne, William refused to take part in the mopping up operation against Free Bezriel. Without William pursuing the guerrillas, well-designed evacuation plans enabled Kaitlin and most of the guerrillas to escape capture.

Kaitlin had quickly gone beyond blaming herself for agreeing to the sorcerer's duel. The past was past. The only thing she could impact was the future. No matter how bleak that future was, it must be her complete focus. Kaitlin was temperamentally a realist and realistically, the situation for Free Bezriel was hopeless. But Kaitlin's passion for freedom for Bezriel was stronger than her realism. She refused to give up. She began working on two impossible projects, springing her greatest military weapon, the sorceress Ariadne, out of prison, and reassembling the scattered men and women of Free Bezriel into a fighting force. Kaitlin needed a sounding board to work out her ideas. Joshua her usual sounding board at Free Bezriel was in prison.

Her new sounding board turned out to be Marcus. They had both been in the last escape group through the invisibility shield. Despite the fact that Kaitlin had appointed Marcus as first officer for coordinating the use of sorcery and despite the fact that he had been her liaison with Ariadne, they did not like each other. But they did respect each other, and mutual respect turned out to be enough for them to work together on Kaitlin's hopeless projects.

Freeing Ariadne and the other Free Bezriel prisoners was the most pressing concern, since it was probably a mere matter of weeks before they would be tried, and then most likely convicted and executed. They discussed four possible ways of trying to free the prisoners.

The first was an armed raid. Soren had used that tactic to free the three witches being tried by Baron Frederick. This possibility was discarded as soon as it was raised. Not only were Free Bezriel guerrillas hopelessly scattered, hence no viable attack force could be assembled in time, but the prisoners were being held in a fortress in the capital, so impregnable that free Bezriel at its strongest could not have successfully stormed it.

The second was to use sorcery to free Ariadne and the other prisoners. Was a sorcery-powered escape possible? Theoretically, yes, said Marcus. But, he said, the only Free Bezriel sorcerer powerful enough to give it any chance of success was Ariadne. And surely Ariadne was confined in a way that prevented her from using her powers. There were known methods, both drugs and charms, by which a confined sorceress could be prevented from using her powers. With reluctance, Kaitlin agreed. There was no chance that Soren would keep a sorceress as powerful as Ariadne prisoner without blocking her powers.

The third possibility, enlisting the aid of Ariadne's guards in an escape, looked more hopeful, but not by much. It was more hopeful because it was very probable that some of those guarding Ariadne felt sympathy for the young girl, seeing her as both a hero and a martyr. She was a hero because she had been willing to fight the invincible necromancer William for a cause she believed in. She was a martyr because she was betrayed by one she thought a friend. But it was not much of a hope, because even if some of the guards did sympathize with Ariadne, it was hardly likely that any of them could be persuaded to risk almost certain arrest for treason, which would very quickly be followed by court-martial and execution. Persuasion of Soren's trusted guards to take such a treasonous risk would require a powerful mind control spell. And here again the only Free Bezriel sorcerer who could cast such a powerful spell was Ariadne. And even if she were in position to try it, which she was not, she had vowed to never again mess with the mind of another human.

Reluctantly agreeing that they had no idea how to bust their comrades out of prison, Kaitlin and Marcus focused on the fourth possibility; mobilizing enough public support for Ariadne and the other prisoners that Soren would be persuaded to release them before trial, or bowing to public pressure, the jury would acquit them, or the jury would convict but Soren would then try to reclaim his reputation as noble and fair by pardoning the convicted rebels. Each of these legal paths to freedom seemed far more likely to succeed than escape from prison.

Sympathy for the prisoners, especially Ariadne, was already widespread, not only among the common folk of Menkara, but also among the nobility. Pro-Ariadne sentiment was especially strong among the Vesparians, the only church that had dared to stand up against Soren. That church was especially strong in the provinces that had fought against Soren in the two decades of civil war before his ascension to the throne. Another important factor in favor of this strategy was that Menkara's powerful neighbors had made it clear they would like to see Soren declare a general amnesty. Kaitlin and Marcus decide to try to increase public pressure for Soren to pardon Ariadne and the other guerrilla prisoners.

Following up this decision, they discussed whether there was any way to use sorcery to increase pro-Ariadne and pro-Free Bezriel sentiment throughout Menkara? Perhaps. After all the growth of support for Free Bezriel had begun with the impressive aerial display of Bezrielite resistance and self-identity at The Temple of Origins. A new spectacular public display of Bezrielite self-identity and pride might be very useful. But such a display of resistance might be a terrible two-edged sword. Even if it helped the rebuilding of Free Bezriel, it might also enrage Soren and become a virtual death warrant for Ariadne and the other prisoners. Fearing this, Kaitlin and Marcus agreed that until Ariadne and the other prisoners were freed or executed, propaganda should focus on Bezrielite spirituality, not Bezrielite resistance. Likewise it would focus on the courage and dignity of Ariadne and the other prisoners, not their military value.

William was a proud man. He had felt publically humiliated when Soren aborted his duel with Ariadne, creating the impression that he was afraid to fight the powerful young sorceress and had connived in the deceit that had led to her capture and arrest. There was no doubt, at least in William's mind, that Soren knew that if the duel had proceeded, William would have slain the rebel sorceress. Thus the point of Soren's treachery could not have been to destroy the rebel group Free Bezriel by arresting Ariadne; because defeat by treachery was much less effective than defeat in open battle. The point of the treachery could only have been to announce to the world that the mighty King Soren did not need the services of the necromancer William to defeat his enemies. The king had proclaimed as clearly as possible "I, King Soren, am in full control. Those who credit my success to William are fools. He is simply my servant, a tool that has sometimes proved useful. But he is far from a necessary tool."

Continuing to work for Soren was an abasement that William could not endure. He would not crawl back like a whipped dog and beg for favors. But what were his options? Use his powers of sorcery to wage war on Soren? Once he had thought he could topple Soren through sorcery alone, but he now realized that one man, no matter how powerful cannot defeat a king and his armies. Acting alone, the most he could do would be to kill Soren and then be hunted down and tortured until he was dead. Emotionally tempting as it was, killing Soren was not a practical option for a man like William who craved power.

Resigning was an even worse option. If he resigned, he would lose not only his high position and the perks that came with it, but he would also lose access to the rare and expensive resources needed to carry out his ongoing experiments in the uncharted regions of necromancy. Furthermore, if he resigned, could there be any doubt that Soren would have him assassinated to guarantee that he would not sell his powers of sorcery to some rival lord?

William was certain that Soren had not yet issued an assassination order. The king no longer really needed William to clean up the few remaining areas of discontent within Menkara. But he was still heavily dependent on William for success of his increasingly ambitious plans of territorial expansion and regional hegemony. Assassination, he thought, was surely an 'only-if-needed' option for Soren, who, no doubt, believed that the sorcerer would have to come crawling back, would have to trade his sorcery for perks only the king could furnish. Soren felt confident that he would win this battle of wills with William; his confidence arising from his assumption that the sorcerer needed the king more than the king needed the sorcerer. But the king was wrong. Surely, thought William, there are other monarchs, desiring his services and willing and able to pay him adequately.

Although alone, William spoke aloud, as if he were addressing Soren. "You would murder me, King Soren, if I do not return to work for you. I know that is your plan, but it will not work. O mighty Soren, you sit on the throne I gained for you, hoping I will come crawling back to serve you. Deceitful Soren, do not deny that if I do not crawl back, you will give the order for my assassination. Do not deny it, for I know you all too well. But pathetic Soren, you plot in vain. By the time you decide to act I will be out of your reach. I will flee to a place where you cannot reach. I will flee to one of the many powers that hate and fear you. Once I am with your enemy, they will still hate you, but, o feeble Soren, after I have switched sides, they will no longer fear you. You will fear them, because you will fear my revenge."

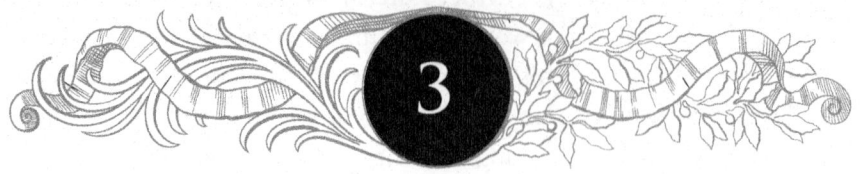

CHAPTER

After the arrest of Ariadne and other Free Bezriel rebels, King Soren wanted to forbid them lawyers and visitors. He wanted to hold Ariadne in solitary confinement before her trial and execution. But he was told by Chancellor Mentaxes that under Menkaran law, all those awaiting trial had a right to both lawyers and visitors. Mentaxes added that given widespread admiration of and sympathy for Ariadne, denying her and the other Free Bezriel prisoners these traditional rights would be a political blunder doing serious harm to the king's popularity with both commoners and aristocrats, a popularity already at a low ebb.

Soren grudgingly conceded the point. He ordered that it be proclaimed throughout his realm that the king's justice and mercy were so great that even traitors were permitted defense attorneys and given fair trials. Visits by family members were also graciously granted by his royal majesty King Soren.

Eight days after Ariadne's arrest, her parents were finally allowed to visit. Sarah was hopeful that public support for Ariadne would eventually persuade the politically astute Soren to pardon her daughter. Daniel had no such optimism, feeling certain that the pride of the king demanded vengeance for the public humiliation that the fleeting victories of the young sorceress had caused him.

Despite the king's promise of a fair trial, Daniel believed the king would stage a show trial with no opportunity for Ariadne to defend herself. A guilty verdict and public execution would quickly follow.

When they met, the mood of Ariadne surprised her parents. Rather than being angry at the treachery that had put her in a dungeon and terrified at a likely death sentence, she radiated peaceful acceptance of all that had happened. She had not fulfilled the prophecy by saving Bezriel. She had failed, but she had tried. After her evil bewitchment of Cerberus, she had acted honorably in her efforts to free Bezriel. Even when she agreed to the duel to the death with William, she remained true to her reverence for life. Much better that one should die in battle rather than many, especially if that one would likely be herself!

And yet, behind that peaceful acceptance of her fate, she remained unyielding to her enemies. Whether she had a few weeks to live or many years, she would challenge Soren by doing what she could in support of the struggle for freedom for Bezriel, even if all she could do would be make a defiant speech at her trial. With that speech, she would strive to turn the struggle for Bezriel's freedom into a struggle to identify Bezrielite sorcery with reverence for life rather than William's identification of it with power over all creation, including power over the life and death of others.

Having been formally charged with treason, Ariadne had the right to a defense attorney and to meet with that lawyer twice a week. Ariadne had not asked for a lawyer when she was arrested nor during her imprisonment. But her parents, horrified when they learned that she did not have a lawyer, insisted to Ariadne that she must have a lawyer and strongly recommended

Bernard, the Bezrielite lawyer who had defended Sarah, Abigail and William at their trial for witchcraft. Ariadne meekly accepted their suggestion but thought that having a lawyer was irrelevant. By joining the guerrillas, she had committed treason. What she wanted was not a lawyer, but the chance to speak at her trial.

When they met, parents and daughter were overwhelmed by emotion. After ten minutes, Daniel's anguish, which he tried to hide, was sensed by Ariadne and disturbed her. Without asking, she knew his anguish was because he believed that she would be tried, convicted, and executed as a traitor. She spoke trying to console her father. "You gave me life, father. I love you for that, but even more I love you as the good man who taught, protected and loved me. I know that you grieve because I will die young. I know that you will do all that you can and more to save me from execution. But if you fail, do not blame yourself and do not grieve. I have had a good life. I tried to do what was right. I have been loved by those that I love: you, mother, my brother Jonathan, my second mother Abigail, my soul mate Marcus, and my comrades in Free Bezriel. If I die young, I die content." With these words Ariadne tried to console her father, but her words were ineffective. Her calm acceptance of death did not move Daniel to likewise calmly accept his daughter's impending death. Nonetheless, seeing Ariadne's serenity and defiance in captivity was a great consolation to Daniel.

But Sarah who could read people's hearts sensed that her daughter's serenity was a surface calm over a boiling caldron of self-doubt and anger. Sarah believed in openly confronting one's buried emotions, but feared what would happen to Ariadne if and when those buried emotions broke through and revealed themselves.

Peter was the main irritant in Ariadne's attempt to be at peace with her situation. Rather than hatred of Peter for his betrayal, she blamed herself for creating such hatred and resentment in a friend who had loved her. She knew that unrequited love was what had led to Peter's betrayal. They had been childhood friends, who had worked together in the struggle to get her mother released from prison on the charge of witchcraft. But then after being reunited at the Free Bezriel base camp, she had played the hussy, enjoying being courted by both Marcus and Peter. And when it was clear that her heart had chosen Marcus, she had done nothing to soften the blow to Peter. She had had no inkling of how angry and resentful he had become. "How could I have been so blind? So stupid? So cruel?" were questions she repeatedly used to torture herself.

When this self-doubt, this belief that she was responsible for Peter's treachery, returned after the visit from her parents, Ariadne's hard gained serenity quickly slipped away. If she could lead a friend who loved her into the darkness into which she had led Peter, what right had she to believe she had anything positive to offer Bezriel? Maybe it would be better, if the death sentence were passed and she were executed. Those were the dark thoughts with which she fell asleep the night following her parents visit.

Ariadne's gloom dragged on. Two night later, the Seeker Esther, for the first time since her arrest, appeared to Ariadne in a dream. In previous dreams Esther had brought words of encouragement, saying that Ariadne had been chosen to lead Bezriel back to the path of enlightenment opened up by the Seekers. It was Esther who had taught Ariadne how to build the invisibility shield. But this time, with Ariadne locked in a dungeon waiting to stand trial for treason, and full of self-doubt and self-loathing, Esther came not to offer aid or comfort, but to express her anger.

"So, Ariadne," she said in a mocking voice "you have decided that you are a god!"

"Me! Think myself a god? Why do you who should be my comfort, mock me?"

"Mock you? You think yourself responsible for Peter's treachery and all the evils that have befallen Bezriel. Only a god could have such power, therefore you must think yourself a god."

The argument with Esther was bitter. When Ariadne awoke from her dream in the middle of the night she was covered in a cold sweat. The thin blanket provided to prisoners was a little help warming her body, but no help to her soul, which needed warmth more than did her body. Ariadne meditated long and deep on the dream and gradually she began to understand and in understanding, a small measure of peace. The mockery of Esther saved her from walking further down a very dangerous path. That mockery taught her to see that even if she had treated Peter badly, she was not responsible for and could not have anticipated his extreme reaction to disappointment in love. Peter betraying Free Bezriel to Soren for whatever reward he got was his self-damning act not hers. She also recognized that night that although she was sometimes selfish and often confused and wrong, that did not mean that she should withdraw from the world and crawl into a corner. It did not mean that she had nothing of value to offer Bezriel. It simply meant that she was human.

Technically, since her parents and her lawyer were allowed to visit, Ariadne was not in solitary confinement. But she was alone with her thoughts for all but a few hours each long week. Man is a social animal. Therefore such solitude is often terrifying and debilitating. But after the dream Ariadne accepted and even welcomed the enforced solitude as a chance to take stock of her life; review the choices she had made, and examine who and what she had become.

The decisive events in her life, events that sent her stumbling or running down a new path towards new goals, were easy to pinpoint. Her life had been going down unexpected new paths ever since the shocking discovery of her powers of destructive sorcery, a discovery triggered by anger at her parents for treating her as a mere child. Very shortly thereafter she had learned of her mother's prophetic dream when pregnant. The prophecy if true meant Ariadne had a unique historic role to play. Ever since then, she had oscillated between rejection of the prophetic dream as impossible nonsense, acceptance of the prophecy with exultation at her importance, and, more commonly, acceptance of the prophecy with fear and trembling, fear that she would fail and by her failure doom Bezriel. Her teens were years of being shielded from the world by her parents and Abigail, combined with training to follow in her mother's footsteps as a healer. Even with her knowledge of the terrifying prophecy, her years of gradual transition from childhood to womanhood, were by and large peaceful and happy, despite the storm cloud of the prophecy hanging over her head. But such peace could not and did not last.

The next decisive event in Ariadne's young life was her decision to join the guerrillas fighting for independence for Bezriel. During her time with Free Bezriel she had changed dramatically. For the first time she was trained in sorcery by an expert. Under guidance of Gwydian her powers of sorcery became disciplined and very powerful. She became the source of the expanding significance and influence of Free Bezriel. She had been both thrilled and terrified by her newfound importance. On a personal level, two comrades fell in love with her, and although she remained true to her vow of chastity, she had had her first experience of romantic love and sexual lust.

Then tragically out of anger at the massacre of Gwydian and other comrades by Cerberus, Soren's elite anti-guerrilla brigade, she had cast the confusion spell that caused the troops of Cerberus to slaughter each other. In the mental and emotional turmoil that followed she had wanted to totally forsake military sorcery. But after talking with her parents, she had decided to use her powers of sorcery to protect her comrades in Free Bezriel from the wrath of Soren and William, but not use them in guerrilla offensive actions. Her refusal to join guerrilla raids alienated her from most of her comrades who could not understand or sympathize with her halfway commitment to their cause.

The next, and probably last, turning point in her life had been her decision to accept Soren's challenge of a duel with William to decide the fate of Bezriel. Because of the treachery of Soren, that sorcerer's duel had never been fought. But showing up for the duel had led to her arrest and the destruction of Free Bezriel.

The most important common threads Ariadne discovered in these decisive events were the central role of her powers of destructive sorcery and the welling up within her soul of strong emotions that she could not control and that overwhelmed her. The emotional outbursts had begun with her anger at her parents triggering the first eruption of her powers and had reached an apex or nadir in the cold fury that had led to her devastation of Cerberus. Her decision to fight a duel with William to end the bloody civil war and, if she won, create self-determination for Bezriel, was seemingly altruistic. But she knew in her heart that she had agreed to the duel not in a spirit of self-sacrifice and out of love for Bezriel. No! Her agreement to fight the duel had resulted from her blindly striking out against William's mockery of her original refusal to fight the duel as the predictable response of a scared little girl.

Fortunately for Ariadne's peace of mind, after struggling through long days of solitude, she gradually began to see that her life was more than that set of negative-emotion driven decisions and responses to events. Her short life had had two very different stages, first, childhood and adolescence with her extended family and, second, life as a young adult fighting for freedom for Bezriel and meeting and falling in love with Marcus. In both stages she been surrounded by love and respect and she had loved and admired those around her. She and her friends had tried to do what was right, even at great risk to themselves. That she hoped was the core of her life, not those negative-emotion driven decisions that had ended so badly.

Ariadne's reflections about turning points in her life eventually quieted the turmoil in her soul. When calm had been restored, Esther once again appeared to Ariadne in a dream. This time the Seeker did not mock Ariadne. Rather she praised her distinction between the core of her life and her tendency towards negative emotion driven decisions. But she also wanted Ariadne to examine in depth the reasons for three turning point decisions in her life: her decision to join the guerrilla struggle, her decision to cast the confusion spell on Cerberus, and her decision to fight a sorcerer's duel to the death with William.

Happy that Esther had returned and was no longer angry or mocking. Ariadne readily agreed. She examined the decisions in order, beginning with her decision to abandon the peaceful path of her parents by joining Free Bezriel. Voluntarily joining a guerrilla army went against the grain both of her innate tendency to strive to resolve conflicts through peaceful compromise and of the faith which she had absorbed from her parents that the essence of Bezriel was harmony not discord, peace not war. She had ardently desired to follow in the footsteps of her mother and become a healer. Despite the prophecy and the eruption of her awful powers of destruction, she had gladly spent her teen years as an apprentice learning her mother's craft.

But then the guerrilla war for independence had begun and her older brother Jonathan had joined Free Bezriel, breaking the hearts of their parents. The young Ariadne who loved and trusted her brother was thrown into intellectual and emotional turmoil. She shared her parents' pacifist belief that all warfare, especially civil war, was a poisonous tree that destroyed the spirit of Bezriel. Even before her brother left to join the guerrillas, Ariadne had believed in the cause for which Free Bezriel fought, self-determination for Bezriel, but not in their violent means. Ariadne felt like a coward and hypocrite, sitting safely at home, while others risked their lives fighting for freedom for Bezriel. After her brother joined the rebels, that feeling of hypocrisy intensified.

What she had wanted more than anything was to help the spirit of Bezriel flourish. She believed that history had proven that the spirit of Bezriel could survive while Bezriel was a subject people, but it could not flourish under those conditions. Survival was not enough. Her brief life under the tyrant Baron Friedrich had convinced Ariadne that even though violence contradicted the spirit of Bezriel, freedom, even freedom gained through violence, was better for Bezriel than subjugation. There was no way she could help free Bezriel sitting at home. Given her powers and the prophecy, she had decided that she must cast aside her pacifist emotions and join the struggle for freedom and independence for Bezriel.

Had joining Free Bezriel been the right choice? It had eventually led to disaster. Nonetheless, after long meditation, Ariadne decided that joining Free Bezriel had been the morally right choice because staying passively on the sidelines would have been shirking her duty. But then doubt returned. Her parents, had striven to restore the true spirit of Bezriel through nonviolent protests. Her brother had rejected non-violent protest as ineffective against ruthless tyrants like Baron Friedrich and Soren. Shortly thereafter she herself had reached the same verdict (non-violence is ineffective) and made the same decision (join the armed insurrection of Free Bezriel). But now the violent path of Free Bezriel had also failed. Close to despair, Ariadne asked "Is there any path that can restore Bezriel to health?"

Fortunately that night, seeing the depression into which Ariadne was falling, Esther again came to her in a dream. She told her young charge that she was experiencing a dark night of the soul. As scary as it was, the only way back to the light was to continue the journey. This would be hard because the next stage would be the worst, reliving her decision to wreck revenge on Cerberus for the slaying of her mentor Gwydian.

It was self-torture for Ariadne to examine in detail her devastation of Cerberus, but bearing in mind the warning of Esther that the only way out of her dark night was to push on through it, she forced herself to relive those terrible events. She remembered her grief when Cerberus overran one of the guerrilla camps slaughtering those defending the camp including Gwydian. As bad as that was, much worse was memory of the rage that had led her to cast a spell befogging the minds of the troops of Cerberus, causing them to mistake friend for foe and in this black fog kill their friends and comrades. That confusion spell was hailed as a great victory by Kaitlin and her comrades in Free Bezriel. But for Ariadne it was an unforgivable misuse of her powers of sorcery.

The focus of her agonizing review was to examine why her reaction to the tragedy at the rebel camp was not just grief for her friends who had been slaughtered, but rage at the enemy soldiers who had done the deed. In her rage she had committed senseless slaughter that was much, much worse than the evil done by Cerberus because she had used her powers of sorcery to make the soldiers of Cerberus kill their own friends and comrades.

Why had she who believed so strongly in the Bezrielite doctrines of universal brotherhood and the need for forgiveness committed such an atrocity? Her anger and rage were the surface explanations. But she now saw that what made it possible for her rage to get so out of control that she could commit such an atrocity was that her belief in universal brotherhood was abstract, at least with respect to the enemy forces that Free Bezriel was fighting. As the war lengthened, she had more and more thought of them simply as the enemy, and less and less as fellow humans. Forgetting that the enemy is human explained both the massacre committed by Cerberus and the self-annihilation of Cerberus that she had caused.

Any tool can be misused by a mad woman. She had become a mad woman. Sorcery like medicine, like carpentry, was a tool that could be used for good or misused for evil. She had misused it for evil. Misusing her sorcery she had controlled enemy soldiers like puppets, stripping them of their humanity. Manipulating the strings of the puppets she had turned the enemy soldiers into, she had caused them to kill their friends and comrades. The root evil was not her sorcery, but that she had ceased to see the enemy as human.

Before going to sleep that night, a distraught Ariadne implored Esther to talk with her that night. But Esther did not come. When she awoke, her first thought was "Esther, why have you abandoned me?" The sound of her own voice startled her. She had not realized she had spoked aloud.

The next day, Ariadne tried to carry out the third and last of the introspective tasks required of her by Esther—to reflect on why she had she agreed to fight a kill-or-be killed sorcerer's duel with William. Having renewed her commitment to non-violence after her devastation of Cerberus, why had she agreed to fight a duel to the death?

The world believed she had agreed to the duel to end the civil war and, if she won, gain independence for Bezriel. She had been told that because of her willingness to fight William, the most powerful sorcerer in modern times, fight him in order to liberate Bezriel, she had been hailed as a heroine ready to die to liberate Bezriel. But two days earlier, in the loneliness of her dungeon, awaiting the trial that would end in her execution, she had admitted to herself that it was her petty anger at William's taunt that her refusal to fight was all that could be expected of a scared little girl that had triggered her acceptance of the duel. Wounded childish vanity, not love of Bezriel, was why she had agreed to the duel.

Because of her betrayal by Peter and the treachery of Soren, the duel was aborted and ended in disaster. What else, she now thought, could be expected of a decision made in a childish temper tantrum? The ugly repercussions were expanding. Hatred between Bezrielite patriots and the occupiers and collaborators who now ruled Bezriel was greater than ever, and her comrades from Free Bezriel were being hunted down like dogs. She and those comrades arrested with her would most likely be condemned and executed.

Her final turning point decision, her decision to fight the duel, had been motivated by injured pride and had led to disaster for herself, her comrades, and for Bezriel. Nonetheless even now she believed or at least wanted to believe that albeit for bad reasons, she had made the morally right choice, a choice that offered a path to freedom for Bezriel with minimal bloodshed.

But then she thought, how could it have been the morally right choice since it had led to disaster? Bezriel taught that the world was a living masterwork of wondrous organic harmony and beauty. In despair, she now thought "how can that be true?" Did not recent events lend credence to the view that the world was a chaos of warring elements? Was her faith in Bezriel, her faith in the goodness of the world, childish naiveté?

After completing her remembrance and analysis of the sequence of her decisions, a project demanded by Esther that had left her close to despair, Ariadne desperately wanted to discuss her dark thoughts about herself with Esther. But Esther did not appear. Waking in the middle of the night, Ariadne's restless mind turned repeatedly to what seemed to be the one constant in her turning point decisions; they all flowed from her emotions at the moment rather than from rational thought. Emotion as a guide for her actions must be wrong she reasoned, since the result had been disaster.

She had joined Free Bezriel because she had felt like a coward and hypocrite standing on the sidelines while others were risking their lives trying to free Bezriel. She had caused the devastation of Cerberus because of her out of control rage at Cerberus for slaughtering her friends and comrades. She had agreed to a to-the-death duel with William because of her petulant anger at his mockery of her as a scared little girl. And now she also remembered that her powers of sorcery had first erupted when she was furious at her parents for not taking her ideas seriously because in their eyes she was still a child.

It seemed to Ariadne that her entire life as a sorceress had been circumscribed by out-of-control emotion. Was the danger of strong emotion, the lesson that Esther wanted her to learn? That would imply that she should use her mind and not her heart when making decisions. But what was the point of learning such a hard truth a few short weeks before being executed?

Mid-morning, while Ariadne was still running in circles around those questions, she was informed that her parents had just arrived for their scheduled visit. She had become so used to solitude that she was irritated that her meditations were being interrupted. She remained in this foul mood while being escorted under guard to the visitor's meeting room. Even after she entered the room with her parents, her bad mood remained.

Sarah and Daniel were very careworn. Sarah had hoped that Soren would see that pardoning Ariadne, who had become a folk hero, would help him regain public support. But Soren's ever harder line on those who had taken up arms against him had subverted that hope and confirmed Daniel's pessimism about their daughter's fate. The fact that the start of the trial was now just ten days away was turning their anxiety into despair.

Sarah immediately noticed the look of a tortured soul on Ariadne's face. Stifling her own fears, while trying and succeeding in keeping her voice calm, she said "Do not lose hope, daughter. Bezriel willing, you will be acquitted or pardoned."

"Bezriel willing! Mother, you know as well as I, that it is not Bezriel that will decide my fate. Rather it is Soren, a man who hates me. But that is not what bothers me. Long ago I accepted that I would be condemned. Rather I am distraught because of what I am learning about myself on my journey of self-understanding."

"I do not understand. What is this journey?"

Ariadne than told of the Seeker Esther's command that she meditate on why she joined Free Bezriel, why she had induced the self-massacre of Cerberus, and why she agreed to fight a duel to the death with William. After briefly summarized her meditations, she said "I finally understand why I failed in the mission for which I was born. It was because I trusted my emotions that I made so many bad decisions, and why even when I made a right decision, I did so for the wrong reasons. I learned …"

In a strident voice, Daniel interrupted his daughter. "Those damn self-righteous Seekers. It is outrageous that while you are imprisoned and vilified by the enemies of Bezriel for doing what the Seekers told you to do, they lay the blame for Bezriel's troubles on you and ask you to meditate on your failings."

"Please, father! Esther asked me to reflect on my mistakes not to torment me but to help me understand myself. Self-understanding is a necessary journey. If what I find makes me unhappy and ashamed, it is because I have made bad decisions, done bad things, made decisions based on emotion rather than reason."

"Is emotion such a bad thing?" asked Sarah. "Love and compassion are emotions, and at its heart Bezriel is love and compassion."

In a burst of frustration, Ariadne replied. "You understand nothing, mother. If you had seen comrades slaughtered like animals, you would see that love and compassion are not enough! They are not enough to save Bezriel, since to Soren and the powers of this world the only value of Bezriel is military sorcery. To save Bezriel we need power, military power greater than Soren's; military sorcery stronger than Williams."

Wounded in her heart and soul by her daughter's words, Sarah asked, "Oh, Ariadne, have you really become so cynical?"

"It is not cynicism to be realistic."

An outraged Daniel then spoke. "If the Seekers, supposedly the guardians of Bezriel, teach power rather than compassion, it is not surprising that Bezriel is losing its soul. Ariadne, apologize to your mother for your insolent words!"

When Ariadne did not speak, he commanded "Apologize now!" When Ariadne still did not speak, he said "Sarah, let us go. This wretched girl is not our daughter."

Crying, his wife replied, "No, Daniel. Do you not see she speaks out of misery and confusion; she speaks words she does not believe."

Then without warning the dam burst. Fearful that her parents were about to abandon her, Ariadne's defiance collapsed. With head bowed, unable to look either her mother or her father in the eye, she sobbed. "I am so confused. Please forgive me. Please help me."

After being soothed and comforted in her mother's strong embrace, Ariadne tried to explain. "I have been so angry at everything and everyone, most of all angry at myself, that when you said that at its core Bezriel is love and compassion, a doctrine that has failed me and failed Bezriel, I went crazy. I want to believe in the power of love and compassion to solve all problems, but I can no longer believe."

Despite being shocked and unprepared for Ariadne's crisis of faith, Sarah and Daniel did not reproach her. They did not have the answers Ariadne was seeking, but the love and wisdom they offered comforted their daughter.

Her father said, "Bezriel is not an external god, but the true soul within us. We do not pray to Bezriel to solve our problems, but rather we try to plumb our true soul for insight into ourselves and others. In this way we try to bring out the best in ourselves, the best being deeds expressing love and compassion."

Daniel's thought was continued by Sarah. "'Bezriel' is our name for the goodness in our soul. But no soul is all good. Everyone, even the best of us, does bad things. We must learn from our mistakes and moral failures. That means that you must try to understand what weaknesses within you led you to do bad things. It means you must try to understand what weaknesses within your enemies led them to do bad things. Understanding is part of love and compassion. We must not abandon Bezriel because the bad in people is now winning, rather we must find the courage to continue the struggle."

That night Esther did come to Ariadne. In her dream, Ariadne saw herself sleeping. She saw Esther enter the cell and wake her up. "Your parents are wise, Ariadne" she said. "Listen to what they say."

Her dream-self replied. "How can you say that when my parents and you have contradictory views on the nature and meaning of Bezriel. My parents believe love and compassion are the heart of Bezriel and opposed my joining Free Bezriel and their guerrilla war to liberate Bezriel. Whereas you supported me when I was with the guerrillas and using my sorcery in military combat."

"You are right, your parents and I gave you contradictory advice on joining the guerrillas. But people who share the same values, can make different decisions on how to live by those values."

"But how can you advocate war if love and compassion are your highest values?"

"Do you believe that only pacifists really have love and compassion? Were your comrades in Free Bezriel without love and compassion?"

"No. Of course not. We had love for each other and for Bezriel. But we had no love for Soren and William, nor for those in Soren's armies. Whereas my parents preach love and compassion for everyone."

"They preach the ideal. I hope that humanity can someday reach that ideal. You and your comrades in Free Bezriel chose to fight for more modest, more attainable, goals. That does not mean you forsook the ideal."

Then as often happens in dreams, the scene shifted. Ariadne was no longer watching her dream-self talking with Esther. Suddenly she was simply in her cell talking with Esther. She was no longer an observer, she was now a participant. It began with Esther opening a new topic.

"Did you think seriously about the three turning points I asked you to reflect on?"

"Yes."

"What conclusions did you reach?"

"That those decisions were based on emotion, rather than rational thought."

"And …?"

"And since those decisions based on emotion ended in disaster, I now see that reason rather than emotion is the proper guide to action."

"Are you sure?"

"What else could it mean?"

"Think, Ariadne! You want to believe that the heart of Bezriel is love and compassion. And yet you conclude that the lesson to be learned from your self-analysis is that it is wrong to base decisions on emotions. But love and compassion are emotions."

"Are you saying that the lesson I should learn is that decisions based on emotion are okay, if the emotion is love or compassion. My bad decisions were based on rage and petulance. But when I was boiling with anger at Cerberus and when I was feeling humiliated and insulted by William, I do not see how I could have summoned up love and compassion for either Cerberus or William."

"True. Rage and compassion are incompatible. What conclusion do you draw from this?"

"That Bezriel asks the impossible. It is not possible to love those that are trying to destroy what we love."

"Let us take a step back, Ariadne. Love and compassion is too simple a description of the heart of Bezriel. Your mother had a deeper understanding when she spoke of love, compassion, and understanding. You repented your decimation of Cerberus? Why?"

"Because I came to see that the soldiers in Cerberus acted out of the intense hatred generated by war. In casting my confusion spell I also acted out of hatred generated by war."

"That insight is an important step on your journey. The next step is much harder – developing the discipline to achieve understanding before acting. You have a long spiritual road to travel. I will help you. We will begin tomorrow. Since you are emotionally exhausted, I will begin by helping you to sleep peacefully through the night and to wake refreshed."

Ariadne did sleep peacefully and did wake refreshed. She remembered both parts of her dream. She now realized that making emotional decisions was not itself the problem. All human actions have their genesis in emotions. The problem was her lack of discipline, her failure to see that in those three situations, perhaps in all turning point situations, different emotions pull us in different directions. Often the strongest emotion of the moment does not reflect our best self. That is why we need to cultivate discipline, so that when important decisions must be made, we can force ourselves to consider all aspects of the situation before deciding what path to take.

CHAPTER 4

It was inevitable that Lord Lucien and Lord Soren would become became bitter enemies. Each began as a powerful provincial lord in the fragmented feudal kingdom of Menkara. But in every other way they were opposites. Lucien loved the flourishing of distinct regional traditions and cultures that had been made possible by the collapse of centralized authority in Menkara. He loved the fact that in his native Caxtonia, commoners felt free to come to him with their hopes and problems, for example to ask for special training for a musically talented daughter or to settle a boundary dispute with neighbors. He loved the unique religious and cultural heritage of Caxtonia where his family had lived and ruled for countless generations. He loved the fact that the aristocracy was a society of equals with no higher authority demanding their subservience. Lucien disliked and feared the growing strength of modernization in all aspects of life, cultural as well as political and economic, and especially distrusted the centralization of power that came with modernization. Thus Lucien distrusted and feared Soren, the harbinger and agent of modernization and centralization in Menkara.

By birth Soren was hereditary lord of Thorheim, the largest and most powerful province in Menkara. But Thorheim was much too small a stage for the ambitions of Soren, hence he waged a long campaign to become king of a reunited Menkara. He built a powerful military equipped with the most destructive modern weaponry and led by officers trained in modern techniques of strategy and command. But after twenty long years of military campaigns, he controlled only half of Menkara. He created a vast, efficient bureaucracy to administer the territories he controlled, including collecting the high taxes he imposed. He grudgingly admired the ancient and diverse cultures of Menkara, but dismissed them as outmoded remnants of a superstitious past and dreamed of supplanting them with a modern unifying culture based on science and the ideal of endless progress.

The forces opposing Soren and fighting to maintain the decentralized feudal system, gradually became more organized and effective under the leadership of Lucien. Then it all rapidly changed after Soren recruited the Bezrielite necromancer, William. No army, no other sorcerer could hold up against his dark conjuring. Within two years, Soren was crowned king of a reunited Menkara. There were, however, still small pockets of armed resistance.

With ill-grace Lucien acknowledged Soren as king, but turned down all offers of position in the new government. He refused to move to the capital and continued to live in Caxtonia. Soren, who disliked Lucien, had very serious doubts about his loyalty, and was looking for a pretext to arrest or exile him.

Soren's suspicions were well-founded. Even before the coronation, Lucien began organizing a not-so-loyal opposition faction. His most important initial recruits were Lord Menjaro and the high priestess Grassic. Menjaro was the feudal lord of the remote mountainous province of Altaria. He still controlled a provincial army. The Altarian army was formally part of Soren's national army, but in reality remained loyal to Menjaro. Grassic was the universally respected leader of the Vesparians, the largest and most powerful religious group in Menkara.

At first united only by distrust of the new king, gradually a few issues came to dominate the discussions and political activity of these dissidents. The first issue that galvanized them was distrust of the centralization of power in Menkara that Soren was effecting. Their second galvanizing issue was dislike of the blurring of ethnic and provincial differences created by Soren's policies. Their distrust of cultural homogenization led to the selection of a name for the group. They settled on Society for the Preservation of Provincial and Regional Traditions (SUPPORT) and referred to themselves as SUPPORTERS. They chose this bland acronym precisely because it was bland and did not reveal the depth of their opposition to King Soren.

Soon thereafter, a third issue, opposition to the ongoing militarization of Menkara fueled by Soren's obvious expansionist ambitions, came to dominate both SUPPORT's internal discussions and public activity. It seemed only a matter of time before Soren would use his powerful military and the sorcery of William to try to gain hegemony over, and possibly conquest of nearby states.

Members of SUPPORT used their positions of power and influence to delay and hobble King Soren on all three of these fronts. But they did so cautiously, knowing full well that if they went too far, Soren would crack down hard on them. For now he tolerated SUPPORT as a mere gadfly. But how long would toleration last? Due to fear of its members being arrested and the organization dissolved if its demands went too far, SUPPORT at first advocated only modest reforms. At that time, Soren viewed SUPPORT as a minor nuisance, albeit a nuisance whose legality served the useful propaganda function of demonstrating that that he was no tyrant.

Lucien and the others in SUPPORT saw the impending treason trials for Free Bezriel guerrillas, especially the trial of Ariadne, the popular young sorceress, as a golden opportunity for blackening the public image of Soren. The popularity of Soren which had soared to new heights when he proposed a sorcerer's duel between William and Ariadne to peacefully end the Free Bezriel insurrection, had sunk to new lows when he arrested Ariadne before the duel could begin. Lucien hoped to use the upcoming treason trial of Ariadne as a propaganda weapon to demonstrate the arrogance of Soren and to portray him as a coward who won his battles through treachery. This would be done through intermediate organs of public opinion in order to avoid SUPPORT becoming the object of Soren's wrath.

This led to a fracturing of the opposition group when Grassic spoke against Lucien's plan. She pointed out that Ariadne and her Free Bezriel comrades about to go on trial for their lives were fellow soldiers in the battle against Soren. Following Lucien's plan would subject Soren to public opprobrium and for that very reason would certainly lead to death sentences for Ariadne and her comrades. The counter plan Grassic advocated was a propaganda campaign emphasizing the valor and dignity of Ariadne and her comrades, rather than focusing on the treachery of Soren. Grassic's goal was to save the lives of the brave guerrillas, not embarrass King Soren.

Grassic carried the day. Lucien, seeing that sentiment was swinging strongly in favor of Grassic's plan, rose and endorsed it. As a result, Grassic's motion for SUPPORT to join the movement to pressure King Soren to pardon and free the Free Bezriel prisoners passed unanimously.

As discontent with King Soren grew, those opposed to his policies and growing power gravitated to SUPPORT as both the most powerful and safest place to make their discontent known. The power came from the powerful provincial lords such as Lucien of Caxtonia and Menjaro of Altaria and influential religious leaders such as the high priestess Grassic of the Vesparians that had founded SUPPORT. The safety came from the fact that King Soren still strove to be a popular monarch rather than a tyrant. Nonetheless members of SUPPORT recognized there was a limit to how far their opposition could go, because as much as Soren wanted to be popular, praised and loved, he valued his power even more. If he were ever to feel really threatened by SUPPORT, he would close it down and arrest its leaders.

But as William's absence from court lengthened, Lucien organized a secret inner group of influential men and women within SUPPORT to discuss deposing Soren as king. First, at the insistence of Grassic, they discussed legal maneuvers to declare his kingship and many of his proclamations unlawful. In the great epic poem of Menkara, describing an age long before kingship became hereditary, kings were not only elected by the clan leaders, but could be deposed for actions contrary to the ethos of their people.

A moral case cold certainly be made to depose Soren on those grounds. But not a legal case. A scholarly member of that inner circle of plotters informed the group that the text of the sacred poem carried no legal weight. Three kings had been deposed in Menkaran history, two by civil war and one by palace coup. In each instance, the legal ruling validating the transfer, came after, not before the transfer of power. Without a military coup, the only result of SUPPORT starting legal proceedings to strip Soren of his kingship would be the arrest of everyone in SUPPORT. In the early days of SUPPORT, even Lucien was hesitant to initiate discussion of either armed insurrection or a palace coup d'état. For if even one member of the group was a spy or would panic if such treason was contemplated, they would all be doomed.

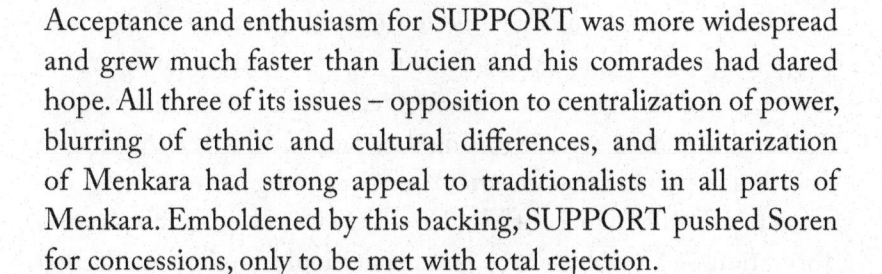

Acceptance and enthusiasm for SUPPORT was more widespread and grew much faster than Lucien and his comrades had dared hope. All three of its issues – opposition to centralization of power, blurring of ethnic and cultural differences, and militarization of Menkara had strong appeal to traditionalists in all parts of Menkara. Emboldened by this backing, SUPPORT pushed Soren for concessions, only to be met with total rejection.

Meanwhile, William's continued absence from the capital and insider rumors of the emotional depth of the split between Soren and William, encouraged the radical wing of SUPPORT led by

Lucien, to believe that a successful coup d'état might be possible. With William defending him, Soren had been invulnerable to domestic discontent. But with the current level of discontent among both the aristocracy and commoners and with William no longer willing to come to Soren's aid, Lucien came to believe that at long last the tyrant Soren could be defeated, believed that a coup d'état if attempted could succeed. But could the moderate wing of SUPPORT led by Grassic be convinced? Without support of the moderates, any coup attempt would fail.

To win support from the moderates for a coup, Lucien had to convince them of three points. First, there was no hope for meaningful reform while Soren was king. Second, the rift between William and Soren was so deep that if a coup were attempted, William would not come to Soren's aid. Third, if SUPPORT were to set up a rival government and announce its popular reforms, then with William on the sidelines, a majority of provincial lords and many important figures in the central administration would abandon Soren and support the rival government. The coup would succeed with a minimum of violence.

Lucien's propaganda campaign succeeded. Among the first to be convinced was Grassic. With her help, the radicals convinced the moderate majority that a coup was justified and given William's abandonment of Soren that there was an excellent chance it would succeed. Shortly thereafter SUPPORT endorsed the plans for a coup d'état presented by Lucien.

Ideally Lucien would have liked to arrest Soren, and to announce the change of regimes as a done deal. But given the heavily armed palace guard that protected Soren everywhere he went, there was no feasible way to arrest the king. Instead, SUPPORT decided to coordinate public announcements of the rival government on the same day in all provinces of Menkara. They would also announce the formation of a revolutionary junta that would implement needed reforms such as lower taxes, the end of forced conscription into the army, and decentralization of power on many issues. Finally, a committee of representatives from all the provinces would draw up a constitution for Menkara including a bill of rights and rules for the election of a constitutional monarch, a king bound by the constitution. A list of prominent Menkarans who supported the new regime would be published. Appeals would be made for all others to join in that support.

The plotters counted on support from three powerful aides of Soren: Chancellor Mentaxes, General Danton, and the arch-sorcerer William. To their shock, when they announced their coup, none of these power players, joined the rebellion, not even Mentaxes, who agreed with their ideology, nor William who hated Soren. Mentaxes said that the declaration of a rival government was treason. Worse, it would restart the civil wars that had devastated Menkara for twenty years. As good as the reforms the rebels advocated were, the method they had chosen was indefensible.

After Mentaxes denounced the rebels, General Danton, who would have defected if he had been sure the rebels would win despite the fact that his rise to prominence was solely due to Soren, declared his undying loyalty to the king and promised to crush the rebellion.

William was silent. He made no public comment on the coup. He did not reply to the plea of Soren to resume his old positions in the government and army. He did not reply to the plea of the rebels for his help in overthrowing Soren. The common explanation of the rejection of both sides by William, an explanation that I accept, was that William despised Lucien almost as much as he hated Soren for publically humiliating him by aborting his duel with Ariadne. He had never forgiven Lucien for insulting him repeatedly during the time he was clearing Soren's path to the throne.

The result of these important rejections of the coup d'état was that once again Menkara was on the brink of civil war.

CHAPTER 5

William was consumed by his need for revenge on Soren. He had long contemplated defecting to one of the neighboring kingdoms threatened by Soren's increasingly obvious expansionist ambitions. But he had not taken that decisive step because he doubted that he could persuade any of the rulers in those kingdoms to make the dangerous move of invading Menkara to depose Soren. So great was their fear of Soren, that if he offered to defect, they might even try to arrest him and hand him over to Soren.

But now the situation was very different. Soren's arrogance had provoked an attempted coup d'état. Because of the loyalty of Mentaxes and Danton, instead of a new government with Soren under arrest and dethroned, the coup attempt had resulted in rival governments claiming legitimacy, a situation that would surely result in a bloody civil war. Soren had not been deposed, but he had been greatly weakened. Both sides had tried to recruit William, but he had not been tempted. The only possible reason for accepting Soren's offer would have been to get close enough to assassinate him. But that was not the type of revenge that William craved. He wanted to not merely slay Soren but to publically humiliate him. Assassinating Soren while working for him would in the eyes of history make Soren a martyr and William a cowardly murderer of a benefactor Fighting with the rebels, he could defeat and slay Soren in battle. Why not then accept the offer from the rebels? Because defeating Soren that way would be to aid Lucien, Menjaro and the other rebel leaders who were his bitter enemies, proud lords whom he had previously defeated in battle. They hated and feared him. He had no doubt that if with his help, Soren was defeated, they would latrer order his own assassination.

William's preferred scenario for revenge would be to take advantage of the current chaos in Menkara caused by the coup attempt that had pushed Menkara to the brink of civil war, and slip unnoticed out of the country and defect to a powerful neighboring kingdom. The kingdom he would defect to must meet two conditions – it must have a powerful army and an ambitious king who felt threatened by King Soren. He would paint a portrait of the power and dominion the ambitious king could attain with William working for him rather than for their mutual nemesis, King Soren. With William on his side, the ambitious king would not fear reprisals from Soren. Later, after he had become invaluable to the king, he would claim that Soren was plotting revenge against himself and the king who had granted him asylum. He would then argue that the safest option was to launch a preemptive strike against Menkara to depose Soren.

William thought long and hard about which kingdom met those conditions. The options for defection were Nesa, Mittani, and Galatia; the three kingdoms bordering Menkara. Their kings, he was certain, had been deeply impressed by the power of his military sorcery, sorcery that had cleared away the many obstacles blocking Soren's path to the throne. Possessed of strong conventional military forces, these kingdoms were now trying to recruit sorcerers to develop military sorcery of their own. But they were hopelessly far behind; far less powerful in sorcery than Menkara would be even without William. Hence until the outbreak of unrest in Menkara they had been trying to conciliate and appease Soren.

The strongest of these apprehensive neighbors was Galatia, currently ruled by King Radames VII. Radames was reputed to be a proud man who would like nothing better than to stand up to Soren if there was any chance of success. If Radames was a man that he could mesmerize and eventually dominate, Galatia would be his ideal destination. After much deliberation, William decided to risk everything by defecting to Galatia and offering his sorcery to King Radames VII of Galatia.

Both lords and commoners of the neighboring kingdoms had been troubled by the rapid sorcery-backed rise to power of King Soren in Menkara. Now that Soren had reunited Menkara, his increasingly obvious expansionist ambitions was creating fear and panic in these kingdoms. Galatia and Menkara throughout history had been bitter rivals for hegemony on the continent. In modern times, because of the feudal fragmentation of Menkara, Galatia had been the undisputed dominant regional power. But then the alliance of Soren with William had changed the balance of power on the continent. Galatia had nothing to match or combat the devastating power of William's sorcery. When rebels announced a coup d'état in Menkara, most Galatians assumed that with the aid of William, Soren would quickly crush the rebellion.

Two days after the coup was proclaimed, William came uninvited and without official protocol to Sardis, a large Galatian town near the Menkaran border. Government officials in Sardis were very surprised by his arrival and disconcerted when he asked to be taken to the capital city of Xanthos to meet with King Radames. The mayor of Sardis asked the sorcerer the purpose of his visit and why it was unofficial and unannounced. In peremptory tones, William replied that such information was for the king's ears only. Frantic with concern at the arrival of Soren's powerful sorcerer, and unsure whether the king would want to grant or deny his request for an audience, the mayor dispatched messengers to the capital to get instruction from the king.

Months earlier, King Radames had sent an agent to observe the sorcerer's duel between William, King Soren's necromancer, and Ariadne, the young sorceress representing the rebels. That agent had reported to Radames both the arrest of Ariadne and William's anger at Soren. Why had William now traveled to Galatia? The most likely reason was that the rift between King Soren and his sorcerer had been healed and King Soren had sent the sorcerer across the border to ask for the help of Galatia in crushing the uprising of the Menkaran nobility. But asking for help was not Soren's way of confronting difficulties. If King Soren had sent William, the crisis created by the rebellion of the Menkara nobles must be very serious.

Anxious to know for certain why King Soren's sorcerer had travelled to Galatia and even more anxious not to anger Soren by refusing to see his secret envoy, King Radames decide to meet with William. But Radames was a cautious man. The messengers returned to Sardis with the king's order that William was to be treated courteously and brought to the capital to meet with the king. But since his visit was unofficial he was to be surrounded by armed guards at all times and the windows of the carriage that would bring him to the capital were to be covered with dark cloth so that no one could identify the unexpected visitor. Only approved government officials would be allowed to talk with William. When the carriage arrived at the capital, the sorcerer was to be taken straight to the royal palace where he would meet first with Diamant, chancellor of Galatia and chief political advisor to King Radames. Only then if Diamant saw no danger in such a meeting, would William be allowed to meet with the king.

William was amused rather than offended by these precautions as they unfolded. All that mattered to him was that he would soon be meeting with Radames, the king of Galatia.

After arriving at the royal palace, William was escorted to Chancellor Diamant's office. The head of the security team that had escorted

William on the trip from Sardis announced "Chancellor, this is William, head of military sorcery for King Soren of Menkara. It has pleased his majesty, King Radames to grant him a royal audience." What the escort did not say, but Diamant knew and William correctly guessed was that William would have an audience with the king if and only if Diamant approved.

In the placating language he had decided to adopt, the chancellor addressed the visitor he thought was Soren's envoy. "Royal sorcerer of Menkara, we are honored, but puzzled by your visit. Can you tell me what message you bring from King Soren? Or may only the king of Galatia hear that message?"

William had thought long and hard about his opening statement. But he immediately realized that the phrasing of the chancellor's question had given him an even better opening. In a proud and angry voice, he replied, "Chancellor, I am no man's messenger, least of all King Soren's."

Diamant was so startled by William words and anger that he paused to reconsider the situation before replying. He focused on the contemptuous way the visitor had spit out the surprising phrase, "least of all King Soren's." That was promising, for it could only be good news for Galatia if the rift between King Soren and his powerful sorcerer persisted. On the other hand if the rift had been healed then the sorcerer's proclamation of hostility was a trap, probably laid by King Soren, himself. Was Soren trying to trick Galatia into demonstrating its hostility to himself in order to justify a Menkaran attack on Galatia?

It was essential to learn the true motivation of the sorcerer's visit. After a long hesitation, Diamant finally replied. "You are a bold man, William of Bezriel. You say you are not in Galatia as Soren's messenger. By what right then do you demand an audience with the king? And why should his royal highness King Ramades VII grant a private audience to a mere commoner?"

"As you well know, chancellor I am very much more than a mere commoner. I am a sorcerer with unique talents. As Galatia is in need of sorcery, I come to offer my sorcery to King Radames."

Diamant needed all of his lifetime of training in self-restraint to avoid showing his extreme surprise and uncertainty. The sorcerer's words seemed to imply that he was offering to defect to Galatia. If that were true, it would change the balance of power on the continent. That was Diamant's greatest wish, but such good luck was surely too good to be true.

"William, working with King Soren has brought you wealth and fame. Why do you now offer to desert and betray your benefactor. And why should King Radames accept the services of a man willing to desert and betray the king who has lifted up him from poverty and obscurity? Why should he not fear that you will also desert and betray him?"

William's reply was arrogant. "Know this, chancellor. I am not deserting and betraying Soren. Soren deserted and betrayed me on the fields outside The Temple of Origins where I was to fight the sorceress Ariadne to determine the fate of Bezriel. On that day, Soren publicly betrayed and humiliated me. I cannot work for such a man."

Diamant liked that answer, but still feared that the sorcerer's offer was part a devious plot by King Soren to test the goodwill of the king of Galatia. Accepting the sorcerer's offer might lead to war with Menkara.

Diamant's dilemma was that the sorcerer's offer to defect might or might not be sincere. He tended to believe it was sincere, for even if William and Soren had again become allies, why would Soren send his powerful military sorcerer on a relatively minor diplomatic probe just as civil war was breaking out in Menkara?

Ever the realist, Diamant recognized that if the sorcerer really was offering to defect, there could be no doubt that giving sanctuary to the turncoat would incur the wrath of Soren and lead to war between Galatia and Menkara. But if the offer to defect was sincere, rejecting William's offer would be to pass up the chance of a lifetime to make Galatia the dominant power on the continent. What advice should he give the king?

"William," said the Chancellor ending the meeting, "only King Radames can decide whether or not to accept your offer. I will go now to inform the king of the purpose of your visit. Then you will be summoned to meet with the king."

Chancellor Diamant informed the king of William's seeming anger at King Soren and his offer to defect to Galatia. Both men were acutely aware that the offer if sincere would change the balance of power on the continent. But both knew there was a very real possibility that the offer was insincere, part of a devious trap being laid by the notoriously cunning King Soren. They discussed in detail how the king should handle the interview with the sorcerer.

After a wait that seemed eternal to William, but was actually less than an hour, he was escorted to the royal receiving room to meet with King Radames and three of his advisors: Chancellor Diamant, General Ptolemy, and Archbishop Khofu. General Ptolemy despite his lack of battlefield experience was the officer in charge of the Galatian military. He yearned for a war so that he could prove himself in battle. Archbishop Khofu, a very old man, was a high official in the Ventaxian Church and a good friend of the high priestess Grassic, one of the conspirators who had plotted to dethrone Soren. Archbishop Khofu was a universally liked and respected religious leader and long-time advisor of King Radames. After William entered the room and was standing respectfully at attention, Diamant introduced him. "Your majesty, I present to you William, head of military sorcery for King Soren of Menkara. It has pleased your majesty to grant William a royal audience." In his introduction, Diamant said nothing about William's offer to defect to Galatia. After a few minutes of polite formalities, King Radames rectified that omission.

"William, I have been informed by Chancellor Diamant of your offer of your services to Galatia. Does King Soren know and approve of your offer?"

This was the decisive moment. If William admitted Soren knew nothing of his visit, the die was cast and there was no turning back. But his talks with his escorts and what was revealed when he was questioned by Chancellor Diamant had convinced him that Galatia would prove a fertile operating station for his plans to launch an invasion of Menkara to vanquish his archenemy King Soren. It was clear to William that both King Radames and Chancellor Diamant feared Soren, but under the changed circumstances, his own defection and civil war in Menkara, he was confident that he would eventually persuade king and chancellor to invade Menkara. He was already confident that Diamant relished the opportunity.

William's reply to King Radames' question was direct and implied more than was directly said. "No, your majesty. King Soren knows neither of my visit, nor my offer. If it please your majesty, let us not waste time with cautious diplomatic fencing. Soren has mortally offended me and I can no longer work for him. I offer my services to Galatia in return for Galatia financing my research expanding the limits of sorcery."

"William, your offer is very tempting. But you are proposing to defect from Menkara to Galatia. Given your importance to Soren's war machine, he will regard your defection as treason. In fact, my acceptance might mean war between Menkara and Galatia. I am not prepared to go to war with the mighty war machine that King Soren has built up."

William was unhappy with the king's reply, but in his reply, he hid his disappointment well, knowing it was far too early to suggest war with Menkara. "Your majesty is correct that King Soren will be very displeased with my defection and with you granting me asylum. But know this, after Soren publically humiliated me at The Temple of Origins, he and I have become deadly enemies. I will never work for that vainglorious king again. Know also that before the insurrection of the Menkaran nobility, he was preparing to expand his reign beyond the Menkaran borders. The rich kingdom of Galatia would have been one of his first targets. But after my defection, your power will be greater than his. Soren will, indeed, be unhappy. But he will be powerless to effectively vent his anger on me or on you."

King Radames was very pleased with William's answer. But he wanted to confer privately with Diamant, Khofu, and Ptolemy, before finishing his questioning of William and making a decision. Even the bold declaration by William that he and Soren were now bitter enemies did not prove that the whole visit by the sorcerer to Galatia was not a farce written by Soren and performed by William. Hence the king asked the palace guards to escort William to another room while he consulted with his advisors.

After William was escorted from the room, Radames spoke. "If William truly defects from Menkara to Galatia, military dominance in the region moves with him. That seems an unexpected gift from the gods. But I am sure we all share the same doubt. Is William's offer what it seems? Or is it a trap laid by Soren to justify an invasion of Galatia? Give me your honest opinions. Hold nothing back. I need to know what you really think."

General Ptolemy replied first. "Your majesty, I hope the rift between King Soren and his military sorcerer has persisted and that the sorcerer is truly abandoning the Menkaran king and enlisting in your service. I hope this because that would not only seriously weaken Menkara as an external threat, it would make Galatia the strongest power on the continent. That is what I hope. But I share your majesty's fears that the sorcerer has been sent here by Soren as part of some devious plot. I share your fears, but do not know whether those fears are justified."

"I am disappointed by your uncertainty, Ptolemy, but I thank you for your honesty. Hopefully Diamant or Khofu can resolve our uncertainty."

Chancellor Diamant rose to speak. "Your majesty, in my long career in politics, I have frequently been lied to by ambitious knaves seeking favors and foreign diplomats seeking to gain concessions or an edge. Survival instinct and experience has taught me to know when I am being lied to. I am not infallible, but I am usually right. In my opinion, the Menkaran sorcerer is telling the truth when he says that his quarrel with King Soren is deep and real. He truly hates King Soren and wants to defect to Galatia. This is confirmed by the reports of our agents in Menkara, reports that Soren and William quarreled bitterly after Soren aborted his duel with the sorceress Ariadne and that the rift has never been healed. William has not been seen at court since that day. In my opinion, William's offer to defect is real and should be accepted."

"Thank you, Diamant. Khofu?"

The old bishop rose slowly to his feet. The physical pain it cost him was obvious to those who knew him. "In my opinion, your majesty should reject the sorcerer's offer. Reject him, not because he has made you a deceitful offer. I agree with Diamant, that the sorcerer really does want to defect to Galatia. Reject him not because employing him will anger King Soren. Of course, defection will anger Soren, but as William himself said, after the defection, Soren will be powerless to wreck vengeance on Galatia. I say reject him, because once he is in your employ, he will betray you just as his coming to you betrays his current master. My friend Grassic, high priestess of the Ventaxian church in Menkara knows William. She is an excellent judge of character. She tells me that William does not know the meaning of loyalty and cannot be trusted."

The discussion that followed was heated and lasted more than hour. The most important points in persuading the king made were made by Diamant. First, he drove home the point that both he and Khofu had already made that after the defection of William, Soren would not dare attack Galatia. Second, he pointed out that sorcery had many uses other than military. William's powers could be used to improve the economy of Galatia and make it the most prosperous nation on the continent. Diamant's points mollified Khofu somewhat, but did not change his mind, since his objections were based on his negative evaluation of William's character.

Radames was unhappy that he had received contradictory recommendations. But he had nonetheless reached a decision.

Bishop Khofu was his closest friend, but Radames like Diamant and unlike Khofu was most impressed by the power shift that the defection of the sorcerer would create. His decision was that William would be granted asylum in Galatia and would with no public fanfare be appointed as king's minister in charge of both military and economic sorcery. But until his transfer of allegiance was definitively verified, he would be kept under round the clock surveillance and would be arrested if it were learned that his defection was a ploy engineered by Soren.

CHAPTER 6

The coup had failed but important regions of Menkara no longer recognized Soren as king, no longer recognized his right to rule. In the short run, Soren's grandiose plans of territorial expansion had been replaced by the prospect of renewed civil war.

Even though, William had refused an appeal by King Soren to resume his duties and help crush the rebellion, Soren was not at first worried by the sorcerer's prolonged intransigence. He was sure that he could squash the rebels with his powerful conventional army and a more than competent group of loyal military sorcerers, all of whom had been recruited and trained by William himself. He was confident that poverty and isolation would eventually overcome pride and force William to return to duty.

Before learning of William's defection, Soren, even though confident he would crush the rebels, had been in a foul mood because of the treachery of lords he thought he had tamed. He also cursed the extra time and money that would be needed to crush the rebels without William's sorcery.

Three days after the botched coup, King Soren learned that William had disappeared. Incessant probes yielded no information. It was another four days before the king learned from one of his foreign agents posted in Galatia that William had defected to that neighboring kingdom. That news sent Soren into a towering rage. He screamed to his attendants about the ingratitude of a man he had rescued from being burned at the stake. After his rage exhausted itself, he instructed his attendants to find Chancellor Mentaxes, General Danton, and the sorcerer Petrov, and tell them to report immediately to the strategy room to meet with the king. Petrov did not have the lofty rank of the others summoned, but he had been one of William's most skilled assistants. Soren had need of a sorcerer who understood the range and depth of William's sorcery at the emergency strategy conference.

Soren was now angry at himself for wrongly assuming that William would have to come crawling back. It was inexcusable that he had not seen treason coming. That made life miserable for everyone who had business with the king; for when Soren was angry at himself, it was his subordinates who suffered.

Civil insurrection and the William's continued refusal to return to work had been bad for King Soren, but the sorcerer's defection to a rival kingdom was far worse. William's military sorcery had revolutionized warfare and made Soren not only king of Menkara, but the most powerful and feared king on the continent. Even now after the defection, Menkara still had the best equipped and largest conventional army. But other kingdoms had very powerful armies, even if not quite as big, and certainly not as battle-tested. Unfortunately Soren's dream of empire stemmed not from the edge in power provided by his battle-proven conventional army, but from the unrivaled military sorcery of William. The sorcerer's defection to Galatia radically changed the balance of power on the continent and Soren knew it. Whatever kingdom had the use of William's military sorcery had a decisive military advantage. That advantage had now shifted from Menkara to Galatia, from King Soren to King Radames.

Because of this one act of treachery, Soren's vaunting but realistic ambition of empire was dead; replaced by a newborn fear that he might be overthrown by the new alliance of William with Galatia. But in all honesty, Soren had no right to complain of treachery, since he had long considered having William assassinated if the threat that the sorcerer posed ever became greater than his usefulness. Soren and William, despite being extremely useful to each other, had never trusted each other. Each man recognized and feared the overweening pride and ambition of the other. Soren had only himself to blame for his current dilemma. Renowned for his ruthlessness, he had committed the cardinal political sin of letting pride overbalance realism in his treatment of William.

The meeting that day of Soren with his aides was grim. The political and military crises caused by the defection were so serious that the emotional blame-assigning analysis of how William had managed to slip unnoticed out of the country was postponed until a later day.

The discussion of how the defection would impact the campaign to squash the rebellion was short. Immediately after Lucien's announcement of a rival government, Soren had sent Mentaxes to ask William to return to duty with full restoration of his rank and privileges. The sorcerer had coldly said no. That gave rise to anxiety that William might join the rebels. But a day later Soren learned that William had also turned down an invitation to join the rebels. As a result, King Soren, in consultation with General Danton, had developed a strategy to defeat the rebels without the help of William. Whether and how that strategy would have to be modified because of William's defection to Galatia would depend upon military requirements to deal with the increased power of Galatia and whether Galatia and William would provide aid to the rebels.

After learning of the defection of William, the most important issue confronting Soren and his advisors was whether Galatia, emboldened by William's transfer of allegiance would try to invade Menkara. The practical associated question was whether Soren's forces could repel a William-aided attack. Soren asked the foreign affairs expert Chancellor Mentaxes to open the discussion of whether the Galatians, drunk with their new power, would dare to invade Menkara.

Mentaxes reply was comprehensive. "The Galatians surely knew that granting asylum to the renegade William would create a very tense and hostile relationship between Galatia and Menkara. Why then did King Radames grant him asylum? In my opinion because the defection of William presented him with an unexpected opportunity to dramatically weaken Menkara and strengthen Galatia. Will King Radames be content with shifting the balance of power in Galatia's favor? Or will he choose to actually use the military sorcery of William against Menkara? At this time, it is only possible to make an educated guess as to what they will do. What I am certain of is that William will urge King Radames to invade Menkara and depose Soren as king. Will Radames acquiescence and invade? Based on what I thought I knew of the cautious sovereign Radames, I would have said "no." But the cautious Radames I thought I knew would never have granted asylum to a dangerous renegade such as William.

"King Radames has no experience of war and reportedly is more interested in creating a legacy of economic prosperity and cultural brilliance for Galatia than in increasing the military power of Galatia. Nevertheless the sorcery-aided rise to power of you, your majesty, must have worried him greatly. Responding to the pleas of General Ptolemy he has approved major increases in the Galatian military budget, He also ordered an intensive hunt to locate and recruit military sorcerers. There are many in Galatia that yearn for Galatia to reassert its dominance on the continent. Both General Ptolemy and the chancellor, Diamant, are known to be of that mind set. The civil war now beginning in Menkara weakens us and is encouraging to those that yearn to reassert the glory of Galatia. The defection of William will embolden the Galatian war-hawks and bring declaring war on and invading Menkara to the top of their agenda.

"Fortunately other factors work against such a militant policy. King Radames is a cautious man. Even if war-hawks persuade him that Menkara must be invaded and you, King Soren, driven from power, there are three complex issues, that Radames must deal with that will lengthen the time before he will be ready to order an invasion. First, Radames, I believe, will insist that before he orders an invasion of Menkara that his strategists work out a safe and detailed strategy that makes maximal use of the sorcery of William.

"Second, Radames and the Galatians must figure out how to effectively use William while guarding against the possibility that the sorcerer who has just betrayed Menkara will also betray Galatia. Third, Radames and the Galatians must decide how to relate to the other nations on the continent in the suddenly transformed military/political context. With William working for Galatia, will Galatia be content with being recognized as first among equals? Or will King Ramades or the powers behind his throne seek hegemony, strive for Galatia to become the new dominant power, perhaps with an ambition stretching to continental conquest? Fortunately for us, resolving these three issues that will take a lot of time.

"An important factor that works against us is the incipient civil war in Menkara. The fact that it weakens us undoubtedly will hasten the onset of a Galatian invasion. Even worse would be an alliance of Galatia with the Menkaran rebel lords. An alliance of Radames with Lucien's rebels is possible. But I believe both the rebels and the Galatians will reject such an alliance. Even if Radames promises and William guarantees military victory for Lucien and the rebels, alliance with Galatian invaders would destroy the claim to legitimacy that the rebels are desperate to claim. Hence most likely the rebels would reject such an alliance. Much more certain is that William who haughtily declined an offer to join the rebels before defecting will surely try to dissuade Radames from forming such an alliance.

"Unfortunately, a much more powerful and much more likely alliance against Menkara is likely to be formed, an alliance of Galatia with Nesa and Mittani, the other two kingdoms bordering

Menkara. All three of those kingdoms fear you, King Soren. With William on their side, sooner or later an alliance between them to invade Menkara is all too likely.

"It is much too early to be certain, but in my opinion, for Galatia, the value of building an anti-Soren regional alliance in which its voice is dominant will outweigh the advantage of striking quickly to take advantage of the defection of William and the outbreak of civil war in Menkara. In my opinion, if and when an anti-Menkara regional alliance under the hegemony of Galatia is created, an all-out allied attack on Menkara, heavily dependent on the sorcery of William will be launched."

Soren nodded grimly while Mentaxes spoke, but when the old man was finished, he made no comment. He simply called upon General Danton to assess the transformed military situation.

Danton began by noting that if an anti-Menkaran alliance was formed, the allied invading army would be significantly larger than the defending Menkaran army, but inferior in the quality of its armaments. More importantly, whereas Menkaran officers and troops were battle-tested veterans, the officers and troops of Galatia and its likely allies would be full of academy trained officers with no experience of making decisions in the chaos that is war and of green recruits untested as yet in battle. Danton was confident that the conventional army of Menkara could repel an invasion by the conventional armies of any Galatian-led alliance.

"But, King Soren," he continued, "as your unification of Menkara proved, wars are no longer decided by conventional armies. The military sorcery introduced by William, has changed everything. Your majesty, in your campaign to reunify Menkara, no army that we faced was able to hold out against your armies aided by William. The question now becomes 'Can your armies and the military sorcerers who remain loyal to you repel an invasion aided by William?' Even with the treasonous defection of William, your Menkaran army is much stronger in both conventional armaments and military sorcery than any enemy William has ever confronted. But is it strong enough to fend off a powerful foreign army supported by William? I humbly apologize, your majesty, but I simply do not know."

"Thank you general. That is why I invited Petrov, one of William's assistant sorcerers to this meeting. Petrov, can you answer General Danton's question. Can you and my other loyal sorcerer's repel an attack by William?"

Petrov, a foreign mercenary, had never before given a report directly to the king and hence was extremely nervous. Nevertheless, his reply was courageously blunt. "Your majesty, I and the other sorcerer's working for you have learned much from our training by William. Our skills have developed beyond what we dared dream possible. But even so, individually we are no match for William. Collectively we might hold him at bay for a short time, but eventually he would break through our resistance as he did against every opponent he fought against when working for you."

"Not every opponent, Petrov," interposed Soren. "William was not able to penetrate the invisibility shield erected by the Free Bezriel sorceress, Ariadne."

Petrov was flustered, unsure how to respond. Finally he said, "It is true your highness that William could not penetrate the invisibility shield. But not because of the Free Bezriel sorceress. She is naught but a young untrained wizard incapable on her own of defeating William. William has told me that it was the ancient Seekers of Bezriel that frustrated him, not the young sorceress. And he was sure he would soon learn how to defeat them."

Soren lost his temper. "Are you a fool, Petrov? The sorceress Ariadne is young and untrained you say. Yes, she is young, but she was well enough trained to transform Free Bezriel from an irrelevant gadfly into a dangerous guerrilla threat. It was not she but the Seekers, you say, that erected the shield for her. So what? It is still the case that with the help of the Seekers, she frustrated William! If we recruit her to work for us against William, the Seekers will join her. If they helped her against William with the invisibility shield, why will they not do so again? With the sorceress Ariadne and the Seekers on our side we can defeat William!"

Only the old man, Mentaxes, had the courage to try to dampen the king's new found optimism. But he tried to do it diplomatically. "Your highness focuses on the crucial fact that even if Ariadne is young and her powers borrowed, she may with the help of the Seekers be William's equal. But problems remain. She is now your prisoner awaiting trial for treason. She has openly avowed her hatred of you personally and sees Menkara as the oppressor and enslaver of her people, Bezriel. I doubt that we can persuade her to fight for us."

Soren was still angry, but his voice was calm. "Failure is not an option. We are in a crisis. We will pursue, two very different strategies for dealing with the crisis. First, we must try to assassinate William. We have undercover agents already in Galatia. Today I will send agents trained in assassination across the border. If those agents succeed, we will invade and conquer Galatia. If those agents fail, we must find a sorcerer capable of resisting William. The only sorcerer with that kind of power that we know of is Ariadne, the Free Bezriel witch in our dungeons awaiting trial. We must convince her to join us.

"To repeat, failure is not an option. Mentaxes, it is your duty to convince her to join us. You will use your vaunted powers of diplomatic persuasion to convince her to fight with Menkara against William. How difficult can that be, since if she says no, she will be tried for treason and executed, but if she says yes, she will be freed and given rank, privilege, and wealth? Meet with me after dinner this evening to discuss how to persuade the witch to join us; the rewards I will give her if she joins us and the penalties for herself, her family, and Bezriel that I will inflict if she refuses."

A long and heated discussion followed, focused on how to deal simultaneously with both William's defection and the traitorous rebels. Soren simply did not have a big enough army, nor enough military sorcerers, to both crush the rebellion and prepare for a William-led Galatian invasion. Danton argued for focusing first on crushing the rebellion, since an invasion had not yet begun, and might never occur. Mentaxes argued that although it had not yet occurred, a William-led invasion from Galatia was by far the more dangerous threat and must take absolute priority. For now he advocating ignoring Lucien and his rebel government unless they were foolhardy enough to launch an attack on Soren's forces. Mentaxes repeated his assertion that because of William's hatred of the rebel lords, an alliance between those rebels and King Radames was extremely unlikely. Soren sided with Mentaxes and that settled the issue. Their priority would be preparation for war with Galatia.

Political and diplomatic aspects of the struggle could not be ignored. It was decided that tomorrow the king would publically announce the defection of the traitor William. The role of William in the reunification of Menkara would be downplayed. Long term threats from Galatia to the peace and prosperity of Menkara would be emphasized. A strongly worded protest alleging domestic interference would be sent to Galatia, but diplomatic ties would not yet be broken. In drawing up this strategy, hope for success rested on the ability of Mentaxes to convince Ariadne to join in the defense of Menkara against William and Galatia.

How to obey Soren's command and persuade the young Bezrielite sorceress, Ariadne, to use her powers of sorcery to help defeat the threatened invasion? That was the problem that Chancellor Mentaxes wrestled with between his two meetings with Soren that day. He knew that Soren's suggestion of bribing her with wealth and honors had no chance of working. It was clear to the old man that he had to cast his offer in terms that appealed to what mattered most to Ariadne – her love of Bezriel and her deeply ethical sense of right and wrong. Reports of her remorseful withdrawal from military duty after her devastation of Cerberus implied she would never again try to free Bezriel by what she regarded as immoral means. Hence she would never agree to help Soren, a ruler she regarded as cruel and immoral, no matter what the reward.

But if he presented her with a chance to win freedom and independence for Bezriel in return for using her sorcery to protect the people of Menkara from a brutal invasion by an army led by the Bezrielite turncoat, William, she might see acceptance of that offer as her ethical duty. Surely that was an offer the moralistic sorceress could not refuse! A tougher task for Mentaxes would be to convince Soren to allow him to make such an offer.

That night Chancellor Mentaxes met with King Soren to discuss the recruitment of Ariadne. To his surprise, the king was already in the conference room when he arrived ten minutes early. As soon as Mentaxes entered the room, the king spoke. "Old friend, you have had all day to think. What strategy will you employ to recruit the witch?"

"Indeed, sire, I have thought of nothing else. What strategy has the best chance of working depends on Ariadne's character, on her values and goals. I recalled the times that I talked with her. I reviewed the dossier we prepared on her in preparation for her trial for treason. And without giving away what was at stake. I summoned and talked with Bernard her defense attorney. I did not meet with Peter, the Bezrielite who betrayed her. Peter knows her much better than Bernard, but he is so consumed by anger and hatred that I do not think anything he might say about Ariadne could be trusted."

Despite this long preface, Soren listened patiently and made no effort to force Mentaxes to get to the point faster. For once, he appreciated the old man's systematic approach. The chancellor continued. "How can we persuade Ariadne to use her powers in our fight against William and Galatia? Threats in my opinion, would have no chance of success. What could we threaten? She is already charged with the capital crime of treason. If we were to threaten preordained conviction and burning at the stake, that would only appeal to her martyr-syndrome. Even if she were weak and in her weakness agreed to work for us to save herself, she might have a change of heart at any time and would not be reliable in the fight against William. Threatening her family would be even more certain to backfire. She would hate and despise us, and the hatred would be personal. We would not dare rely on her."

After a pause, in which he waited for questions from Soren which did not come, the old man continued. "Bribes, such a monetary rewards and honors would be better than threats since we want to win her goodwill or at least her willing cooperation. But according to those who know her and our own experts who have studied and interrogated her, monetary rewards and honors would have little if any chance of persuading Ariadne to act against her principles. The only thing we can offer that would induce Ariadne to willingly fight for us is to offer what she most wants: independence for Bezriel and freedom for her Free Bezriel comrades. She was willing to die for that when with Free Bezriel. I think she would be willing to live and join with us in the fight against William for those same goals."

By the time Mentaxes finished, Soren was glowering. "You are a brave man, Mentaxes, to tell me that to save my kingdom from destruction from without, I must tear it apart from within. Fortunately for you, I know you speak the truth. I agree with your analysis. I am convinced that a William-led invasion by Galatia is coming. That invasion must be defeated and the sorcery of the Bezrielite witch gives us our best chance. Therefore, promise her what you must to gain her cooperation, even autonomy for Bezriel."

"Excuse me, your majesty. I said that she wants independence for Bezriel. You give me authority to offer autonomy. What if autonomy is not enough, and she demands independence?"

"It is your job to make sure it is enough. If she sees that we are unyielding on this point, she will agree. If she thinks, we are desperate, she will insist on independence. Be sure that she knows that while we will grant autonomy to Bezriel within a unified Menkara, we will never sanction the dissolution of the kingdom that we unified at such great cost!"

Mentaxes hoped that the king's emphatic rejection of independence for Bezriel was just the bluster of a proud man trying to save face. But he feared that soon he would have to put his belief in the pragmatism of Soren to the test and tell him that a sine qua non for Ariadne's help was independence for Bezriel.

The immediate tactical issue for Mentaxes was whether to let Ariadne learn of William's defection by the prison grapevine or from a visit from her lawyer or to himself break the news to her. That was a no brainer. By breaking the news himself, he could frame for her the issues posed by William's defection. Whereas if she learned of it beforehand, when he did meet with her, she might already understand the new situation in ways incompatible with accepting Soren's offer. He therefore ordered her held incommunicado until his visit when he would break the news of William's defection and of Soren's offer.

He would do it himself, but not for another day yet. Before speaking with Ariadne, he would speak with her parents to try to enlist their support in persuading their daughter to accept the offer. If they were in favor of acceptance, persuading Ariadne would be much, much easier. But the parents were in Bezriel, a half day's ride away. He had already sent a convoy led by an officer known to Sarah and Daniel to bring them to the capital to meet first with himself and later with their daughter. He would meet with the parents early tomorrow morning and then later in the day, present Ariadne with the offer. He would tell her that before making a decision, she could discuss the offer with her parents who had been brought to the capital.

Sarah and Daniel were tired after their stagecoach ride to the capital. But anxiety overrode their exhaustion. Shortly after they heard the startling announcement that William had defected to Galatia, couriers from King Soren had arrived with orders to escort them to the capital. It seemed clear that the two events were related, but the connection between them was obscure. Did the defection of William bode ill or bode well for their daughter? Since both were possible, Sarah and Daniel were bundles of nerves. The little sleep they got before being escorted early the next morning to a meeting with Chancellor Mentaxes was restless and hagridden.

They had previously met Mentaxes in the days after Cerberus had aborted the witchcraft trial by overpowering the military convoy escorting Sarah, Abigail and William to court and then brought the freed prisoners to safety in Thorheim. Sarah and Mentaxes had met again during the diplomatic negotiations between the Free Bezriel guerrillas and King Soren. Sarah and Daniel were relieved to be meeting with Mentaxes, who had impressed them as an ethical man, rather than with Soren, a man they feared and mistrusted.

After preliminary formalities, Mentaxes got straight to the point. "You have, no doubt, heard of the defection of the king's sorcerer William to Galatia?"

"Yes, sire" said Daniel. "The news reached Bezriel very shortly before we were summoned to the capital."

"William's defection is bad news for Menkara, but may be good news for your daughter."

Again it was Daniel who replied. "Good news? In what way, sire?"

"King Soren wants to improve his military. He has graciously decided to grant pardons to all who fought against him in the late wars, if they enlist in his military regiments now. Thus your daughter has a chance to avoid trial and regain her freedom."

"Ariadne will never buy her freedom by fighting for an enemy of Bezriel," was Sarah's angry reaction.

"Control your temper, Mistress Sarah, and hear me out. I summoned you to the capital to give you the opportunity to save your daughter by convincing her to use her powers not to protect Soren, but rather to protect the people of Menkara, people she has known all her life"

Mentaxes shrewd rephrasing of the looming conflict had the desired impact of making Ariadne's parents more receptive to further discussion. In the dialog that followed Sarah and Daniel saw through the diplomatic subterfuges of Mentaxes and got him to admit that a general amnesty was part of Soren's strategy to enlist their daughter, a very powerful sorceress, in his looming fight against William and a Galatian-led coalition.

Finally Daniel brought up the decisive point. "Both Soren and William are deadly enemies of Bezriel. Why should Ariadne, why should any Bezrielite, take sides in an oncoming battle between our enemies? Better for us if our enemies destroy each other. We are sorry for the misery and devastation that the common people of all the warring nations will suffer, but Bezrielites have no reason to take sides in the war that now seem imminent."

Mentaxes had been waiting for this moment. "No reason! There is every reason for Bezriel and Ariadne to takes sides. King Soren has instructed me to inform Ariadne and to inform all of Bezriel that if she uses her powers to defend Menkara against William, he will grant full autonomy to Bezriel. Do you think there is any chance that Galatia and William will treat Bezriel so gently?"

From that point on Sarah and Daniel went from opposition to Soren's proposal to qualified approval, liking its basic terms, but with serious concerns about the exact details of the offer. There were two sticking points. First was the need for guarantees that Soren would honor his promises to Ariadne and Bezriel if the invasion were defeated. That was major, since Ariadne and her Free Bezriel comrades were in prison because they had believed and relied on an earlier solemn promise of Soren, a promise which the king had ruthlessly cast aside. The second problem was that Soren had promised autonomy to Bezriel, not independence. Sarah and Daniel were among those Bezrielites who that believed that autonomy within a strong Menkara was a better option. But would Ariadne, a member of the outlawed Free Bezriel, ally herself with the king she despised in order to obtain mere autonomy?

Sarah and Daniel conveyed these reservations to the Chancellor. They found a simple solution that hopefully would be acceptable to all interested parties, including both Free Bezriel and King Soren, on the question of independence for Bezriel or autonomy within the kingdom of Menkara. A binding referendum of Bezrielites would settle the issue.

The second issue was more difficult. What possible safeguards could there be to guarantee that if the invasion were defeated that Soren would keep his word and honor his promise of independence or autonomy to Bezriel? The solution the three agreed on relied on diplomacy, public opinion, and realistic threat of reprisals. The deal, independence or autonomy for Bezriel as well as full pardons for Ariadne and the other Free Bezriel guerrillas in return for the help of Ariadne and the guerrillas in the fight against the threatened invasion would be embedded in a widely publicized compact between Menkara and Bezriel, signed by Soren, Kaitlin, and the chair of the Bezrielite Council of Elders. Another, perhaps more important safeguard was that if the invasion were defeated, Soren would not dare to renege, because if he did, Ariadne would withdraw her support, leaving Soren alone to face a new William-backed invasion, an invasion that would probably succeed.

It was agreed that Mentaxes would meet with Ariadne later that day, tell her of the defection of William and Soren's offer of and amnesty for all Free Bezriel guerrillas who volunteered to fight against the William-aided invasion and also tell her of Soren's promise of autonomy or independence, for Bezriel, if she accepted the offer. Ariadne would be given a day and a night to decide and would be allowed to discuss the offer with her parents. But before presenting the offer to Ariadne, Mentaxes must first meet with Soren to try to get his approval of both the binding referendum and Daniel and Sarah's demand for guarantees that he would honor his promises to Bezriel.

Soren's reaction to the condition that Sarah and Daniel were placing on acceptance of his offer to free their daughter was predictable. How dare mere commoners question and impugn the integrity of their king! How dare commoners doubt that their king would keep his promise of a binding referendum on autonomy or independence for Bezriel! How dare petitioners for mercy for a daughter who had committed treason demand an iron-clad guarantee that he, the king, would honor his promise! How dare lowly subjects of the realm question and impugn the integrity of their king!

Mentaxes knew better than to remind Soren of past promises he had broken. The king knew full-well that not only was he capable of breaking a promise, but that he would break this one if it became profitable to do so. The king's anger was over the fact that mere commoners dared to voice doubts about his integrity, even when their daughter's life hung in the balance. Hence Mentaxes reply focused on two aspects of the reality of the crisis. They needed Ariadne and assistance of the parents would be very helpful in gaining Ariadne's consent.

Fortunately, the threat of an invasion employing William had restored pragmatism and realism to Soren's decision making and with one condition, he agreed to the terms of Sarah and Daniel. The condition was that since the crisis was immediate, Ariadne must agree to join the fight against William now even though it would take time to negotiate details for the referendum to settle the question of independence or autonomy for Bezriel.

By the time the deal was finalized, it was late evening. That necessitated modifying the time schedule: early tomorrow Mentaxes would meet with Ariadne, tell her of William's defection and the king's offer, and inform her that she would be allowed to talk with her parents and lawyer before replying to the offer.

The next morning, Ariadne was very surprised when she was told she was being taken to meet with Chancellor Mentaxes. She knew that such a meeting meant an important new development, and although she liked the old man, she feared that a summons to meet with the chancellor probably meant bad news, possibly a decision to execute her without a public trial in which she could defend herself.

The meeting took place in a comfortable but austere conference room, not in the dungeon-like room where prisoners usually met approved visitors. After Ariadne was escorted into the room, Mentaxes dismissed the two guards that were her escorts and told Ariadne to take the seat to his right. After the guards left, using humor to hide her fear, Ariadne said "Are you not afraid to be alone in a room with a witch who is your avowed enemy."

Mentaxes' reply was grave. "I am not afraid, Ariadne. We are not enemies."

"Since I mean you no harm, I am pleased that you are not afraid. But how can you say that we are not enemies, when you are chancellor to the king who wants to execute me as an enemy of the state?"

"Much has happened, Ariadne, since you were arrested. Please listen carefully as I tell you what has happened, the new situation that exists, and how these events affect you and affect Bezriel." Mentaxes then told Ariadne of the attempted coup d'état, the probable renewal of civil war in Menkara, and the defection of William to the neighboring kingdom of Galatia.

Ariadne interrupted the story being told. "I did not anticipate these events, but they all flow naturally from the overweening arrogance of Soren. He made the proud independent lords of Menkara, his vassals. That they should respond by rebelling and reasserting their traditional rights once William withdrew his support from Soren is not surprising.

"Nor is the defection of William surprising. In agreeing to work for Soren, the enemy of Bezriel, William proved that his only allegiance is to himself. His defection from Menkara to Galatia, merely proves that point again. I can see why that rebellion and that defection upsets Soren and yourself, but I do not see why it brings you to visit me in prison."

"I think you are being disingenuous, Ariadne. I think you know or at least can guess the reason for my coming to talk with you. Galatia would not have accepted William as a defector, knowing that would infuriate King Soren, unless they intended to use him to attack Menkara and overthrow Soren. Given both the anger of William at Soren and the rampaging of an invading army, the resulting devastation of the people and lands of Menkara, including the people and lands of Bezriel will be horrifying. You are the only sorcerer who has ever been able to thwart William. You were arrested when about to fight a duel with William. I am here to appeal to you to use your powers to try to thwart this attack on our homeland by your sworn enemy, the renegade Bezrielite, William."

Ariadne hesitated before replying. "You speak eloquently to my heart. But my common sense tells me that it was not the people of Menkara who sent you to ask for my help. It is Soren who is asking my help to save his sorry hide. I am of peasant stock and do not have the cunning mind of a politician for whom buying the aid of an enemy is normal everyday commerce and who assumes that switching allegiance is a practical question of advantage not an ethical issue of right and wrong. Behind your pretty words that I would be defending the common people, you are offering me the job of defending Soren against William. Why should I a prisoner of Soren wish to oppose those who want to depose him? You have misjudged me as a mercenary and wasted your time and mine."

Mentaxes was unhappy about Ariadne's first response, but did not lose heart. "It is true," he said, "that it is Soren who sent me to recruit you. But my appeal begging you to protect the common folk of Bezriel and Menkara against the vengeance of William and the depredations of a marauding army is no pretext. You have a difficult decision, Ariadne. If you accept the commission I offer you will be both protecting innocents and protecting your enemy, King Soren. You cannot do one without doing the other. You cannot refuse to do one without refusing to do the other."

"You are a cruel logician, Mentaxes. What you say is true, and therefore I must seriously consider Soren's request. I assume his request is the offering of a deal. What is my payment if I accept? My freedom and money?"

"I am not here to buy your skills, Ariadne. I know you are a woman of principle.

King Soren does not admire that, but I do. The king is desperate. There are two more parts to Soren's offer. First, if you accept, he will issue a general amnesty to all the Free Bezriel guerrilla who took up arms against him."

Ariadne had been ready to refuse Soren's offer on principle. She had not anticipated a general amnesty. But she held firm. "I cannot speak for my Free Bezriel comrades. They may accept or decline as they think fit. But I will not buy my freedom by helping the tyrant Soren stay in power."

"It does not work that way, Ariadne. General amnesty was offered only to help gain your acceptance. If you refuse, general amnesty is off the table."

"How like the tyrant Soren. Even his offer of clemency is a blackmail threat. If I stick to my principles, my comrades will suffer. That makes refusal harder, much harder. But it changes nothing. I will not use my powers to help Soren, the enemy of Bezriel. Please call the guards to escort me back to my cell."

"Wait, Ariadne. You have not yet heard the most important part of what Soren is offering to win your cooperation. If you join the fight against William, Soren will grant, what Free Bezriel fought for: freedom for Bezriel. If you join with Soren, Bezriel will be granted autonomy within Menkara, which means the right to self-governance. Within a year, a referendum of Bezrielites on whether to take a further step to national independence will be held."

That offer more than surprised Ariadne, it left her speechless. Eventually, she regained her composure. "That is a very tempting offer, but I am still not sure. When I was with Free Bezriel, I was ready to fight a duel with William for those stakes. The new situation is very similar. But it is not identical. The duel would have ended the war and no one other than William or I would die. But this new fight with William that Soren proposes would be the opening of a new and much bloodier war. I need to think before giving you an answer."

"A wise reply, Ariadne. And to help you think wisely, I have brought your parents to the capital to talk with you. After I leave, they will be brought to you. You will give me your decision tomorrow. I have just one final comment to make before leaving. You correctly point out the difference between the aborted duel to end a war and the current situation which threatens to be the start of a very bloody war. I know that at heart you abhor violence. What you must consider is whether the violence will be greater or lesser if you accept the offer? Whether the people of Bezriel and Menkara will suffer more or suffer less?"

With those hard questions, Mentaxes left the room, leaving Ariadne to ponder the toughest and most important decision of her life.

CHAPTER 7

While Ariadne waited for her parents to be brought to the conference room, both her mind and emotions were in a state of shock. Instead of trial and execution, she was being offered not only freedom, but a chance to liberate Bezriel. But accepting that chance meant allying herself with and taking orders from the tyrant Soren. Irony of ironies, liberating Bezriel now meant, not defeating Soren, but saving his sorry hide.

Her mind was in turmoil over agonizing questions. Was the prize worth the cost? Could she defeat William and succeed? If by some miracle she did succeed, would Soren honor his promise? Would her soul survive once again engaging in military sorcery? Ariadne had no answers, only hopes and fears.

That meeting of Ariadne with her parents began with long embraces, wordless demonstrations of love trying to hold off fear. Ariadne finally broke the silence with a blunt question "Have you been informed of Soren's proposal?"

It was Daniel who replied. "Yes. We had just heard of the defection of William, when agents of Chancellor Mentaxes arrived to escort your mother and me to the capital to meet with him. He told us of Soren's fear of a William-led invasion of Menkara and beseeched us to try to convince you to win freedom not only for yourself, but for Bezriel. He promised autonomy and possibly independence for Bezriel, if you help defend Menkara against William."

Fearing that her parent had agreed to act as agents of Soren in order to gain permission see her, Ariadne's voice cracked as she asked, "Is that why you are here – to persuade me to accept?"

Aware of the tension in her daughter's voice and body, Sarah knew she had to try to allay the fear behind her daughter's simple question. "Mentaxes tried to persuade us that accepting Soren's offer would be good for you and good for Bezriel and asked us to try to convince you to accept. But we promised nothing. Our counterproposal was that if we were allowed to meet with you, we would try to help you understand the consequences of accepting and the consequences of rejecting his offer. Mentaxes had hoped for more, but must have found our reply satisfactory, for he gave us permission to see you."

Ariadne's body tensed when she heard what Mentaxes had asked her parents to do, and relaxed when her mother reported "but we promised nothing". When her mother finished speaking, Ariadne simply said "Thank you, mother. Thank you, father."

The discussion that followed was complex, long, and meandering. I have prepared a compact account based on surviving journals and memoirs of Ariadne, Daniel, and Sarah. The following topics were discussed: Will Galatia invade? Why did Soren made his offer to Ariadne? Could the promises of Soren be relied on? If Ariadne rejected Soren's offer, what would happen to Ariadne and Bezriel, first from the anger of a frustrated Soren and later at the hands of the invading Galatian army and a vengeful William? If Ariadne accepted Soren's offer, could the invasion be defeated? What would happen to Bezriel, if Ariadne accepted Soren's offer, and the invasion succeeded? And finally, a question very important to Ariadne, if she used her sorcery to help Soren resist the invasion, would the level of violence in the war be greater or lesser?

Will the defection of William eventually lead to Galatia invading Menkara?

Daniel was the first to address that issue. "King Radames must have known that giving sanctuary to the renegade necromancer William would infuriate Soren, a powerful and vengeful king. Sooner or later, war between Galatia and Menkara is inevitable. Knowing this, if Radames did not have power ambitions of his own, he would never have given sanctuary to William. Over time, as Radames becomes drunk with the intoxicating power of William's sorcery, he will be drawn down the path of wars of aggression which he will justify as self-defense. For both Radames and William the most important target will be Soren and his powerful army and sorcerers."

The Sarah spoke. "If King Radames acts as you predict, then he has learned nothing from the mistakes of Soren. William's sorcery promises and delivers great power to kings. What is equally true, but not as obvious is that William's power combined with his arrogance and ambition creates a deadly danger for any lord foolish enough to believe that when employing William they are in control. The truth is that no one can control William. He is always a deadly danger to the lords who hope to gain wealth and power by using him."

Having agreed that William would always be a deadly danger to the lords who relied upon his powers, Ariadne and her parents sadly concluded that King Radames, blinded by William's promise of power and riches, very probably would not see the danger. Since the main obstacle to the power and wealth promised by William would be Soren lusting for revenge, Hence, they decided that a William-inspired Galatian invasion of Menkara would sooner or later occur.

Why did Soren made his offer of amnesty to Ariadne?

The three quickly agreed that Soren's offer of amnesty to Ariadne was based on his knowledge of her creation of an invisibility shield that William could not penetrate. Soren clearly believed that Ariadne's sorcery was his best hope of defeating the coming attack on Menkara by William.

The offer to Ariadne also meant that Soren knew of no other sorcerer that had any chance of defeating William. If he had any other options, Soren would not be trying to recruit Ariadne, a Free Bezrielite he had publicly denounced as a terrorist, a rebel that he had accused of treason, a sorceress he had sought to publicly humiliate and execute. If he had any other options, Soren, who had vowed to wage relentless war on separatist groups, would never have agreed to free a Bezrielite heroine and hold a referendum that would likely lead to independence for Bezriel.

Could the promises of Soren to Ariadne and Bezriel be relied on?

This was an issue on which consensus was not reached.

Ariadne had been arrested and imprisoned after she had relied on Soren's promise of a fair duel to decide independence for Bezriel. Using that fact and other examples, Sarah argued that Soren's promises were worthless. If Ariadne fought and the invasion were repelled, then Soren would renege on his promise of a binding referendum on independence for Bezriel.

Daniel, however, argued that the current situation was very different from the one that had led to Soren's deceiving Ariadne to come of hiding to fight a sorcerer's duel with William. Rather than dealing with a ragtag group of rebels, Soren was now confronting a powerful army aided by William. He was desperate. Therefore Daniel was confident that adequate language guaranteeing compliance could be put into a written document signed by Soren. But, he said, since contractual promises can be broken, Bezriel must not only get such a contract, it must also wage a publicity campaign both within Menkara and in foreign capitals that would make the political and diplomatic cost of reneging on his pledge to Bezriel so high that Soren would not be tempted to renege on his word. Daniel believed that the combination of a contract and high powered publicity campaign would force Soren to keep his promise.

Emotionally Ariadne agreed with her mother. But she saw the power of her father's argument that the current situation where Soren was threatened by a powerful kingdom aided by William was very different than when Soren aided by William was being annoyed, not threatened, by ragtag Free Bezriel. But that did not prove that Soren would keep his promises to Bezriel if, somehow with Ariadne's help, the invasion were defeated.

If Ariadne rejected Soren's offer, what would happen to Ariadne and Bezriel, because of the anger of a frustrated Soren

When this question was raised, Daniel was ready with an answer. "Soren will be furious. There will be a show trial of Ariadne and the other Free Bezriel prisoners. The trial will be used to stir up hatred against Bezriel. Inevitably, all will be convicted and publicly executed. Staring at his own immanent doom, Soren will wreck vengeance on Bezriel and Ariadne. Oppression of Bezriel will intensify. Our religious practices will be outlawed and our taxes doubled. It will be a replay of what happened when Baron Frederick was in power, but worse, much worse."

Sarah was not so sure. "Perhaps Soren will execute Ariadne and the other Free Bezriel prisoners if she refuses, but I doubt it. The king is evil, but he is no fool. He needs Ariadne. If she rejects his offer, he will redouble his efforts to recruit her. If there is a show trial, its purpose will be to use fear of execution of herself and her friends to change her mind."

Finally Ariadne spoke. "You both speak persuasively, but arrive at opposite conclusions. We do not know but can only guess at what Soren will do if I refuse to fight for him." They agreed that further speculation on what the megalomaniac Soren might do if Ariadne rejected his offer was pointless.

If Ariadne rejected Soren's offer, what would happen to Bezriel at the hands of the invading Galatian army and a vengeful William?

This time Sarah spoke first. "King Radames has no quarrel with Bezriel. If Ariadne and Bezriel refuse to join the fight against him, will that not convince him that Bezriel is not his enemy? Radames will not grant us independence, but surely he will treat Bezriel no worse than other parts of Menkara. And since Radames fears and hates Soren, I believe he will free the political prisoners of Soren. If Ariadne refuses to fight and Radames wins, Bezriel will certainly be no worse off than we are now and most likely will be better off."

Ariadne thought that her mother's points were good, but her father did not.

"Sarah, you see goodness in everyone and are far too trusting. Bezriel will be for King Radames, exactly what it is now for every powerful lord—a rich source of militarily useful sorcerers. Our culture and customs mean nothing to these people. King Radames will treat Bezriel in whatever manner he thinks will maximize the supply of powerful sorcerers to himself and minimize access by his enemies. Following the logic of power, he will hold Bezriel on a short lease. As for Ariadne and the other Bezrielite prisoners who fought for freedom, Radames probably hopes Soren will convict and execute them all now, so that he will not have to perform that unpopular task himself after the conquest. I am sure that he sees Ariadne and the other Bezrielite prisoners not so much as enemies of his enemy Soren, but as enemies of authority and hence his enemies.

"Why are you so pessimistic, father?" asked Ariadne.

"I am not pessimistic, Ariadne, I am realistic. Unfortunately for Bezriel, the power lust of King Radames is not the worst aspect of a Galatian invasion. The worst will be William's lust for vindication and revenge, not only against Soren who humiliated him, but against you and your Free Bezriel comrades for thwarting him. His power and influence will be great and that bodes ill for all of us. His pride will insist upon death for you and for all who fought for Free Bezriel against him."

After a long pause, Ariadne spoke. "My heart agreed with what you said when you spoke mother, but father has spoken what I know to be true about William and all those who love power. Victory for Radames and William means disaster for Bezriel. But the question remains -which would be worse for Bezriel – life under Soren or life under Radames and William. If I knew, my decision would be easy, but I do not know."

Sarah did not concede the point. "You both assume that Bezriel will be treated badly by Galatia whether or not we fight against the invasion. But to me that is a bad assumption. King Radames is a pragmatist. Pragmatists seek to turn neutral parties into friends, not enemies. You speak of the corrupting influence of power and the quest for power. But the pragmatism of Radames may be stronger than his love of power. And pragmatism dictates that he treat Bezriel fairly."

Daniel had a ready reply. "Soren was a pragmatist before he began to rely on William and became king. He ended up power-mad. The same will happen to Radames."

How much influence would William have on the decisions of Radames? They knew that both with respect to the prosecution of the war and treatment of the defeated enemy if Galatia won, William would be far harsher than Radames. Daniel argued that after war broke out, King Radames would become so dependent on William that he would sanction the necromancer's harshest revenge on Bezriel and Ariadne.

If Ariadne accepted Soren's offer, could the invasion be defeated?

The most important question for Ariadne and her parents, and the most difficult to answer, was what would happen militarily if Ariadne agreed to Soren's offer and then spurred on by William, Galatia invaded Menkara. Were Ariadne's powers strong enough to stop an invasion of Menkara fueled by the sorcery of William? Sarah and Daniel deferred to Ariadne on this point, but she was reluctant to venture an opinion.

Upon being pressed, she finally replied. "Can I defeat William? On my own, certainly not. With the aid of the Seekers, I do not know. Will the Seekers help me, even though I will be helping Soren stay in power? In most circumstances I am sure they would not. But if their help will avert thralldom of Bezriel to William and gain autonomy for Bezriel, then perhaps, yes. Hopefully Esther will come to me in my dreams tonight, and if she comes, I pray that she will tell me. I need to know."

They then agreed that no decision should be made until after Ariadne met with Esther and learned whether the Seekers would aid her in battling against William and the Galatian invasion and if the Seekers believed that with their aid Ariadne could defeat William.

What would happen to Bezriel, if Ariadne accepted Soren's offer, and the invasion succeeded?

At an emotional point during the long day, Ariadne asked that question.

Sarah quickly replied. "Earlier I said that if you refused to fight, Bezriel would not suffer if the invasion succeeds. But, if you fight and the invasion succeeds, I fear the worst. Radames will identify you as the standard bearer of Bezriel and say Bezriel has declared itself an enemy of Galatia and he will make us suffer accordingly, perhaps military occupation of Bezriel. That is why, you must not fight for Soren against Galatia."

Then Daniel spoke. "It is true that if you fight and do not win, things will go very badly for Bezriel. The retribution of a victorious Radames and William will be fierce. But we must weigh that disaster against the wrath of Soren if you refuse to fight."

It was then for the only time that day that Ariadne cried.

If Ariadne used her sorcery to help Soren resist the invasion, would the level of violence in the war be greater or lesser?

The most agonizing issue for Ariadne was how much and in what direction would her fighting for Soren change the level of violence. Although in general she thought that judging whether an action was morally good or bad based on results, she nonetheless intuitively believed that it would be morally right to use her sorcery to aid the defense of Menkara only if that would reduce the death and destruction of the war. She did not want to use her sorcery in warfare again, even if it led to independence for Bezriel, if doing so would lead to an escalation of the carnage in the coming war. That was a clear decision criteria, but unfortunately there was no way of knowing in advance the impact of her sorcery on the level of violence.

"It is possible," her mother said, "that you will be able to use your powers to mute the violence as you did when you erected the invisibility shield to protect Free Bezriel from the onslaughts of Cerberus and later William."

"Unfortunately mother, an invisibility shield, while adequate to protect a small group, cannot possibly shield a large nation. If war breaks out, both sides will desperately strive to win and, unfortunately hope of winning and fear of losing tend to escalate the violence and brutality of war."

Daniel had a very different perspective than his daughter. "For anyone who goes to war, the objective has to be winning, not minimizing violence. That is certainly Soren's goal, and you will be working for Soren."

Again, as so often that day, Ariadne, Daniel, and Sarah were forced to admit that it was only guesswork whether Ariadne's sorcery would increase or decrease the suffering caused by the war.

The family council went on until the wee hours of the morning. Near the end of that agonizing meeting, Ariadne spoke from the depths of her heart. "I must answer Soren, but I do not yet know what answer to give. I do not want to kill again, hence my heart, I do not want to go to war again. But the prophecy and my soul tell me that I must strive to help liberate Bezriel."

Daniel tried to put Ariadne's dilemma in historical perspective. "William defected because he now hates Soren. He chose Galatia because Galatia gives him his best chance of exacting revenge on Soren. King Radames accepted the defector because the defection puts an end to the threat to Galatia posed by Soren and enables him to turn the tables on Soren. Because of the defection, war between Menkara and Galatia is inevitable. Bezriel as part of Menkara cannot avoid the coming war. Even worse, because of the military value of its sorcerers, Bezriel is now forever trapped within the power struggles of the mighty of this world. All outcomes for Bezriel are bad. But which will be worse: life under Soren or life under Radames and William?"

Before her parents left, Ariadne asked them to summarize their views on whether she should accept Soren's offer.

Sarah advised against accepting. She believed that William would triumph even if Ariadne fought against him, but her fighting would escalate retaliation against Bezriel both during the war and when it was over. And even if Ariadne's sorcery did succeed in repelling the invasion, she totally distrusted Soren and believed that a triumphant Soren would renege on his promise and Bezriel would remain in thrall to present and future kings of Menkara.

Daniel strongly recommended that Ariadne accept Soren's offer. He too distrusted Soren, but believed that safeguards against betrayal could be worked out. But no safeguards against the wrath of a victorious William were possible. He was sure that William hated Bezriel for rejecting him and making him an outcast. The only hope for Bezriel was to defeat William and the armies of Radames. And the best hope of such a military victory was the sorcery of Ariadne.

Ariadne then ended the marathon session. "My dear parents, thank you for helping me think through the issues. I doubt that

William can be defeated and I fear the wrath of a triumphant William directed at his own people. But if by some miracle we defeat William, I do not know whether Soren will keep his promises to Bezriel. My heart and conscience tell me that I should follow the path that will minimize the violence to come. But which path is that? I do not know. I hope and trust that Esther will come and give me guidance tonight."

An aide to Mentaxes came when summoned to escort Daniel and Sarah back to their guest quarters. Minutes later guards came to lead Ariadne back to her dungeon.

That night, Ariadne dreamt that she was trying to ascend a steep path to the top of a mountain. In the dream she had gotten so tired that she had begun to doubt that she could complete her journey to the mountaintop. Then she lost her balance and slid back down the hill, halting her plunge a few feet from a precipice that she did not remember being there on her climb up the hill. Lying on the ground, in pain and close to despair she wondered if she should continue the climb or give up and start back down.

"Daughter of Bezriel, get back on your feet." Those words, spoken from what seemed to be the void, startled Ariadne. Looking around to locate the speaker, she saw an old woman, standing at the very edge of the precipice, a stone's throw away.

Fearing that the old woman was perilously close to cliff's edge, Ariadne tried to caution her "Be careful, grandmother. You are too close to the edge. Move away."

"It is you, daughter of Bezriel, that is in peril, not me," said the old woman. She stamped her cane on the ground. Then waving her cane threateningly in the air, she slowly tottered towards Ariadne, yelling "Get up! Get up and try to finish your journey!"

Given the weakness of the old woman, the implied threat of the cane was absurd. But her belligerence angered Ariadne. In a hostile voice she replied. "Hag of Bezriel, do not tell me what to do. I do not need advice from such as you. I am in pain and need to rest. I will get up when I am ready to get up!"

"So, Ariadne, you have spirit enough to insult your elders, but not spirit enough to finish your journey. How pathetic!"

Shocked that the old woman knew her name and now very angry, Ariadne replied. "Age is not wisdom, hag. I do not need your help to decide what to." The old woman stopped moving towards Ariadne. She said nothing. The frustrated Ariadne spoke again. "Who are you and how do you know my name? What concern is it of yours, whether I go forward or turn back?

Looking intently at the girl on the ground, the old woman at last replied. "I see now that in your youthful pride, you have fully understood the wisdom of Bezriel which is that each man, each woman, even each child is sufficient onto himself to handle all problems without any meddling help from their elders. I know when I am not welcome!" Having said this, the old woman snapped her fingers and Ariadne woke from her dream.

The young sorceress awoke in a cold sweat. She remembered every detail of the dream. Dreams had always been very important to Ariadne. They were how she communicated with the spirit of Bezriel, how she communicated with Esther, how she accessed her deepest and darkest aspirations. As she lay in bed, she was pervaded by a sense of loss. It was as if she had been tested and had failed the test. She had been very disrespectful to an old woman who had told her to stop feeling sorry for herself and to get up from where she had fallen. All her life she had been taught respect for the elderly. But in her dream she had been angry and very rude. If, as she had been taught, dreams told the truth, then she, Ariadne, was not a good Bezrielite. Her parents would be shamed by her behavior.

Who was the old woman? The answer came to her like a slap in the face. She had implored the Seeker Esther to come to her. Surely the old woman was Esther. Alas, in her dream, she had told Esther to keep her advice to herself.

With a heavy heart, Ariadne laid back down. In the morning she had to give Mentaxes her answer. She now knew that her answer must be "no". She was an unworthy daughter of Bezriel. Any new attempt by her to save Bezriel would surely once again end in disaster.

After much tossing and turning Ariadne fell asleep for a second time that night and for a second time dreamt. And for a second time, Esther appeared to her. But this time she appeared in a form that Ariadne was familiar with and recognized. Esther began by saying in a calm voice, neither friendly nor hostile, "Hello, daughter of Bezriel."

In this new dream, Ariadne remembered both her earlier dream, and her waking remorse over her behavior in that earlier dream. "You call me by a title I do not deserve. No true daughter of Bezriel would heap scorn on an elder who offers advice."

"It was but a dream, Ariadne. Interpret that dream for me."

Ariadne paused to think before replying. "Mentaxes has offered me much to fight for Soren against William. Before sleep I was wrestling with my decision. In my dream, I was climbing a mountain and became very tired. I assume that continuing the climb means accepting Soren's offer and trying to fight off the threatened invasion of Menkara by William. Going back down means declining Soren's offer and refusing to fight William."

"Perhaps. Tell me about the old woman, 'the meddling old hag', I think you called her."

"I am so ashamed. I did not recognize you."

"Was it me? What difference does that make? Do you think it is okay to be rude to an old woman who is not a Seeker?"

"Of course not. It seems that everything I do and say betrays Bezriel."

"Stick to the dream. Why did you become so angry at the old woman?"

"Because she urged me to continue a climb that had become too difficult for me."

"You mean a climb that you thought had become too difficult for you!"

"Is there a difference?"

"There is a big difference between a task that is too hard for you and one that seems too hard, but can be accomplished with enough effort."

Ariadne was close to tears as she said "Are we talking about climbing a mountain or saving Bezriel?"

"Once again, does it matter? The same distinction applies to any difficult task. Surely you know that"

"In the dream I was too tired to continue the climb. That is why I got angry and was rude when you told me to do it anyway."

"No, Ariadne, you were only told to try."

"What is the point of trying when you know you will fail? I was proclaimed as the savior of Bezriel. But my whole life proves I am not worthy to carry out such a sacred mission. When I try, people die, and Bezriel grows weaker. Therefore I must abandon my imposture."

"So the answer that you will give Soren is that you will not fight."

"Since I do not have the ability to succeed and seeing the disaster my first attempt at fighting to save Bezriel led to, I am loathe to try again."

"Does the prophecy mean nothing to you?"

"It means everything to me. It is why I dare not accept Soren's offer. The prophecy said I would lead Bezriel to freedom or to destruction. Since I am not worthy to lead Bezriel to freedom, my trying would lead to its destruction. By not fighting I cancel out the prophecy and let Bezriel decide its own fate."

"That is too easy, daughter of Bezriel. The Seekers saw the future unfold up to the point where your actions would decide the fate of Bezriel. But we could foresee neither what you would do, nor the results of your actions. Your choosing to fight might lead Bezriel to freedom or might lead Bezriel to destruction. Likewise your choosing not to fight might lead to Bezriel's freedom or might lead to Bezriel's destruction. Your choosing not to fight does not negate the prophecy. It simply fulfills it in another way."

Ariadne was horrified. "Are you saying I am a slave to a destiny that I cannot escape?"

"No. I am saying just the opposite. You are free to choose your path in life. But you must bear the heavy burden that what you do will impact not just yourself, but all of Bezriel. This is equally true whether you choose to fight against William or choose not to fight against William."

This time Ariadne could not hold back her tears. "It's not fair," she sobbed.

"Yes, daughter of Bezriel, it is not fair. But it is the reality you face. I promise that the Seekers will always be there for you, providing what help we can, helping you think through problems and revealing sacred knowledge long forgotten by the living. I cannot promise victory if you choose to try. Even with our help, you may fail. Facing an unknown future, you who must decide what you will do."

Ariadne was not happy with the new knowledge that her second dream that night had brought. She now knew that despite her doubts about her worthiness she must continue to try to climb the mountain, to devote her life, however short or long it was, to fighting for the true spirit of Bezriel. But that resolution, as important as it was, did not tell her whether she should accept or reject Soren's offer. With all her heart she wanted to make the choice that would be best for Bezriel, but she did not yet know which choice that was. She had the sense that Esther was also as yet uncertain. The last thing Ariadne and Esther agreed on that night was that Ariadne would ask Mentaxes for one more day to consider her answer to Soren's offer.

The next morning, Mentaxes who had feared immediate rejection, made a pretense of being annoyed by the requested delay, saying that Soren would never approve. But Soren, as Mentaxes knew full well he would, granted the extra day. The day was spiritual agony for Ariadne. Hope that the Seekers would teach her a way to defeat William pushed her towards accepting the offer. Fear that her sorcery would intensify and prolong the brutal conflict which would still end in William's inevitable triumph pushed her even more strongly towards rejecting the offer.

That night Ariadne received an unexpected boon. She slept restfully for several hours before once again she met the old woman who the night before had confronted her when she fell while climbing up the mountain.

"Greetings, daughter of Bezriel."

"Greetings, honored grandmother. I humbly apologize for my rudeness yesterday."

"I accept your apology. Is there anything you want to ask me?"

"Yes, grandmother. Tell me what answer I should give King Soren!"

"Why make that request, Ariadne? You know that you yourself must decide what path you will take."

Ariadne surprised herself by saying. "Then I will decline the offer. My fighting might lead to victory for Soren and independence for Bezriel. That is possible but unlikely. My fighting will certainly increase the intensity of the conflict, will increase death and devastation on both sides. That is certain. Since the good is only a small possibility and the bad is certain, I choose to decline Soren's offer."

"If that is your decision, daughter of Bezriel, so be it."

"Do you approve, grandmother? I must know."

"I trust your heart and soul Ariadne. If your heart and soul tell you not to fight Ariadne, then you are making the right choice."

That reply terrified Ariadne because while her heart told her not to fight, her soul told her to fight. But it was too late to tell the old woman that, because she had already vanished.

Ariadne, formally, informed Mentaxes that morning that she was rejecting the offer. The old man said he would convey her refusal to King Soren who would be very unhappy with her decision.

Late that morning Mentaxes met with Soren. Unhappy with the refusal, Soren, as Sarah had predicted, calmly decided to not yet threaten reprisals, but to play a waiting game, hoping the sorceress would change her mind.

CHAPTER 8

Even before the granting of asylum to William, the power structure in Galatia was complex with many obscure webs of intrigue and multi-level struggles for influence and dominance. As the peace of the region was disturbed by King Soren of Menkara, the importance of the Galatian army and the generals who led the army increased dramatically. The rise of military influence in Menkara and other nearby kingdoms had inspired in chief of staff General Ptolemy a desire to create a military strong enough to keep Galatia free from outside domination. He had succeeded in doing so, until William's military sorcery had multiplied the power of King Soren, who clearly had ambitions for regional hegemony, and perhaps even conquest. General Ptolemy became greatly worried, until the defection of William to Galatia put those worries to rest. The Galatian army regiments were loyal to General Ptolemy and only to Ptolemy. Therefore at the time, William became part of the Galatian power structure, King Radames no longer had the power to remove Ptolemy as head of the army. Being king, Radames could dismiss Ptolemy as chief of staff. But if he did, since the troops would remain loyal to their general, dismissing Ptolemy would provoke a rebellion that would depose Radames as king.

Radames was a good man and a well-intention king. But he did not understand power. He had devoted his life to the good of Galatia, striving to keep the economy prosperous and to help the arts and sciences flourish. He spent his free time creating landscape paintings and going to concerts and lectures. Over time, real power in Galatia gradually shifted away from the king to the generals, but power also shifted to the competent and ambitious bureaucrats who understood and controlled the complex machinery of the state apparatus and to the entrepreneurs and technical specialists capable of efficiently running a modernizing economy more and more dependent on large scale production and foreign trade. At the control center of this bureaucratic apparatus was Chancellor Diamant, a man with the personality of a spider, constantly spinning webs to trap the unwary and to expand his control of key positions. Even though Radames was king, real power was split between General Ptolemy and Chancellor Diamant. Fortunately for the king, his general and his chancellor neither liked nor trusted each other. That distrust between them worked to keep Radames on the throne.

The combination of William's extraordinary powers of sorcery with the conventional military might and growing imperial ambition of King Soren had disrupted the continental balance of power and the peace and stability that balance had led to. It had been widely believed that Soren would soon launch sequential Menkaran invasions of Galatia, Nisa, and Mittani, the three kingdoms bordering Menkara. With William powering Soren's offensives, those invasions would probably have reduced those three kingdoms from their historic status as powerful independent kingdoms to mere vassal states of Menkara.

Thus both General Ptolemy and Chancellor Diamant were delighted by the attempted coup of the rebel lords that had separated about a third of Menkara from Soren's rule and were ecstatic about the defection of William to Galatia, since under these new conditions, an invasion of Galatia would be so foolhardy, that even Soren would not attempt it. General Ptolemy and Chancellor

Diamant easily overcame King Radames aversion to the coup and defection, acts that defied authority, by emphasizing that both developments weakened King Soren, whose ambitions threatened Galatia and whose right to rule Menkara was the result of waging war against the legitimate king of Menkara.

But not everyone in Galatia was happy that asylum had been granted to the powerful sorcerer. The most prominent among those who thought it a mistake was Archbishop Khofu. Khofu was pleased that William had defected from Menkara and thereby put an end to the serious external threat to Galatia posed by the power-crazed King Soren, but he was not happy that the sorcerer had defected to Galatia. Khofu became even more discouraged as the sorcerer's influence over king, general, and chancellor grew steadily in the weeks and months after he was granted asylum.

It seemed obvious to Khofu that William was trying to instill in King Radames, the same vaunting ambition for power and lust for riches that had driven his former master, King Soren. A crucial difference, however, was that such ambition and lust were the defining part of Soren's character, but had to be planted and nourished to life in Radames. Khofu recognized the sad fact that both Chancellor Diamant and General Ptolemy were helping William nourish the seeds of ambition for power and lust for riches in King Radames. If successful, the result would be the same in Galatia as it had been in Menkara – militarization of the kingdom and endless wars.

Acquaintance with William had led Khofu to believe that topping William's personal list of ambitions was not wealth and not honor, but revenge. First and foremost, revenge on King Soren, the man William hated for publicly humiliating him by aborting his duel with the Free Bezriel sorceress, Ariadne. Also high on his list of priorities was revenge on Ariadne, the young sorceress who had frustrated his own sorcery, thereby weakening his reputation and causing his feud with Soren.

Khofu feared that William, aided and abetted by Ptolemy and Diamant, would try to convince Radames to launch an invasion of Menkara to remove Soren from power. Because of the poison dripped into his ears by William, Ptolemy and Diamant, King Radames would be receptive to the argument that through William's sorcery, Galatia now had a golden opportunity to turn the tables on Soren the powerful upstart warlord who had been casting covetous eyes on Galatia.

But would war stop with deposing Soren? If William, Diamant and Ptolemy succeeded in planting and nourishing the poisonous seed of imperial ambition in Radames, then after defeating Soren, other Galatian wars of domination and conquest would surely follow. Archbishop Khofu, with his knowledge of history, saw the insidious social and political damage wrought by imperial ambition: lust for power displacing concern for the public good as the motivating force of the aristocracy; sycophancy displacing honorable service as the pathway to success of the middle classes; a variety of vices (idleness, greed, envy) displacing traditional virtues (hard work, thrift, good fellowship) among the peasants and artisans. That is what Khofu foresaw, but he doubted that he could get King Radames to see the same future. And even if the king could be brought to see that future, would he reject it?

As bad as that vision of imperial decay was, Khofu's fears went deeper. The defector who had won the ear and confidence of the king was both a very powerful sorcerer and a very ambitious man. King Radames, General Ptolemy, and Chancellor Diamant believed that William was merely a convenient tool to be used to further their own ends. But was not that also how William saw them? As convenient tools to further his own ends? Khofu felt sure that William aspired to be the master in his relationship with the king, general, and chancellor of Galatia and he feared that William would succeed, would bend that trio to his own will and ambitions.

What were those ambitions? The archbishop sensed that the sorcerer aspired to much more than revenge against Soren. William often spoke of expanding the limits of sorcery. This from a sorcerer who could already raise and control the dead. Khofu's deepest fear was that William aspired to develop his sorcery to the point where he could control the living as well as he could control the dead. Both would be mere puppets in his hands.

William vowed that this time would be different. He would not make the same mistakes in Galatia that he had made in Menkara. Achieving his goals through an alliance with Soren had failed, because from day one it had only been an alliance of convenience on both sides. As soon as pursuit of Free Bezriel led to their first failure, the relationship had degenerated into mutual suspicions, mistrust, and recriminations. With the alliance already on life support, Soren's treachery of publicly humiliating William by aborting his duel with the Free Bezriel sorceress had led William to believe that his only options were to crawl back to the capital and cravenly accept Soren as his lord and master or to flee from Menkara. He had chosen flight, but not a flight of submission and despair. Rather a flight to give him opportunity to mobilize for a triumphant return to Menkara.

William was determined that the same disaster would not happen in Galatia. King Radames, he believed was a weaker man than Soren, a man he would be able to bend to his own will and desires. Soren had always seen William as both his greatest weapon and his greatest threat. The sorcerer's goal was to make sure that King Radames never saw him as a threat. William was confident he could do it. Especially since both General Ptolemy and Chancellor Diamant, the king's two most important advisors, clearly wanted to use William's sorcery to eliminate Soren as a threat to Galatia. The main obstacle to success was Archbishop Khofu, who was not only a man who saw William as a threat, but also was a respected spiritual leader who had the ear of the king. Khofu would doubtless try to poison the king's mind, warning him not to trust the sorcerer.

William began his campaign to push Galatia into war by telling King Radames and his top advisors that plans for an invasion of Galatia were already being made at Soren's court before the partially successful coup had split Menkara in two. But, William told the Galatians, the splitting of Menkara had not put an end to Soren's plan of foreign conquest; it had merely delayed its implementation. After Soren crushed the rebel lords, he intended to resume his aggressive expansion of Menkara. By telling the Galatians of Soren's plans, William was trying to manipulate the fear, anger, and resentment of Soren already present. In this way he hoped to convince King Radames that a Galatian invasion of Menkara to depose the tyrant Soren would not be aggression but simply rational and justified self-defense.

But convincing Radames that deposing Soren was desirable was not enough He also had to demonstrate to him that invading Menkara and toppling Soren was feasible and would succeed. The best way to do that would be to demonstrate just how awesome his powers of sorcery were,

Cautious King Radames would not risk going to war unless he believed both that the cause was just and victory was guaranteed. William decided to begin his campaign to persuade the king to go to war by demonstrating his awesome powers of military sorcery to the king and his advisors, Demonstrate powers great enough to prove that his sorcery would be enough to enable King Radames at the head of the Galatian army to ride triumphantly into Menkara and depose the upstart Soren. His demonstration of powers would be in three parts over three nights; mass hypnosis, creating explosions at a distance, and finally raising the dead. King Radames, General Ptolemy, Chancellor Diamant, and Archbishop Khofu would be the witnesses at these demonstrations. They were the men that William needed to impress to forestall opposition and create support for his ambitious and aggressive plans.

The first night's demonstration was at an army barracks three miles from the capital. The site had been picked by General Ptolemy as the barracks of a unit that had a very good record for tight discipline. William cast a spell that hypnotized the soldiers in one of the barracks, all of whom were sleeping. He suggested to eight of the soldiers that they announce to the barracks they were sick and tired of the hard life of a soldier, that they then would go AWOL and blend unnoticed back into civilian life. William hypnotically suggested that all the other soldiers in the barracks make no effort to stop those going AWOL. Instead they would wish them good luck before going back to sleep. William's suggestions were obeyed. Eight soldiers flaunted regulations and walked out of the barracks. The other soldiers wished them good luck and went back to sleep. No one tried to stop them.

Ptolemy was outraged. "Sorcerer, how dare you use your unnatural powers to suborn desertion." William replied, "General, it is not desertion. Not free will, but my mesmerizing of their minds made them leave their barracks and go AWOL. They will soon return to their and barracks and tomorrow will not remember their strange actions this night. My intention is to demonstrate the chaos I can create through mass hypnosis. I will of course use this power on the enemy, not on loyal Galatians. But since the enemy is not here I had to use your loyal soldiers to make my point."

Twenty minutes after the eight AWOL soldiers exited the barracks, William issued new hypnotic commands; the eight returned to barracks, climbed into their bunks and went to sleep. William then issued a post-hypnotic command to everyone in the barracks that erased their memory of that night. Interviews the next day with those in the barracks revealed that no one remembered anything.

The Galatians were impressed. But whereas king, chancellor and general rejoiced at the awesome power now working for Galatia, the archbishop shivered in apprehension of the unknown intentions of the powerful sorcerer that had been accepted into their midst.

The second night's demonstration of William's powers was at an army munitions depot where cannons, muskets and gun powder were stored. The same observers were again present, not at the depot, rather at an observation post about a half mile to the southwest. William asked for permission to blow up the munitions depot. The Galatians knew that sorcerers could cause explosions at close quarters, but an explosion at that distance seemed to them impossible. Diamant voiced this disbelief.

"To all but me, it is impossible!" was William's arrogant reply. "I stationed us at such a great distance from the depot in order to demonstrate just how mighty my sorcery is."

"If you succeed, losing that supply of weapons and gunpowder will be a very expensive night for Galatia," said the king, "But if you can do it, the loss of the depot supplies is a small price to pay for the services you bring me."

William took fifteen minutes to prepare. He then unleashed a savage spell. Nothing happened for thirty seconds. As the seconds ticked by, Diamant made the mistake of snorting derisively. It was a mistake, because within seconds, the depot exploded with the loudest sound the Galatians had ever heard. When at last conversation again became possible, the king exclaimed "Such power belongs only to the gods. Or so, I believed, until tonight."

The third night's demonstration was in the burial chambers of the royal palace. William began by telling the Galatians that in warfare calling forth apparitions of the dead could be used to
inspire one's own troops or to panic and terrorize the enemy. An example of terrorizing the enemy, would be calling forth ghosts of one's own dead soldiers dressed in battle to make the enemy believe the forces opposing them were larger and fiercer than they were in reality.

To begin, William asked the king to name a dead ancestor he wished to talk to. The king chose an ancestor he had known, his grandfather, because he wanted to be able to test if the apparition called forth was the man William said it was. When the spirit of Radames V appeared, he reproached the sorcerer for disturbing him, but calmed down when introduced to his grandson, who had been a child of ten, when the old king had died. The old king promised that if called upon in a time of crisis for Galatia, he would rouse the Galatian troops to fever pitch before they went into battle.

That first ghostly demonstration was impressive, but William wanted to show a far greater power. He wanted to prove that he could summon and control large numbers of the dead in ways that could impact large scale battles. He requested the presence the next night of forty Galatian soldiers, half of whom should be dressed in Menkaran uniforms, at the cemetery adjacent to the old Damascene battlefield where centuries ago the Galatian army under the command of King Radames I, had defeated an invading Menkaran army.

When all were assembled the next night at the cemetery, William addressed King Radames. "Your majesty, my demonstration tonight will be in two parts. First I will raise long dead Galatians and use them to inspire today's Galatians. Then, I will raise long dead Menkarans who died in battle and show you how I would use them on a real battlefield to demoralize living Menkaran soldiers.

The first demonstration stirred the hearts of all the Galatian witnesses. The sorcerer awoke five Galatians who had died bravely defending their homeland at Damascene. As ordered by William, they told the living Galatians that there was no finer life, and no finer death than a life and death dedicated to the glory of Galatia.

The second demonstration was terrifying. William awoke seven Menkarans who had died horrible deaths at Damascene. Obeying William's commands, they addressed the twenty living men dressed as Menkaran troops. They cursed the commanders who once had ordered them to cross the Galatian border. They described the horrible agonies awaiting those who died on enemy land. They implored those they believed to be living Menkaran troops to desert and return to their home land.

Dear reader, please excuse me, Bartholomew, the narrator of this history, for inserting my own views here on William's raising of the dead. William was a necromancer who controlled the dead he awakened. In my opinion the words they spoke did not express their own emotions and beliefs, but were simply the words William forced them to speak. In my opinion there is no reason to believe anything the dead Galatians or the dead Menkarans said that night. They were forced to mouth what William wanted the king and his advisors to hear.

The hearts and minds of King Radames and his three advisors were overwhelmed by what they witnessed over the four nights on which William demonstrated his powers of sorcery. But their reactions were very different.

King Radames was doubly pleased. The powerful sorcery of William would not only make Galatia safe from attack by King Soren but undoubtedly also provide invaluable technical aid to all parts of the economy, not only to the traditional base of agriculture, but also to the expanding industrial and transportation sectors.

General Ptolemy exalted in the fact that such an extremely powerful military resource was now working for Galatia. He was sure that made Galatia the mightiest military power on the continent. He was no longer worried that the power mad Soren would use William and his powerful army to invade and conquer Galatia. If Soren was foolish enough to try, he would be soundly defeated.

Chancellor Diamant was pleased in a far more ambitious manner. He had sensed from his first interview with William that the sorcerer not only wanted revenge on King Soren, but also wanted to use his sorcery to dominate nations. By letting William exercise his sorcery, Galatia would become the most powerful kingdom on the continent. Diamant would ride on the sorcerer's shoulders to become the most powerful man, not only in Galatia, but on the continent. He just had to make sure that in the internal politics of Galatia, William was aligned with the chancellor and not with the king or with the army.

But the enthusiasm for what William and his sorcery could do for Galatia was not unanimous. Archbishop Khofu, who had opposed granting asylum to William, was terrified by what he had witnessed those four nights. William was far more powerful and far more dangerous than he had previously suspected. It was clear that the sorcerer exulted in his power. Could such a man be content with being the agent of others, such as King Radames? Would he not aspire to personal dominion?

Three days after his mass summoning of the dead, William requested an audience with King Radames, asking that Chancellor Diamant, General Ptolemy and Archbishop Khofu also be present. The king readily agreed. At the appointed time, the king entered the conference room and recognized William.

"Your majesty, as you know, by accepting me as a defector, you have made a deadly enemy in Soren, who will seek revenge not just on me, but on you. We assumed that with my defection and civil war against his rebellious lords looming, he would not dare attack Galatia, but we were wrong. Even after defections resulting from the provincial secessions, his army is not only larger than yours, but it is better armed and has been honed into an efficient attack force by two decades of civil war. Whereas your troops have little experience of actual combat.

Also Soren still has seven powerful sorcerers trained in military sorcery by me. He has issued an order that I be assassinated. Once I am out of the way, he will invade Galatia and he will conquer Galatia. The only way to avert this disaster is to strike at Soren first. I advise an all-out invasion of Menkara as soon as General Ptolemy with my assistance can work out the best strategy and your troops can be equipped, mobilized, and prepared. If you strike first, you will win. Galatia will be the dominant power on the continent."

All present were shocked by this speech of William. The first to speak was the archbishop. "Your information, *if true*, William, changes everything. *If true,* it makes a Galatian attack on Menkara nothing other than rational self-defense. Before the coup attempt split off part of Menkara from his control and before you defected, King Soren could have attacked Galatia with odds heavily in his favor. Yet he did not attack. Today, if Soren were to attack, the odds would be heavily against him. Yet you say that now when his chance of victory is much less, he has decided to attack. You paint the strategic genius who against all odds reunified Menkara as an irrational fool. Thus to support your absurd claim of an imminent Menkaran invasion of Galatia, you claim he first plans to have you assassinated. I have two questions for you, sorcerer. What proof do you have that Soren has ordered your assassination? And given your awesome powers of sorcery, is it even possible that an assassin could succeed."

"You have all but called me a liar, Khofu! But rather than sinking to name calling, I will give you and all here present, my evidence. First is logic. Soren is ruthless. He never accepts defeat, and he always plots to destroy those who threaten his power. Can you doubt that at the top of his enemies list are myself for defecting, and King Radames for giving me asylum? His revenge can only take the form of having me assassinated, and then invading Galatia, and deposing King Radames. If you are not convinced by logic, I will show you a letter I received from a high-ranking sympathizer in the Menkaran army that Soren has ordered highly skilled sorcerers to work with professional hit men to sneak into Galatia and assassinate me. The letter goes on to say that after I am assassinated, Soren will launch a full-scale invasion of Galatia."

The letter had been written by Timaeus, a commoner who by skill and hard work had risen in the army ranks to become an aide to General Danton in the feared Cerberus brigade. After Danton was elevated to commander-in-chief of the Mentaxan army, he had not taken Timaeus with him to central headquarters. William, noticing both the high ability and festering resentment in Timaeus, had cultivated him as a friend. Timaeus, who knew that he would be court-martialed if Danton or Soren learned of the letter, sent it anyway, planning in the near future to join William in exile in Galatia. His letter accurately described Soren's plan to assassinate William.

The sorcerer then reached into his robe and pulled out the letter from Timaeus that he handed to King Radames. The letter from a high ranking officer in the Menkaran army said exactly what William claimed it said. The king read the letter, then passed it to General Ptolemy, who read it and passed it to Chancellor Diamant who passed it to Archbishop Khofu.

Finally the king spoke. "Your logic and the letter have convinced me, William. Your assassination followed by invasion is exactly how the warlord Soren would react. We must strike at him, before he strikes at us. General Ptolemy and William I order you to work out strategy and timing for a preemptive strike against King Soren and Menkara."

Archbishop Khofu did not agree with the king's decision, but knowing that nothing he could say at that time would make any difference, he said nothing. It was General Ptolemy who spoke. "A wise decision, your majesty. We will get to work immediately."

As they left the conference room the Galatians were grim, William forced himself to refrain from smiling.

The defection of William led to the rebirth of King Soren as master strategist. Within days his anger was refined into a burning desire to not only survive, but to turn the tables and exact revenge on the sorcerer who had stabbed him in the back and on the king who would probably try to use the turncoat to try to dethrone him. Soren knew that he was now threatened in three very different ways, all of which he must prepare for: a William-aided Galatian invasion; civil war with the rebellious provinces; and assassination attempts by Menkaran dissidents and Galatian agents.

Civil war and assassination were immediate dangers facing Soren, but, he believed that in the long run, a vengeful William was by far the most serious threat. William, he knew was not foolhardy and hence would not try to strike alone. He would try to persuade Radames, the fool king of Galatia, to order a military invasion of Menkara. To prepare for a Galatian invasion, that he believed to be inevitable, King Soren ordered General Danton to reinforce all defensible positions near the Galatian border and to prepare plans to rapidly move all regiments and military sorcerers to the border once evidence of an imminent Galatian invasion surfaced.

With the threat of William-led invasion on Menkara looming, Soren's troops would be deployed against the traitorous rebels only when the rebels attacked loyalist garrisons or towns. The king's propaganda machine would be kicked into high gear, emphasizing the need for national unity against external enemies. Grand gesture, such as lower taxes, and concessions on local grievances would be used to mobilize popular support.

King Soren met with his internal security personnel and ordered them to come up with plans for infiltrating spies into Galatia with the objective of assassinating William. Soren thought there was little chance of success, but if the assassination plan was surreptitiously leaked, as he planned, it could force William to waste time and effort on personal defensive measures. Soren also worked with General Danton to develop plans both for launching either a pre-emptive strike or a counterattack into Galatia.

Such plans would be adequate if the Galatian army were acting alone, but not against the Galatian army aided by William. The king knew that the odds that his sorcerers would be able to hold off the demonic attacks unleashed by William were not good. Soren knew that his best hope of surviving the crisis was recruiting Ariadne, the young Bezrielite sorceress who had erected the invisibility shield that had frustrated not only Soren's own troops, but the determined efforts of William. He must have her, no matter what her price. She had been tempted by his offer of a referendum on independence for Bezriel, if she fought with him against the rebels, but in the end, she had refused. Soren could only hope that as the threat from their common archenemy William grew more imminent that Ariadne would change her mind.

CHAPTER 9

It had been with great trepidation that the Menkaran rebel alliance had tried to recruit William.

The necromancer joining their rebellion would have guaranteed success. But they feared the negative impact that being militarily dependent on William and his dark powers of sorcery would have on their desire to recreate the traditional Menkara. William's flight to Galatia both ended the faint hope that he might join the rebels to take his revenge on Soren and eliminated the danger that he might rejoin Soren and crush the rebel alliance. But if William's flight immediately eliminated those two scenarios, it soon paved the way for hitherto unimaginable futures for Menkara and its peoples.

After William rejected overtures from both sides, the leaders of the rebel alliance assumed he would stay neutral. They never imagined that the sorcerer would defect to another kingdom. When his defection became known, an emergency meeting of the rebel alliance was called to discuss the implications of William's defection and how the rebels should respond to it.

At first it seemed clear that William, having defected would play no role in the looming civil war between opposite visions of the future of Menkara. Hence the meeting just days after his defection focused on one basic question: were the rebels strong enough to defeat Soren? Their pre-coup optimism had been based on the false assumption that Chancellor Mentaxes and General Danton would join the rebel lords and that Soren would be unable to mount serious resistance. That optimism had proved to be a delusion. The rebels were now staring at a looming civil war that would probably be long and bloody because neither side had a decisive advantage. This led to dissension among the rebels. Many led by Lucien only wanted to discuss ways of winning the civil war that they saw as inevitable. Others led by Grassic were looking for ways to avoid having their homeland ravaged by renewed civil war.

But then rapidly unfolding events in Galatia and Menkara quickly forced the rebel leaders to reanalyze the meaning and significance of the defection of William. The rebels learned from reliable informants in Galatia that William's influence over King Radames was growing. Two month after William's defection, they received reports of troop movements in Galatia indicating preparation for war. Given the voice of William in the king's ear, the only plausible target of Galatian aggression had to be King Soren and Menkara.

That suspicion based on events in Galatia became a certainty when reports were received from rebel sympathizers in the Menkaran capital. The reports were that Soren was frantically preparing for war, but not an aggressive military campaign to try to crush the rebels. Rather the nature of troop movements and the tenure of public announcements indicated preparation to repel a foreign invasion.

Even with William gone, what nation would be foolhardy enough to attack Menkara, the kingdom with the strongest conventional army and strongest military sorcery on the continent? The only possibility was Galatia, the nation that now had at its disposal the awful powers of sorcery of William.

The conclusion that the rebel leaders drew from all these reports was that a William-powered Galatian invasion of Menkara was being organized and that King Soren knew it and was preparing a defense. After these reports of troop movements came in, the rebel leaders reconvened to try to arrive at a consensus on how to respond to the looming invasion of Menkara by Galatia, an invasion assisted by the hitherto irresistible military sorcery of William. They met in Carpanzia the capital city of the province of Caxtonia, the hereditary domain of Lord Lucien's family. Carpanzia had been chosen as the usual meeting place for the rebel leaders because it was centrally located and had natural defenses that made it almost invulnerable to attack.

Lord Lucien spoke first. He emphasized that the rebel goal had been to depose Soren and restore the decentralized Menkara that had existed for centuries before the depredations of Soren. It now seemed that Galatia was about to declare war on Soren. Therefore, he claimed that the obvious path for the rebels was to forge an alliance with Galatia against King Soren, their common enemy.

A cacophony of protests erupted. The oldest of the rebel lords passionately asserted "that if and when the Galatian army crossed the border into Menkara, Galatia would be declaring war not just on King Soren, but on all of Menkara." Another lord rose to say "We are rebels against the King, not traitors. I will not take up arms to aid those who attack my homeland."

Supporters of Lucien replied that the quarrel of King Radames and William was with King Soren, and not with the people and nation of Menkara. The assembly was divided until the high priestess Grassic rose to speak.

"Lord Lucien speaks the truth when he says that the coming Galatian invasion is motivated by distrust and fear of King Soren. That same distrust and fear motivated our rebellion. But the passions of the Galatians are being roused by the sorcerer William who seeks revenge for his humiliation by Soren. Once William and the Galatians have defeated Soren, do you think they will simply hand Menkara back to us on a silver platter? No! William craves power and the Galatian preparation for war proves that he has roused a similar lust for power in King Radames. After their military victory, they will both see Menkara and its riches as well deserved spoils of war. The only thanks we will get for aiding their invasion will be to be treated as lapdogs by the Galatian conquerors." No vote was taken but after Grassic spoke, sentiment in the hall was clearly against allying with the invaders.

Grassic then overplayed her hand and suggested a very different strategy. She argued for abandoning their opposition to Soren in favor of a joining with him in a united front to save Menkara. Despite the universal respect for high priestess Grassic, her proposal never had a chance. Since the rebels had repeatedly been denounced by King Soren as scum and traitors, no appeal to patriotism could persuade the rebels to form a united front with a man they despised.

Menjaro, lord of Altaria, had bided his time well. He had waited until the assembly had revealed its emotional hostility to each of their possible alliances. He then proposed that each of the rebel lords withdraw into his provincial base, thus allowing the armies of Radames and Soren to exhaust each other. The rebel would fight only if attacked. With this strategy, the rebels would avoid the carnage of the large scale war that was about to begin, and when that war ended, the rebels with their armies still whole would be in good position to obtain favorable terms from the war-ravaged winner either by diplomacy or force of arms.

Lord Menjaro's's proposal eventually carried the day. In anticipation of the Galatian invasion of Menkara, each of the rebel lords would hole up with his army in his provincial homeland to await the outcome of the war between Galatia and Menkara. Since many details remained to be worked out, the assembly would meet again in the morning to work out the details of the chosen strategy.

That evening, two weary and uninvited travelers arrived in Carpathia, travelers who would soon persuade the rebel leaders to reconsider their options. The two were Kaitlin, who had led the Free Bezriel guerrillas, and Marcus, her travelling companion.

The coup attempt had given renewed hope to Kaitlin and Marcus. They had decided to find the rebel leaders and add Free Bezriel to those supporting the new regime. Once they learned that the Carpathia was the rebel headquarters they began their long trek on foot from Bezriel to the rebel stronghold. Since they were wanted fugitives with a price on their heads their journey was difficult and dangerous.It was early evening when they arrived in the capital. They went to the palace, introduced themselves and requested an audience with Lord Lucien. The minor official who spoke with them at first denied their presumptuous request. But after learning that they represented Free Bezriel and wanted to join the rebel alliance, he passed their request on to a higher official. Eventually Lucien heard of Kaitlin's arrival. He immediately ordered that the new arrivals be brought to his receiving room.

Lord Lucien and guerrilla leader Kaitlin had never met. But each had long admired the other's principled opposition to Soren. To begin, Kaitlin and Marcus answered questions from Lucien about their life on the run after the arrest of Ariadne. Kaitlin then pledged Free Bezriel to the rebel crusade to rebuild Menkara on the principle of regional autonomy. Lord Lucien graciously accepted their offer and said that Kaitlin would have a seat on the rebel's central committee, even though he knew that the rebel force she commanded was now scattered and no longer much of a fighting force.

Kaitlin then said she had a proposal she would like to present to the rebel high command and expressed the hope that Lucien would support her proposal. "Lord Lucien, the defection of William has changed everything. Soren and William united were a force of evil that was invincible. Now their enmity gives us hope. I am sure it was hope based on that enmity, that inspired your coup d'état. You did not rebel when Soren was backed by William, because you knew that you would lose. William is now with King Radames of Galatia. With William egging him on Radames will soon invade Menkara. If we fight Radames backed by William, we will surely lose. Are we to despair? What hope is there for freedom, if there is no shortage of kings willing to employ William to ensure and expand their dominance? But I do not despair! There is hope! The name of that hope is the Free Bezriel sorceress Ariadne!"

Lucien could restrain himself no longer. "Stop, Kaitlin! My allies and I have made the same analysis. We dreamed the same dream; cherished the same hope. But it is a vain hope. Ariadne, her powers blocked, is held prisoner in a dungeon in Soren's own castle. She will soon be executed for treason."

"Excuse me, Lord Lucien, but your conclusion is too hasty. It is true that Ariadne is held prisoner in a well-guarded castle. But without the sorcery of William, that guard is not invincible. Free Bezriel does not have the resources needed to free Ariadne, but the rebel alliance does. What is needed is a strong attack by rebel troops on Soren' castle to provide cover for a crack team of sorcerers led by Marcus to enter the castle, free Ariadne and bring her here to join the rebel alliance."

They talked long into the night. Eventually Lucien promised that in the morning he would propose to the assembly of leaders that Free Bezriel be accepted into the rebel alliance. He would then introduce Kaitlin and Marcus as the leaders of Free Bezriel and allow Kaitlin to propose her daring plan for freeing Ariadne so that she could use her sorcery to aid the alliance.

The strategy of Lucien and others in the anti-Soren vanguard had changed repeatedly since Soren had become king because the power situation they confronted had changed repeatedly. When William was working with Soren, all they could do was create SUPPORT to mildly protest the king's centralizing and expansionist moves. During the period when William in anger had withdrawn into seclusion but had not yet defected, through SUPPORT they had with increasing aggressiveness openly opposed Soren. Then when certain that William would not intervene, they had declared a rival government pushing Menkara to the brink of civil war. After William defected to Galatia and it became clear that a Galatian invasion of Menkara was immanent, they had voted to hole up in their home provinces, hoping that the William-aided Galatian invaders and Soren's forces would exhaust each other. It was a desperation plan since few if any really believed that Soren would be able to hold off the William-aided invaders.

And now with the backing of Lucien, a new proposal was made by Kaitlin the leader of the Free Bezriel guerrillas that might radically change the relationships in the three way power struggle that had emerged. She proposed a plan to free Ariadne, the Free Bezriel sorceress from her confinement from the dungeon in Soren's castle, where she was being held while waiting to be tried for treason, convicted and executed. Since Ariadne was the one sorcerer who had successfully resisted William the plan was not only daring in what it proposed to do, but, if successful, promised great rewards.

Before Kaitlin arrived, the rebels had not totally forgotten about Ariadne. As Lucien told Kaitlin and Marcus, they had joined the campaign to pressure King Soren to pardon Ariadne. Since it had seemed so obviously hopeless they had never seriously considered trying to bust her out of captivity. Now a daring plan for freeing Ariadne had been put forward by the Free Bezriel leader, a plan that be successful required both the sorcery of Marcus and a well-armed and well-trained raiding party from the rebel alliance. Lucien pleaded passionately trying to persuade the assembly of lords to approve the raid.

The debate on the proposal was intense. Pessimists argued that the rescue attempt would fail to free the young sorceress. That failure would lead to a significant military confrontation between the forces of Soren and the forces of the rebels. That would play right into the hands of William and Radames and make their conquest of Menkara faster and easier.

The pessimists also argued that even if Ariadne were freed, she would be weakened by the months of drugging that had been used by Soren to block her powers and would be unable to fend off the attack on the rebels that would surely come once Radames and

William realized that their most dangerous opponent was now with the rebels.

Optimists argued that freeing Ariadne gave the rebels their best chance to survive and to negotiate favorable terms with Soren, or more likely Radames, whoever won that war. They admitted that failure of the Ariadne rescue plan was possible, but even failure would be a useful small-scale trial run of battle with Soren's sorcerers and conventional army. Since they planned a raid, not a battle, casualties would be light. Hence, if the raid failed and Ariadne was not freed, the rebels would be only a little worse off than they were now. To the pleasant surprise of Lucien, both Menjaro and Grassic supported the plan.

Kaitlin's plan to free Ariadne from captivity was approved, mainly because most of the lords agreed that it gave the rebels their best chance not only of survival, but even a chance of achieving their original goals. The support of Grassic was very helpful, since she was widely acknowledged as the ethical conscience of the group. In this time of extreme crisis, these traditionalist lords wanted to act as their ancestors would have acted and Grassic was their pole star for right action.

CHAPTER 10

When Ariadne remained constant in her rejection of what she regarded as Soren's attempt to buy her powers to defend his kingdom against invasion by William and Galatia, Soren's patience was sorely tried. All that prevented him from ordering her execution was his knowledge that Ariadne, despite her moralistic obstinacy, was his last best hope of defeating the invasion.

Three days after Kaitlin proposed to the rebel alliance, her plan to free Ariadne, an elite rebel guerrilla force, commanded by Ezekiel, a rebel warrior very experienced in small guerrilla operations, infiltrated the castle in which Ariadne was held prisoner. Their plan was elegant in its simplicity. With the aid of rebel sympathizers working in the castle, two sorcerers, one of them Marcus, and six soldiers skilled in close quarter fighting were infiltrated into the castle. That night, after the guard around Ariadne had been reduced to the nighttime minimum of three, the rebel unit attacked. Within minutes the rebel guerrillas were in control of the prisoner confinement area.

Under standing orders, guards in the castle when attacked by a superior force were to sound the alarm to bring in reinforcements before trying to repel the attack. As soon as the rebels attacked, those guarding Ariadne sounded the alarm. The guerrillas would soon be outnumbered and surrounded, but they were prepared for that eventuality and did not panic. Next came the most difficult part of the attempt to free Ariadne. The six guerrilla fighters had to give their two sorcerers as much time as possible to break the enchantment binding Ariadne's powers before the palace guard retook the prisoner confinement area. The rescue team would then rely upon Ariadne's sorcery to enable them to fight their way out of the castle.

If the sorcerer's failed to break the enchantment, the rebel invaders were doomed. But they succeeded because while fighting for Free Bezriel, Ariadne had taught Marcus how to break a power-binding enchantment. Such enchantments are not of people, but of areas surrounding a person. Ariadne could not break the enchantment that robbed her of her powers because she was always within the enchanted circle surrounding her body. Only two or more sorcerers working together outside the circle could break the enchantment. That is why the guerrilla contingent included two sorcerers, one of them Marcus. In just twelve minutes, the rebel sorcerers broke the enchantment blocking Ariadne's powers. The guerrillas then broke open the door to Ariadne's cell. A tearful reunion between Ariadne and Marcus was followed by an explanation of her part in the escape plan. Then the palace guard arrived and all hell broke loose.

Shots were fired, swords and knives were drawn. Within minutes the rebels were outnumbered and the imbalance continued to grow. Marcus led the pleas by the rebels for Ariadne to do something that would enable them to escape.

Ariadne knew she had to help the comrades who had risked their lives to free her. But she saw no way to do so without many on both sides dying. In her heart she had vowed to never kill again. She had gotten to know a few of her guards during her months of captivity. She had come to see them more and more as ordinary people doing their jobs to support their families and less and less as the enemy. She knew that she had strong enough powers of sorcery to main or kill enough of the palace guard to enable herself and her comrades to escape. But morally and emotionally, she could not do it.

Ariadne was paralyzed by indecision until one of the palace guard was shot dead close to where she was kneeling on the floor behind an overturned table. Seeing another young man dying in a ferocious battle over control of her powers of sorcery sent shock waves of self-loathing coursing through Ariadne's body and soul. Without considering the consequences, she

cast a paralyzing spell that froze everyone where they were. Soldiers on both sides could see and hear what was going on around them, but could not move.

Ariadne could not maintain the paralysis indefinitely. It was a mere stop-gap solution. What should she do next? Help her rescuers escape and go with them to join the rebel alliance was what Marcus and her other rescuers wanted and expected her to do. But that meant fighting another civil war and she had no heart for that. In her time with Free Bezriel, she had divided the world into us and them. That had led to her evil deed of bewitching the soldiers of Cerberus into slaughtering their comrades. She would not walk down that path again. But what path would she walk now? There was no course of action for which everything felt right. Suddenly an answer came to her of which her soul approved. Whether it was her own idea or a suggestion from Esther she did not know and for the moment did not care.

Realizing that a negotiated truce was needed she unfroze two of the palace guard and ordered them to find Soren and Mentaxes, and convey to them her demand that they negotiate with her under a white flag promise of safety. The two guards, in awe of her power did not even consider disobedience, but immediately went in search of the king and chancellor.

Both Soren and Mentaxes had been informed of the invasion and developing battle and were already on their separate ways to the battle area. The messengers met Mentaxes first. After hearing of the rebels' freeing of Ariadne, her paralysis spell, and her demand to talk to king and chancellor, Mentaxes quickly agreed to go with the messengers to find King Soren and then meet with Ariadne. Minutes later they met Soren who was rushing to the battle scene and gave him the same information, including Ariadne's demand to meet with him.

Ariadne's demand angered Soren. "No one tells the king what to do. The presumption of this witch knows no limits. I will go with you to speak with the witch, but not because she orders me to. I go not to negotiate, but rather to give her an ultimatum: surrender immediately or all Free Bezriel prisoners will be executed." Then turning and addressing the palace guard that accompanied him, he said. "We separate here. Proceed until the last turn before the battle area. Then wait there for my return or an order from me. These presumptuous traitors will either surrender or be killed by you. Not one will leave the palace alive."

The two palace guards did not dare tell the king that Ariadne, not he, was master of the crisis. They did as ordered and brought king and chancellor to meet with Ariadne. Although the battle area was large, only one figure, Ariadne was not frozen. Hence it was easy for Soren to quickly locate her. Although shaken by the sight of his frozen soldiers, the king spoke before the sorceress could seize the initiative.

"Ariadne, you disappoint me. I offered you wealth, honors, freedom. You refused. I gave you time to reconsider. How do you repay my magnanimity? You smuggle your cohorts into my castle and attack my palace guard. Surrender now, before I order an armed battalion to put down your insurrection. Surrender now and I will merely imprison and not execute the unwelcome guests you have brought me."

"King Soren, you need to learn both manners and humility. I was your prisoner for months, my powers blocked. But now my powers have been restored. With William gone, you have no one who can control me. I will dictate terms not you."

"It is true, witch, that I have no one who is your equal. But I have numbers within a short calling distance. Not even William could prevail against such numbers. Surrender while you still have that option."

"Soren, let us stop exchanging insults and threats that get us nowhere. I have a proposal that I think is in the best interest of all Menkarans. For my proposal to take effect, both sides must accept it, both you and the rebel alliance. I will not fight in another civil war, not for you and not for the rebel alliance. But I will fight to defend a united Menkara against the coming attack by William and the armies of King Radames.

"Both sides, hear me well. I will fight William and Radames only if King Soren and the rebel alliance form a united front against the invaders, only if you both agree to fight only the common enemy and not each other. If you do not establish a united front against the common enemy, I will return to my prison cell to watch with grieving heart, the blood bath that will soon begin."

Ariadne then released both sides from her freezing spell, after warning that they would be refrozen if any hostile action was taken by even one soldier. All present were stunned by her united front proposal. Soren choked down his automatic response that no one had the right to dictate terms to the king. Instead he conferred with Mentaxes until his anger gave way to relief. The infuriating girl had just given him the two things he most needed to stymie the invasion. First, she had given him a sorcerer, herself, perhaps capable of battling on even terms with William. Second, instead of the rebels forcing him to fight a two front war, they were now being pressured by Ariadne to add their troops and sorcerers to the defense of Menkara. How the rebels would be dealt with was a problem that would be addressed if and after the invasion was repulsed. Soren told Ariadne that he would agree to her terms, but only if the rebels also agreed.

How to respond was more complex for the guerrilla rescue team. There was no one in that small band with the authority to speak for the rebel alliance. After much bickering, it was finally agreed by both sides that most of the intruders would be allowed to return to Caxtonia to report Ariadne's proposal to the rebel leadership and that a rebel lord with authority would come to the capital within three days with the rebel leadership's reply. Two of the eight intruders must be left behind as hostages.

Marcus volunteered to be one of hostages. To Ariadne's delight that offer was accepted by both Soren and the rebels.

Two documents were drawn up and given to Ezekiel, commander of the rebel rescue team. The first document signed by Ariadne stated that she would not use her sorcery to aide either side in a Menkaran civil war, but that she would use her powers to help a united front defend Menkara against the threatened William-powered invasion from Galatia. The second signed by Soren and carrying his official royal seal declared his acceptance of the terms proposed by Ariadne and full amnesty for the rebels if the united front was formed.

The rebel intruders were given an official escort by King Soren's troops to the border separating loyalist and rebel-held territory. From there they rode a fast as possible to Caxtonia to

hand over to the rebel high command the documents from King Soren and the sorceress Ariadne. Undoubtedly, they would also have to answer many questions about how their rescue mission had led to such an unexpected ending.

Within two hours of the rescue team's arrival, an emergency session of the rebel high command was called to order by Lord Lucien. As the members filed in they immediately noticed that the rescue team had returned without Ariadne. Before Lucien could called the meeting to order, the booming voice of Lord Menjaro echoed through the chamber. "Ezekiel, where is Ariadne? Explain your failure!"

"My lord, we did not fail. Our sorcerers broke the enchantment spell binding Ariadne powers. We then freed her from confinement in her dungeon. Before we could get free of Soren's filthy dungeons, we were attacked by the palace guard. Ariadne seemed paralyzed by I know not what. We begged her to use her powers to enable us to escape. She did nothing. Eventually she used her powers to freeze both sides. She demanded to meet with King Soren and Chancellor Mentaxes. When they arrived, she declared that if civil war came to Menkara she would help neither side. She said that she would only use her powers for a united front of king and rebels to repel an attack by William and Galatia on Menkara."

An uproar of protest and disbelief followed. Ezekiel shouted that he had signed written letters from both Ariadne and Soren that would confirm his story. Lucien somehow managed to quiet the assembly so that the letters could be read and their authenticity verified. Kaitlin and Grassic verified the signature of Ariadne. Several lords verified the signature and seal of King Soren. It was not enough to read the letters aloud. Each member of the assembly wanted to see the actual letters. That took more than almost two hours. It was a long delay, but it proved useful for in that time, emotions cooled so that the debate that followed was relatively calm and rational.

Lucien argued that Ariadne allying herself with her hated enemy Soren proved that she had been tortured and had made her alliance offer under extreme duress. But he persuaded very few. Those who knew Ariadne best stated that the call for a united front between bitter enemies sounded very much like the Ariadne they knew.

There was little drama in the rebels' debate on whether to accept Ariadne's proposal. A united front with Soren was bitter medicine to swallow, but since it brought hope where before there was none, even Lucien joined in what became a unanimous vote to form a united front.

CHAPTER 11

Ariadne had made a united front of king and rebel lords the precondition of her joining the armed resistance to the threatened invasion of Menkara. Despite both sides quickly agreeing to Ariadne's demand that they unite to try to thwart the William-powered invasion of Menkara, King Soren and the rebel lords remained bitter enemies who did not trust each other. For each side, the alliance was a desperation move, a survival tactic. Each needed Ariadne to have any chance of surviving the coming attack by William. They had agreed to work together only because that was the price demanded by Ariadne for her assistance.

Lord Menjaro was typical of most of the lords who had rebelled against Soren. His heart and soul were invested in the feudal universe in which he had been raised. It was a world in which everyone had a place, had the rights and duties of that place. Menjaro had been highborn, born to rule, born to be obeyed, born to the life of a warrior, fighting to defend his lands and heritage. That world had been destroyed by the power-lust of Soren and the irresistible military sorcery of William. Menjaro could never forgive Soren and William. As did so many others, Menjaro had joined the rebellion in a hopeless quest to restore the feudal order of things that had outlived its time. He agreed to Ariadne's terms, agreed to fight with and not against Soren, because William and any army invading Menkara were more of a threat to his values than Soren.

The lord, most reluctant to signing the accord was Lucien. He agreed to the alliance with Soren only when it became clear that Ariadne' proposal of a united front against William and the Galatians had overwhelming support in the rebel camp. He grudgingly accepted that the short term goal must be defeating William and the Galatians, but his long term objective remained driving Soren from the throne. He saw Soren's acceptance of Ariadne's alliance plan as a cynical move in that tyrant's struggle to hold onto the throne. Lucien vowed to himself that if somehow William and the invasion were defeated, he would continue his quest to drive Soren from power.

The Ventaxian high priestess Grassic embraced Ariadne's plan with joy and gratitude. She had joined the rebel alliance hoping for and expecting a bloodless coup. That dream had turned into a nightmare. Ariadne's plan not only gave Menkara its best hope of defeating William and the invasion, but it also prevented the immediate outbreak of civil war. Grassic hoped that by forcing the two sides to work together, the alliance demanded by Ariadne might not only destroy the animosities that created civil war, but might help forge personal bonds of friendship between those who struggled together in a common cause. That was her hope, but she recognized the immense difficulty of creating an effective unity between proud leaders such as Soren, Menjaro, and Lucien who did not like and did not trust each other. Could the sharing of hardships and dangers lead to friendships, or at least create the mutual trust that might eventually overcome the existing hatred and distrust.

Kaitlin, the guerrilla commander of Free Bezriel, looked at everything in terms of how it affected freedom for her people, Bezriel. Thus for her the threat posed by William was all the worse because he was a Bezrielite and that fact sabotaged any possibility that Soren if victorious would ever accept independence for

Bezriel. Hence she was delighted that Ariadne, also a Bezrielite, had become central to the effort to defeat William. If Ariadne succeeded, Kaitlin hoped that out of fear of alienating his savior, Ariadne, King Soren would honor the demand for Bezrielite independence.

Soren was certain that the rebels would accept Ariadne's proposal. Hence he began to develop war plans based on a united front, before receiving official confirmation that there would be a united front. In wartime Soren trusted only his own judgment. But because of constant reminders from Mentaxes, he finally accepted the fact that the rebels would insist on having a voice in setting alliance strategy for defeating the invasion. Thus to appease his new allies, Soren drew up a plan for a war council to consist of himself, General Danton, two representative of the rebel alliance, and Ariadne. The rebels would have a voice. But, Soren insisted to Mentaxes, every army needs to have a commander, the one man in charge, and since he was both king and the most experienced warrior, it was obvious that he should be the one in charge, the one with the ultimate authority to make decisions.

Mentaxes replied that a war council made excellent sense, but doubted that the rebels would agree to be subordinate to the king they had rebelled against. Thus a dilemma for the alliance had arisen: was there a command structure for the alliance that was both politically acceptable to both sides and made military sense. Mentaxes first suggested that important decisions had to be acceptable to both sides. Soren rejected requiring consensus because it would either lead to paralysis, an inability to react in a timely fashion to enemy actions or it would lead to unsound compromise decisions and disaster.

Mentaxes then suggestion that the defense of Menkara be split into two geographic sectors, with Soren defending the east and the rebels defending the west. Ariadne would be deployed where most needed at any given time. Soren hated the idea of sharing command, but agreed that if the rebel lords rejected giving him supreme command he would propose the two sector defense strategy to the rebel faction.

Mentaxes also proposed creating a national political assembly. The purpose of the assembly would be to discuss the structure of Menkara if and when the Galatian attack was repelled. Membership would include provincial, ethnic and religious leaders. The assembly's resolutions would not have the status of law, but would be presented to a future Menkaran national parliament that would have binding legislative powers. For the duration of the war, the assembly would serve the very useful function of allowing the various factions to publicize their goals and vent their frustrations.

Mentaxes was pleased when Soren praised the proposed wartime assembly as thoughtful and pragmatic. He would allow Mentaxes to suggest the assembly to the rebel lords as soon as they officially agreed to the alliance. As a result, Mentaxes was beginning to have hope that Soren the strategic genius was pushing aside the megalomaniac Soren the Magnificent, on the throne of Menkara.

After the alliance contract had been drawn up and signed by Soren, and after her letter to the rebels had been drafted and signed, Ariadne was formally released from prison and escorted to her new apartment in the royal palace. It was far too luxurious for her simple tastes, but absorbed with more important problems, she raised no objections. She was told that she would meet with King Soren, General Danton and Chancellor Mentaxes late the next morning. She accepted that meeting with dread, very unsure about what she would say to the high and mighty of Menkara. She desperately hoped that Esther would come in a dream that night to advise her.

Her spirits were lifted when she was told that Marcus would be allowed to join her for a catered dinner in her apartment that night. That meeting of Ariadne and Marcus was stiff and formal until after the dinner had been served and the servants had left the room.

Ariadne had crippling doubts about what she had done. Ending the bloodshed triggered by the attempt to free her was of course a good thing, as was pushing Soren and the rebels into an alliance, brief though it might be. What bothered her, nay what horrified her, was that to achieve those end she had committed herself once again use her sorcery in a war soon to begin. To make matters worse, once again she had made an emotional spur of the moment decision. Months of vowing and practicing to become a rational person who thought through all aspects of a situation before acting had changed nothing. She had been so focused on the crisis of the moment, the hatred between Soren and the rebels boiling over into violence over which side would control her sorcery, so focused on the moment that once again she had acted impulsively. Her impulse had been to prevent a bloodbath. In that, she had succeeded. But at what a cost! After the servants left, unable to restrain herself any longer, Ariadne cried out in desperation, "Marcus, I have made things worse!"

Marcus who had sensed her unease, as soon as he entered the apartment, was glad that an honest reply would also be a comforting reply. "Made things worse? Just the opposite! You cut short the violence resulting from our attempt to free you from prison. You brokered a truce between King Soren and the rebel lords, who have long been bitter enemies. You created a chance for Menkara to defeat the attack by Galatia and William that is surely coming. You created conditions under which Bezriel at long last might become free."

Ariadne's response to his words of comfort devastated Marcus. "I admit there is truth in what you say, Marcus. My actions made things better for the moment. But you leave out the deeper truth. The ultimate result of the alliance now being formed, the alliance that I demanded, will be to escalate the level of violence in a war that can no longer be prevented. Galatia will invade. William will let loose his demonic sorcery. The stronger the resistance Menkara puts up, the stronger the resistance they encounter, the greater the violence and destruction that will follow."

"Perhaps. But Ariadne, thanks to that alliance, it is possible that William will be defeated! Possible that common people can once again live and work in peace and security."

"A foolish dream, Marcus! I can hold off William for a time, but there is no way that I can defeat him in what will be an ultra-violent no-holds-barred war."

The heart of Marcus was almost broken, but he did not give up. He was fully committed to violent struggle to free Bezriel. But he hated the death and suffering that resulted from that liberation struggle. Thus he was able to understand and empathize with the severity of Ariadne's angst. After an agonized silence, he spoke.

"You are troubled, Ariadne, because you have committed yourself to the defense of Menkara against William and you know that such a defense will be very violent. Two very different specters haunt you. The first and most obvious specter is that defending Menkara involves breaking your vow to never again use sorcery to kill. Fighting a war violates your very nature, violates your commitment to non-violence. But you are haunted, I suspect, by a more insidious specter. You fear that because of your pacifism, you will lead Menkara to national disaster because you will morally shrink from what needs to be done to win the war.

"I cannot tell you what you should do. You know all too well the ethical reasons why you should not fight in the war that is coming. But I am not sure you fully understand the moral reasons why you should fight. If you decide to keep your promise to Soren and the rebel lords, I don't know whether you can defeat William. But your sorcery is our only hope. Perhaps even more important is that for you to fight alongside a united Menkara will bring spiritual hope to our people who are close to despair."

Ariadne held back her tears.

"Marcus, your words prove that you know my soul all too well. But your words did not penetrate to the depth of my despair. It is more than the fact that I am now committed to breaking my sacred vow to never again use sorcery to kill. It is more than the possibility that I may not be able to keep my promise to king and rebels to fight with them to the end against William and the invaders.

"I will try to explain what that "more" is. When one of Soren's men was killed in the counterattack on your rescue squad, I went out of my mind with guilt that a struggle between lords for control of my sorcery was creating death and destruction. I had to find a way to end the killing. Freezing everyone was my first attempt. But I quickly realized I was only postponing the violence. Pledging my help to a united front of Soren and the rebel lords to repel the common danger of a William-led invasion of Menkara was my solution. Unfortunately I didn't think about the intensified warfare that would result from the united front that I caused to be created. Don't you see, Marcus, that by forcing a united front between Soren and the rebels, and by pledging to use my sorcery to aid that united front I have escalated, not decreased, the levels of death, destruction, and hatred in the inevitable war that is about to begin."

Marcus took time to think before replying. What he said reflected both his concern about Ariadne's inner torment and his fear of the vengeance of William if he were to be victorious. "I hear both your words and your heart, Ariadne. Do you really want to base your decision of what you should do on a utilitarian comparison of the levels of death, destruction, and hatred that will result from your actions? If so, you have to look at long run and not just short run results. If our united front holds and you use your powers against William and the invasion, the short run will be more violent, and we may or may not win. But if you sit back and do nothing, our united front will fall apart, the Galatians will conquer and occupy Menkara, and William will soon be in full control of Galatian policy. That new order of power and oppression will last a very long time. In that long run will there be less death, destruction, and hatred? No. On utilitarian grounds fighting the aggressor is the most moral policy."

Ariadne started to reply, but was stopped by Marcus. "Please let me finish, Ariadne. You are not a utilitarian. You believe in moral absolutes. What is more important in your moral universe? Maintaining your personal purity by withdrawing from the conflicts of the world? Or joining the fight against a world governed by William, a sorcerer of great power full of hate and a lust for revenge."

"You forget, Marcus, that fighting against William, means aiding the power-mad Soren."

"I can never forget what Soren has become. But Soren is not a sorcerer, let alone one with the powers of William. Even at his worst, he cannot match the evil William can accomplish."

Ariadne was physically and spiritually exhausted. "Enough! I am too mentally and emotionally exhausted. I must sleep. I implore Esther to visit me tonight to help me see my way through the nightmare that I am living, through the nightmare that we all are living."

Shortly thereafter palace guards came to escort the hostage Marcus back to the drab room that would serve as his holding cell until King Soren received confirmation of rebel acceptance of the alliance.

CHAPTER 12

After months of near solitary confinement in her dungeon, Ariadne craved the company of friends and comrades. But she had been uncomfortable and ill at ease during her longed for dinner with Marcus. It seemed that she could no longer interact comfortably with the living, not even with Marcus. She needed to dream-talk with Esther, the ancient Seeker who had guided her in the past. But she quickly discovered that she was too emotionally wound up to fall asleep. She summoned an attendant and asked for an herbal tea mixture to help her sleep.

Within minutes of falling asleep, she began to dream. She was back in her family's garden in Bezriel. That was where she had often talked with her godmother, Abigail, her confidante in the formative time after the discovery of her powers and before she left home to join the Free Bezriel guerrillas. But it was Esther, not Abigail, who entered the dream garden and greeted her formally. "Welcome home, daughter of Bezriel."

Ariadne was startled and began by asking many questions at once. "Esther! Do you know all that has happened today? The attempt to rescue me? What I did? The alliance? The coming war with William and Galatia?"

"Yes, daughter of Bezriel, I know these things."

"Do you also know how sore my heart is with grief and doubt? Once again I acted impulsively, acted without thinking of consequences, and made a terrible decision that is setting in motion events that will lead to terrible tragedy for Bezriel. And not just a tragedy for Bezriel, but disaster for all of Menkara. What can I do now to undo what I have done? I beg of you, Esther, tell me what I must do to avert this tragedy!"

"Daughter of Bezriel, You ask for what cannot be. Decisions concerning what to do are for the living. The dead cannot tell the living what to do!"

"Are you telling me that what I have done is so awful that you can no longer help me? Is that why you no longer call me by my name?"

"I am not angry or disappointed with you, Ariadne. I called you 'daughter of Bezriel' to remind you of who you are. I did not say I will not help you. I will help you, help you understand the crisis that has emerged. But I cannot tell you what you should do. Since it is you who must act, it is you who must decide."

"But in past crises you told me what I must do."

"No Ariadne, I did not. I merely helped you see the likely consequences of different choices. But in each instance, it was you who decided."

Ariadne, overwhelmed by Esther's insistence that there was no way of avoiding responsibility either for the future or the past, almost cried. But she quickly got her emotions under control and tried to bravely face up to the hard problems surrounding her. "Esther, you said you would help me understand what is happening. Can we start with the rescue attempt and work our way through to the present?"

"That is as good a place to start as any. So, tell me, Ariadne, why did the rebels send a rescue squad to break you out of prison?"

"That is easy. It was the same reason, why after William defected, Soren kept me alive rather than executing me. Both king and rebels want use of my powers of sorcery."

"And why did you not use your powers to effect an escape from Soren's castle with the rescue squad?"

"I am ashamed to admit it, Seeker, but the truth is that the fighting that erupted left me paralyzed with fear and indecision. When one of Soren's men was killed near where I was hiding. I found it intolerable that once again because of me a man had been killed. So I stopped the fighting the only way I knew how. I froze everyone."

"Can you remember what you were thinking and feeling while everyone around you was frozen?"

"Yes, Esther. Those minutes were so awful, I will never be able to forget them. I knew I could only hold the soldiers and guerrillas frozen a short time and that once I lost control, the killing would resume. Then out of nowhere the idea of an alliance of king and rebels against the coming invasion by William and Galatia came to me. I unfroze two of Soren's men and ordered them to find Soren and bring him to me. The rest was easy. A William-led invasion was the greatest threat to both king and rebels. So I told them that I would help neither side unless they formed an alliance to defeat the invasion. As I expected Soren accepted and I am sure the rebel leaders will also agree to the alliance after they learn my terms."

"Daughter of Bezriel, would you like my opinion?"

"Esther, I beg you to step calling me 'daughter of Bezriel'. My actions prove that I am not worthy of that title. But there is nothing I want more than to know your reaction to what I have done. There is nothing I need more than to know that."

"Very well, Ariadne. During the rescue attempt, you were confronted by a complex and terrible situation in which you had no time to think. You want to know my opinion. In my opinion, you came up with a brilliant solution which not only prevented more bloodshed in the bitter battle that was raging, but also against all odds, created an alliance between sworn enemies. All that seems good to me. So tell me, Ariadne, why are you so unhappy over what you did?"

Ariadne answered immediately, without stopping to think. "Because the end result of my thoughtless action will be greater bloodshed and desolation than would have occurred if I had done nothing. By creating an alliance between Soren and the rebel lords and pledging to use my sorcery for that alliance I have transformed what would have been a quick invasion and conquest by William and Galatia with limited death and devastation into what most likely will be a long nasty war with horrifying levels of death and devastation."

"Are you saying. Ariadne that one should not resist evil, if because of the resistance more will suffer and die because of the resistance? Are you saying that if resistance will increase death and suffering, the good should passively let those who are bad rule over everyone and everything?"

Ariadne felt cornered, but refused to concede. She counterattacked with a vengeance "When the forces of good have a chance to prevail, then resistance is justified. But when there is no chance of victory, then, Esther, resistance is ritual suicide. No army and no sorcerer can withstand William. Soren and the rebels think that I can hold my own against William, because once I created an invisibility shield that for a short time protected Free Bezriel from Soren's army and the sorcery of William. That gave rise to the myth that my powers of sorcery are equal to William's. They are not.

"With your help, I was able to briefly protect Free Bezriel, a small group that could be surrounded by an invisibility shield. But there are limits to the size of such a shield. Such a shield will be of limited use in the large scale war that is about to begin. In all other aspects of military sorcery, William is far more powerful than I am. I can delay the triumph of William and Soren. I cannot prevent it. If I keep my word and join the alliance in fighting against the invasion, I will merely be prolonging the war and increasing its savagery with no chance of preventing defeat. Because the invaders will have suffered higher casualties, the post-war butchery will be that much worse."

Esther saw the pain and despair in Ariadne's face and words. But her knowledge of the strength of Ariadne's heart and character told her that now was not the time for sympathy and comfort. Rather it was the time to appeal to her deepest values and to try to strengthen her resolve to fight for those values. Esther's long silence made Ariadne nervous. After what seemed forever to Ariadne, but was in fact less than a minute, Esther finally replied.

"You want to face the world realistically, Ariadne. That is good. That is necessary. But seeing only the dark possibilities if one were to act is pessimism, not realism. You assume there is no way William and the invasion can be defeated and base your analysis on that assumption. Is your knowledge of military history and the possibilities of sorcery so great that you know for a certainty that against William resistance is futile? It is pessimism not knowledge that leads you to such a bleak conclusion. And even if it is true that William and Galatia will conquer Menkara, is it not also true that struggling for a noble cause strengthens both peoples and individuals even when they are defeated?"

"Are you telling me, Esther, that William can be defeated? Are you saying that I can defeat William?"

"Ariadne, I do not know whether you can defeat William. And neither do you. But I do know that resisting evil makes those who resist better and stronger."

"Perhaps it makes the resisters that survive stronger, but what if most of the resisters die?"

"Are you sure that a war of resistance will lead to more death and destruction than decades of life under a cruel master and exploiter?"

Much more was said that night in the argument between the young sorceress and the spirit of the ancient Seeker. Only briefly did they touch upon the rawest level of Ariadne's anxiety about the war that would soon begin. Would Ariadne be able to live with herself when once again as seemed certain, her sorcery killed enemy combatants and possibly even innocent bystanders? Could Ariadne, a true pacifist who abhorred violence against any living creature, fight in the no-holds-barred war that was coming without destroying herself? Could Ariadne become a warrior again and still fulfill her prophesized destiny of leading the tribe of Bezrielites back to the path of Bezriel?

With respect to the impact of fighting a war on the spirit of Ariadne, Esther knew that she had to offer the over-earnest young woman more than just empathy and consolation. Ariadne had vowed never to kill again as a result of her traumatic experiences in the struggle to free Bezriel from the tyranny of King Soren. Not only did she have a natural revulsion against depriving a person of life, but she had experienced the dehumanizing effects of war that had led her to see those on the other side as obstacles to be removed rather than as humans like herself. That had resulted in her spell confusing enemy soldiers so that they slaughtered each other. With that history, could an argument be found to convince Ariadne that fighting on the front lines against the coming invasion was the right choice not just for Bezriel, but also for herself?

Empathy would not be enough, but Esther chose it as her starting point. "We are not so different, Ariadne. I too had to fight military battles. In those battles I could not avoid killing men and women on the other side. Once I accidentally killed a young child. In every case, especially after causing the death of a child caught in a crossfire, I was distraught. What got me through it was remembering that I was fighting for a noble cause and had done everything I could to minimize the harm that I did. I have never ceased to mourn that I had to do what I did; but I learned how to live with what I did. I learned how to forgive myself."

Ariadne's reply was bitter. "We already know, Seeker, that I do not have the moral restraint that you have. You mourn accidentally killing a child. How does compare with my crime. In revenge for the slaying of my friend and mentor, I confused enemy soldiers so that they slaughtered each other. That was not collateral damage, that was deliberate murder. I have vowed to never kill again. Regardless of my promise to king and rebels, I must keep that vow."

"Listen, Ariadne. Taking part in war can lead anyone to do horrible things they would never do in peacetime. But does that mean that good people who want to live a good life should not fight back when bad people use violence and threats to control the world? Is it better to take no active part in struggles in which innocents will suffer? Or is it better to struggle to create a better word in which there will be less needless death and suffering, even if that means taking up arms or using military sorcery?"

"Have you no mercy Esther. Can you not let me find peace by withdrawing from the storms that buffet me?"

"No, Ariadne, I cannot. You are stronger than that. You are better than that. Even if you do not want to hear it, you are a true daughter of Bezriel."

"You are a cruel friend, Esther. I yearn for a world in which knowing what is right is obvious and doing what is right is easy. But you ask me to look at the real world in which knowing what is right is difficult and doing what is right is next to impossible. I yearn for a world in which enemies settle differences peacefully. But you show me a world in which disagreements about fundamentals can only be resolved by violence. I want to do no evil, injure no one, but you won't let me forget that by withdrawing from social struggles to personally do no evil, I am aiding the triumph of evil, violence and oppression."

"I want to curse you, Esther, for your cruel honesty. But I cannot, because honesty is essential even when it is cruel. I now realize that I must thank you for forcing me to look at what I did not want to see. I must thank you for reminding me that I must look at all the consequences of my actions. I was sorely tempted to become a passive non-combatant in the struggles tearing our world apart. But now I see that trying to keep one's soul and hands clean by withdrawal is not the path to Bezriel. Sitting on the sidelines in struggles over what the future will be has a name, and that name is cowardice.

"I hate my choices, but choose I must. Of my own free will I choose to use my sorcery in the fight against William and the invasion of Menkara. The social good is more important than personal purity. I choose to actively struggle for the causes I believe in. I recognize that William will probably triumph. But better to strive for a better world and fail, than to passively let evil triumph."

Esther was deeply moved by Ariadne's words. But all she said was "Are you now committed, Ariadne, to keeping your promise to aid in the defense of Menkara against an invasion by William and Galatia?"

"May Bezriel help me, yes, I am committed."

"Ariadne, some among the Seekers are totally committed to non-violence. Others, including myself are not. I think you have made the best choice and I will support you as far as I am able. Those Seekers committed to non-violence will not. But they will not hinder you."

"Thank you for that information, Esther. I am curious. Would you have supported me if I had chosen non-violence, chosen not to fight?"

"I do not know. Fortunately there is no longer any need to know. But there is one sad fact I do know. We earlier talked about realism and pessimism. I warned you that it is often easy to mistake pessimism for realism. But I have learned the hard way there are also many times when pessimism is realism. You and many other young idealists are joining the fight against the invasion to try to bring about a world with more justice, mercy, and happiness. But have no illusions; those are not the goals of Soren, Menjaro, and most of the other lords, who will lead the fight against the invasion. Their goal is power. In that they are no different than William and King Radames. The leaders united behind the common goal of repelling the invasion, are people with very different values than yours and very different agendas than yours if the war is won."

"I am not a child, Esther. I am well aware that King Soren and I have very different values and goals."

"Ariadne, you are a child in the corridors of power. You grew up in the house of Daniel and Sarah, good people and idealists. After leaving home, you joined Free Bezriel, a group of young men and women willing to risk their lives to try to win freedom for Bezriel. A very different type of Bezrielites than those you knew in childhood; but also good people and idealists. You are aware that King Soren is cut from a very different cloth. But so are all his inner circle. So are also all the rebel lords. For the first time in your life you will be surrounded by a very different type of people. Most of them are decent people. But they are pragmatists, not idealists. Many are powerful, domineering personalities. It will not be easy for you to be yourself, to maintain your ideals, to remain true to Bezriel, and to function effectively in that atmosphere."

"What is the point of your lecture?"

"Simply to remind you how young and naïve you are. Simply to remind you to be careful, very careful."

CHAPTER 13

King Radames was rattled when he received the news that King Soren and the rebel Menkaran lords were not going to wage a mutually debilitating civil war. Rumors throughout Menkara of an impending William-powered invasion were rampant. It seemed impossible that a divided Menkara could defeat such an invasion. But then the sorceress Ariadne, the same Ariadne who had frustrated William with an invisibility shield, had used her sorcery to paralyze King Soren and the rebel lords and told them they must unite against the common threat of a William-powered Galatian invasion of Menkara. She was the only sorcerer who might be powerful enough to help Menkara withstand a William-powered invasion. She told both sides, she would only fight against the invasion if king and rebels created a united front alliance. That united front had now been created.

King Radames immediately called a war council meeting to discuss Soren's unexpected strength. Those invited were William, General Ptolemy, Chancellor Diamant, and, to William's annoyance, Archbishop Khofu.

As soon as all of those invited were in the meeting room, Radames asked for opinions on whether the invasion, scheduled to begin in two weeks, should proceed as planned, or whether plans for the invasion should be modified. He wanted to hear from everyone and began with General Ptolemy.

The general's words and demeanor were grave. "Your majesty, Soren's military alliance with the rebel lords and their recruitment of the powerful sorceress Ariadne means a bloodier, more difficult war against a stronger enemy. I recommend that to defeat this stronger enemy, we recruit as allies Mittani and Nesa, other nations that feel threatened by Soren, before invading Menkara."

The king did not comment, but simply said "Thank you general". Then he turned his head to look at Diamant. He asked "Chancellor, do you agree?"

"Your majesty, with all due respect, I believe that General Ptolemy is being unduly cautious. Neither problem that he points to is that serious. The alliance between Soren and the rebel lords? Since there is hatred, not trust, between king and rebels, the alliance is no threat and will not survive the outbreak of actual battle. An enemy divided into hostile camps cannot be strong.

"The sorceress, Ariadne? She is not the powerful mage, popular opinion thinks she is. Her fame rests on one conjuring trick, the invisibility shield. There is no chance she can protect Soren against the combined might of your armies and the invincible sorcery of William."

The king said "Thank you, Chancellor," but again did not comment. Turning his head to look at Archbishop Khofu, he said. "Old friend, please share with us your views."

The archbishop began calmly. "Your majesty. I agree with General Ptolemy that the alliance and Ariadne means a bloodier, more difficult war. Chancellor Diamant in my opinion underestimates the increased strength of Soren. Strengthening ourselves by recruiting allies, as the general suggests, is one sensible response. But ..." With that 'but' his voice grew tense. "But, I would suggest that a better response would be to call off the invasion. The united Menkaran army is bigger, better equipped and more experienced than the Galatian army. If, as is likely, Soren counterattacks and pushes some of the fighting into Galatia, the cost to our homeland will be far too high. Many of your subjects, civilian as well as military, will be killed, far too many seriously injured. Our economy will be devastated, our people impoverished. Even if the sorcery of William enables us to win the war, Galatia will be worse off after victory than we are now. For the survivors, it will be a very hollow victory."

Again the king did not comment, but perhaps displeasure could be read into his "Thank you, Archbishop" rather than "thank you, old friend." Turning to look at the sorcerer, he said "William, may we have your views on the new developments?"

In a confident voice, William replied. "I assure your majesty that the army's and the nation's losses will be minimal. I learned in the civil wars I fought for Soren, how to achieve victory rapidly with minimal need for conventional military battles. The Galatian army will have little to do other than occupy a defeated Menkara."

Ptolemy bristled at the implied irrelevancy of his army, but Khofu was first to reply. "An easy victory you boast! As easy as your 'victory' over the rag-tag Free Bezriel guerrillas when Ariadne was their sorceress!"

The reference to his one failure infuriated William. "Do not mock me Khofu! I would have crushed the guerrillas and their damned sorceress soon enough, if it had not been for the treachery of Soren. I was stymied for a short time, not by the guerrillas or the sorceress, but by long dead super-mages known as the Seekers. I was on the verge of destroying their invisibility shield when Soren's abominable deceit ended the battle. But all that is irrelevant, since there is no possibility that the Seekers will interfere again. They hate Soren and will not come to his aid."

William then turned his face from Khofu to the king and said, "Your majesty, I promise that with my sorcery and Ptolemy's army, King Soren will be defeated and either killed or captured in just a few short months."

Now it was Khofu's turn to respond hotly. "William, your boast is absurd. King Soren has in his employ your nemesis, the sorceress Ariadne plus many skilled military sorcerers that you yourself trained. And now because of the unexpected alliance, Soren's mighty army is back at full strength. Given his military resources, you certainly cannot bring Soren to his knees as quickly as you claim. In fact, even your claim that you can drive King Soren from the Menkaran throne is as yet nothing but an idle boast."

Khofu then turned to King Radames. "Forgive my outburst, your majesty. With your permission, I have one more point to make." Khofu paused until the king nodded assent. "Throughout twenty years of civil war, Soren's army was always on alert, always battle ready. Based on Soren's long and aggressive military history. I believe he will counter our invasion of Menkara by counterattacking, by invading Galatia. Indeed, given his renewed confidence and strength, he may attack us before we are ready to attack him. The war may begin with a Menkaran invasion of Galatia."

William began to reply, "What nonsense…" But he was cut off by King Radames who had grown increasingly annoyed by the hostility and bickering between the advisors he depended on. He now asserted his authority. "Enough! I did not call this meeting to listen to the four of you squabble like children!" He paused, then in a calmer voice continued. "We will take a short break. Then I want each of you to present a short rational summary of how you think we should respond to the alliance between King Soren and the rebel lords and to his recruitment of the sorceress Ariadne. After a short, very tense break, during which no one uttered a word, the king called upon the archbishop to state and explain his position.

The king's admonition, reinforced by time to cool down, seemed to have worked, for Khofu now spoke with much more restraint than he had earlier. "Your majesty, King Soren's alliance with the lords who rebelled against his tyranny is a desperation survival tactic to try to prevent your conquest of Menkara. How should we respond to that desperation? If we invade, shared hardships of fighting off a foreign invasion will strengthen the alliance between king and rebel lords and thereby make Soren stronger. But if we do not invade the alliance, having lost its reason for being will fall apart. Soren will once again be looking at a looming civil war, hence he will pose no threat to Galatia. If somehow his alliance with the rebel lords holds and does not fall apart, there will still be no danger for Galatia because Soren would never dare launch an invasion when half his army is commanded by lords who challenge his right to rule. Under existing conditions for Galatia to invade Menkara to depose Soren would be to start a needless and very costly war. Therefore your majesty, I recommend you cancel the invasion."

Radames turned to Diamant. "Khofu has argued eloquently against going to war. What do you say in reply?"

"Your majesty, Soren's lust for power is boundless. William's defection has not changed that. But it has made him angrier and more dangerous. As long as he is king of Menkara, he is a threat to all kingdoms on the continent, especially Galatia, since Galatia has given sanctuary to William, the sorcerer that Soren now hates and fears. Soren has strengthened his hand, by luring the rebel lords into an alliance and recruiting the sorceress Ariadne. Archbishop Khofu believes that this greater power of Soren is reason for us not to invade. He is wrong. Soren's increased power is all the more reason to stop him before his power grows even greater. I believe, your majesty that if we do not invade and drive Soren from his throne, his priority will be lead his army into Galatia, to invade and to conquer. If he succeeds, he will have everyone here today executed."

Radames then addressed Ptolemy. "Khofu and Diamant have defended opposite policies. What does my general say?

"Your majesty," replied General Ptolemy, "I agree with Diamant that as long as Soren is king, Menkara will be a threat to Galatia. Therefore I strongly recommend that we invade as previously decided. But Khofu is right that because of Ariadne and the alliance, the Menkaran army is too formidable for the Galatian army fighting alone to vanquish. Therefore I repeat my earlier plea that we recruit allies, specifically I recommend that we recruit the neighboring kingdoms of Nesa and Mittani, to join us in the invasion. Since they will undoubtedly be Soren's first targets after Galatia, I am confident they will agree to join us in the attack on Soren."

Finally, the king turned to the necromancer. "William, much of the burden of success if we invade Menkara rests on your shoulders. After hearing the points made by Khofu, Diamant, and Ptolemy, do you remain confident of easy victory if we invade without allies"

William had regained his composure and spoke with confidence not anger.

"Your majesty, not only is military assistance from Nesa and Mittani unnecessary, but recruiting them and developing a unified battle plan will force us to postpone the invasion and lose the element of surprise. If we attack now, I guarantee not only victory, but a short war."

King Radames thanked his advisors and called for an hour's recess. During that hour the king remained alone in the conference room pondering his options: take the advice of his old friend, the archbishop, and call off the invasion; trust in the mighty sorcerer's extreme self-confidence and invade now without allies, or heed the advice of his general, invade mighty

Menkara to eliminate the menace posed by Soren but only after recruiting Mittani and Nesa as allies.

After he recalled his advisory council, King Radames addressed them. "The decisive fact is that as long as the warlord Soren is king of Menkara, our beloved Galatia is threatened. Soren's rise to power was rooted in aggressive wars of expansion. The safety of our homeland requires eliminating the threat posed by the warlord Soren. As long as William with his unrivalled sorcery fought for Soren, there was no possibility of ending the threat that Soren posed. But the defection of William to Galatia changed everything. William's unrivaled sorcery gives us the opportunity to destroy the pestilence that is Soren. I have decide that our invasion of Menkara must go forward.

"But I am not yet ready to decide whether William's sorcery and my army is enough to defeat Soren, or if we need to increase the power of our conventional army by forming an alliance with Nesa and Mittani before declaring war on Soren. We will now recess for food and drink. After we are refreshed we will resume our deliberation."

After the adjournment for food and drink, the strategy council resumed with Radames asking important questions to William. "Are you sure you can defeat Ariadne? If she cannot prevent our victory over Soren, can she seriously delay it?"

William bristled at the royal doubt of his superiority implicit in the questions. But he controlled his anger and answered with a pretense of humility. "I repeat, it was not the child Ariadne that delayed my victory over the guerrillas, but the ancient Seekers of Bezriel. They helped her in order to try to free Bezriel from the oppression of Soren. For them to help Ariadne now would be to aid Soren. This they will not do. Thus to answer your question, Ariadne without the Seekers cannot defeat me and cannot delay your victory over Soren."

Even though William said to the king 'your victory over Soren' Khofu, sensing William's unspoken smirk, heard "my victory over Soren" as the sorcerer's real meaning. That goaded him to recklessly challenge the powerful sorcerer on whom the king had become so dependent. "But what if you are wrong, William of Bezriel, and the Seekers do aid Ariadne? Can you defeat that child, as you call her, if she is aided by the Seekers? Does not the invisibility shield they helped her create, the shield that frustrated you, prove that they have sorcery unknown even to you; have sorcery which can defeat you?"

"No, archbishop, it does not," replied William in a voice taut with anger and hatred. The antipathy and distrust between Khofu and William had at long last re-emerged in full and open display in front of the king. "When Ariadne was with Free Bezriel, I was unprepared for the help that the Seekers gave her. Since then I have used necromancy to interrogate many of the dead from the early days of Bezriel. Through such interrogations and through finding and reading very old manuscripts, I have studied ancient sorcery, including the sorcery of the Seekers. The Seekers were mystics rather than warriors. Having studied the military sorcery that they did manage to develop, I have learned how to defeat it."

William then turned from Khofu and addressed the king. "Your majesty, I admit that this Ariadne, despite her youth is a powerful sorceress. But her power and knowledge is shallow compared to mine. I assure you that even with the help of the Seekers, she is not a serious roadblock on your path to the conquest of Menkara. She poses no threat to your triumph over Soren."

Radames was pleased by William's answer to Khofu. But he was not yet ready to decide whether to recruit allies for the invasion of Menkara. Rather than placing full faith in the confidence of William, he turned to the leader of his army. "General Ptolemy, are you satisfied that despite the alliance between Soren and the rebel lords and his recruitment of Ariadne, we can without allies defeat Soren?"

Ptolemy replied after a long hesitation. "Your majesty, in my opinion without allies we can probably defeat Soren, but at a very high cost. But if we recruit Nesa and Mittani as allies in the war, I am sure that we can easily crush the tyrant. I have studied the history of the campaigns of Soren and William. There is no doubt in my mind that the decisive factor in Soren's victories was the combination of the sorcery of William and the superiority of the army of Soren over every provincial lord that he fought. Since becoming king, he has spared no expense in expanding the size of his army by recruitment from the ranks of his form enemies and equipping it with the most modern and powerful armaments. With the defection of William to Galatia, the sorcery advantage is now ours. Unfortunately, after Soren's truce with the rebel lords, he has regained the conventional warfare advantage. And he has somewhat leveled the sorcery battlefront by recruiting the powerful sorceress Ariadne. But because of William, the sorcery advantage is still ours. If we regain the conventional arms advantage by recruiting Nesa and Mittani, then with superiority on both fronts we will certainly defeat Soren. Given how much Nesa and Mittani fear Soren, we can surely convince them to join in our attack on Soren now that William is on our side."

"Well argued, general," said the king. Then turning to Khofu, he inquired, "My old friend, after hearing the pro-invasion arguments of my other advisors, do you now agree? Or do you still believe that declaring war on Soren would be a mistake?"

Khofu knew that this would be his last chance to persuade the king to call off the invasion. "Your majesty, even if the invasion has a good chance of driving Soren from the throne, I am still convinced that invading Menkara would be a mistake. Although Soren's ambition is limitless, the rebellion of the lords has destroyed his ability to pursue that ambition beyond Menkara. He is no longer a threat to Galatia. Furthermore, the united front of king and rebels against our invasion and their recruitment of the sorceress Ariadne who previously frustrated William convince me that even if the invasion drives from Soren the throne, the cost of victory will be too high."

Radames replied quickly and decisively. "William and General Ptolemy may not have convinced you, archbishop, but they have convinced me. As long as Soren is king of Menkara, he is a threat to the tranquility and future of Galatia and all other kingdoms on the continent. We must drive him from the throne of Menkara.

"But my general has convinced me that prudence dictates recruiting allies before attacking. We will make every effort to recruit Nesa and Mittani to join us in the attack on Soren. Since they are equally threatened by Soren's dream of empire I am confident that they will join us. If Galatia joins with Nena and Mittani, we become as strong as ever we can be. Despite the alliance of Soren with the rebel lords, and despite Ariadne, Soren has been weakened, since he must now depend on those he does not trust and who do not trust him. My decision is that we recruit Nena and Mittani. As soon as they are mobilized for war, the invasion of Menkara will begin."

We know now that William spoke against the recruitment of Nesa and Mittani to aid in the invasion even though he knew that cautious Radames, would ask for their help. He did so because he wanted the king to believe he could still reject the advice of the sorcerer he was more and more dependent on. Until the war began, the foolish king must be allowed the comforting belief that he was still in charge.

It is clear in retrospect that William was not only a powerful sorcerer, but also a skilled politician and diplomat, although sometimes the effect of his diplomacy was undercut by his pride and his arrogance. In a very short time, William had gone from being a prisoner on trial for his life in Zandor, a small minor province of Menkara, to Soren's most powerful weapon in his successful campaign to reunify Menkara. Although Soren and William successfully used each other to obtain their goals: kingship for Soren, resources to explore the limits of sorcery for William, they never trusted each other. The first turning point from mutual usefulness to enmity was when Soren publically humiliated William by arresting Ariadne as her duel with William was about to begin. William never forgave Soren. The decisive, irreparable break was the defection of William to Galatia The mutually beneficial partnership between Soren and William had at that point degenerated into mutual hatred and an obsession in each to humiliate and destroy the other.

After defecting to Galatia William vowed to regain a position of power, but this time with a king that he could dominate. Soren's ambition and will-power were as strong as William's. A partnership between two such powerful men was destined to end badly. But William learned from that mistake. Galatia because of its location and prominence was William's first choice for a place of exile. But he did not finalize that choice until after he had sized up King Radames as a ruler with two essential attributes. First, unknown even to himself, buried deep in Radames' psyche was an unquenchable yearning for power. Second, the character of Radames, unlike the character of Soren, was weak enough, that given enough time, William could persuade him to do whatever William wanted him to do. The decisive proof of that came on the day that despite the two-fold strengthening of Soren's power resulting from the formation of united front with the rebel lords and the recruitment of the powerful sorceress Ariadne, King Radames, under the influence of William, rejected the rational advice of his old friend Archbishop Khofu and refused to call off the invasion of Menkara.

CHAPTER 14

Despite the fact that Archbishop Khofu thought the planned invasion of Menkara was a mistake, King Radames kept him in his inner circle of royal advisors, partly because of a long history of good advice from Khofu, but mainly because he trusted the character and spirituality of Khofu. William was unhappy with this decision, but recognizing that arguing for Khofu's ouster would be a tactical mistake, he accepted the king's decision without protest. Khofu, for his part, willingly undertook a commission to travel with the king and Chancellor Diamant on a mission to persuade Nesa and Mittani to join the attack on Soren. He did so because he believed that the coalition would both lessen the burden of war on Galatia and improve chances of victory over Soren. Khofu was against the war, but if the king was determined to wage war on Soren, Khofu was for the anti-Soren military alliance with Menkara's other neighbors

    After his initial protest that allies were not needed to defeat Soren, Diamant quickly came to realize that the proposed alliance would be very good for Galatia. Diamant had always been a nationalist struggling to improve Galatia's position in the region both politically and economically. For him the most important fact about the proposed alliance with Nesa and Mittani was that because of the alliance's military dependence on William, it would be led by and dominated by Galatia. The defection of William to Galatia had had expanded Diamant's nationalist hopes dramatically. He now not only expected regional hegemony, but also dreamed of a Galatian empire. The formation of the anti-Soren regional alliance led by Galatia was an important first step on the road to hegemony and possibly empire. Radames would of course be the nominal sovereign, but, Diamant believed, real power would be in the hands of the chancellor, i.e. himself.

Success in recruiting the two neighboring kingdoms proved surprisingly easy. Both feared the expansionist ambitions of King Soren and the awesome military juggernaut he had created. All ranks in both kingdoms, royalty, lords, townspeople and peasants had been terrified of an attack by the armies of Soren and the sorcery of William. The defection of William, and the splitting of Menkara in two by the failed coup attempt of rebel Menkaran lords had significantly weakened Soren. That reduced fear of an immediate invasion. But fear of the expansionist ambitions of Soren, a military leader who had never been defeated, remained. Hence, it proved relatively easy for the Galatians to persuade the kings and lords of Nesa and Mittani that recent events had shifted the balance of power and that now was the perfect time for invading Menkara and deposing Soren.

The leaders of Nesa and Mittani were pleased that King Radames, despite the ascendant power that the defection of William to Galatia gave him, was recruiting them as allies. They liked his plan of striking while Soren was reeling from the twin shocks of rebellion and defection. Thus Nesa and Mittani agreed to join the invasion. They did, as expected request a delay in launching the invasion to give themselves time to mobilize for war. The agreed to meet in one week in Galatia to set a target date for the invasion and to develop detailed plans for carrying out the invasion and defanging the Menkaran menace.

A week later, coalition strategy for the invasion of Menkara was finalized at an intense two day meeting of William with the kings and top generals of Galatia, Nesa and Mittani. Radames chaired the meeting and made the opening statement. "Soren, now king of Menkara, is not royal by birth. He began as Lord Soren of Thorheim. As lord of Thorheim, he created the strongest conventional army in the vast but splintered feudal kingdom of Menkara. After twenty long years of constant military campaigning and political intrigue, he controlled less than half the country. He then recruited the powerful Bezrielite sorcerer, William. There followed a quick series of lightning fast victories over powerful regional lords who had long held him at bay. It was of course the sorcerer William, not Soren who won these quick victories. But it was vain Soren who crowned himself king of Menkara. He insulted and humiliated William, claiming the conquest of Menkara was his and his alone. He developed the evil plan of creating a Menkaran empire by invading and conquering neighboring kingdoms. True hereditary kings like us would be reduced to the status of mere vassals. But Soren's vanity was his downfall. Humiliating the sorcerer who had made him king was a terrible blunder. The sorcerer responded by fleeing from Soren's Menkara to Galatia. Now the united powers of Galatia, Nesa, and Mittani with the aid of William are ready to march into Menkara to eliminate Soren as a threat to the well-being of the peoples of the region. We meet here today to finalize our strategy for the war about to begin. My sorcerer, William, will now explain to you the nature of his sorcery and how it will aid us in defeating Soren."

William's goal was to impress on the assembled kings and generals that his sorcery had revolutionized warfare, and that only through his sorcery could the three kingdoms defeat the mighty armies and sorcerers of King Soren. He wanted them to see that despite their lofty titles and powerful armies, without him, they had no chance of defeating Soren. He wanted them to see that he, a mere commoner, could with his sorcery defeat Soren for them.

William did not begin by courteously recognizing by name or title the kings and generals in the room. He began and ended by praising himself and proclaiming that he alone could bring them victory.

"Modern warfare has been revolutionized by sorcery, by my sorcery. No longer do the size of armies, the valor of knights, or the accuracy of archers decide who wins and who loses battles and wars. This will be a different kind of war than you have ever fought. I will now explain to you the nature of my sorcery and how it will enable you to cleanse the land of the scourge that is *King Soren*." William said the words 'King Soren' as if he were speaking of the bubonic plague.

"My sorcery made Soren king of Menkara. In battle after battle, the enemies of Soren were helpless against my sorcery. What is this sorcery? Sorcery has three parts; controlling nature, mind control, and necromancy. In all of these, I am the most powerful sorcerer in the world. The sorcerers still with Soren were trained by me. Their skills and powers are naught but pale imitations of the skills and powers of the master who taught them, which is to say naught but pale imitations of my skills and powers."

The audience, composed of men used to deference by their social inferiors, was growing restless. But mesmerized and terrified by William's voice and demeanor, none had the courage to question or challenge this commoner who claimed to be their superior.

After a long pause, William continued. "To you controlling nature, mind control, and necromancy are mere words, names for dark powers you have never witnessed and do not comprehend. I will now explain to you their relevance in warfare.

"My first power is controlling nature. With respect to warfare, this means controlling weather by creating weather ideal for one's own army (for example pleasant weather to march in) and bad weather for the enemy (for example storms to delay or sidetrack enemy armies or sink enemy ships at sea). Controlling nature also means that with my mind I can hurl spears, arrows or rocks at the enemy and block the projectiles they throw at us. Finally I can use my mind to cause things to explode."

"Does not King Soren also have sorcerers who can control nature?" asked Cato, the king of Mittani.

William was not pleased by the question. His reply was polite, but less than honest, since what he said was true of the sorcerers he had trained, but not true of Ariadne. "Except for controlling the weather, which is a rare power, controlling nature is the main power of most sorcerers. But I can control nature far more completely than any other sorcerer. This I demonstrated in my campaigns when working for Soren. This I will demonstrate again in the coming war against Soren."

The lords and generals at the assembly remembered what they had heard of Soren's battles after being joined by William. After a brief silence, King Archon of Nesa requested that William describe your other powers of sorcery and their military significance.

"My second power is mind control. Telepathy, the weakest form of mind control, is the ability to see into the mind of others. It is possessed to some degree by most sorcerers. Typically their telepathy is weak, amounting to nothing more than an ability to do parlor tricks, like telling you what card you are thinking of. But advanced telepaths can actually read the minds of those they focus on, unless the person has strong mental defenses, which is rare. Mind reading of secrets is very useful tool for gathering information that the enemy wants to keep hidden. Several telepaths trained by me who still work for Soren have this ability to read minds.

"But there is a third level of telepathy that only I among living sorcerers have reached. That power beyond reading minds is my ability to control the mind of another, my ability to make an enemy do what I want him to do."

The mind control abilities of William made many of the assembled kings, ministers, and generals very uneasy. Would William dare try to use that power on them? Was he attempting to control their minds even now? Sensing the unease in the room, King Radames vowed to himself to speak to his sorcerer about the need for innocuous diplomatic terminology. But for now, making his irritation, and wanting William to move on to a less disturbing topic he asked him to explain his third power, necromancy."

"Necromancy is the ability to raise and talk with the spirits of the dead. Very few sorcerers can raise and talk with the dead. Only I can go beyond merely talking with them to controlling them, forcing them to reveal long forgotten knowledge they would prefer to keep secret. I can control what the risen spirits will say and to whom they will appear. In my campaigns with Soren, I sometimes used necromancy to raise dead heroes to inspire Soren's men and sometimes to raise victims of past wars to terrorize and panic troops and officers of Soren's enemies."

Having finished his brief account of his powers of sorcery and their wartime uses, William stood silent. Finally King Radames rose and asked "Are there any questions?"

"Yes," said Cato, the king of Mittani. "Why do we need to mobilize and go to war. Can't Wliam just use his powers tomorrow and defeat Soren by destroying his army with a hurricane or gaining control of his mind and ordering him to surrender?"

"No," replied William. "All powers of sorcery, especially weather control and mind control require being physically close to what you want to control. To defeat Soren and his armies and sorceres, I will need the advance of the alliance armies deep into Menkara. Of course, my sorcery can greatly assist and hasten that advance."

General Ptolemy then rose and asked "William, assuming our armies get you close, how confident are you of victory?"

"Just as a conventional infantry or cavalry attack by the armies of the three allied kingdoms will be met by conventional infantry or cavalry defense by Soren, so the sorcery attacks by me will be resisted by Soren's quite powerful sorcerers, who I myself trained. I will defeat them, but it will not be easy."

"Do you guarantee victory?"

"Yes!"

Having sufficiently awed the assembled kings and generals, William had little difficulty getting the three king and their ministers and generals, all of whom were anxious to oust Soren as king of Menkara to approve his preferred strategy. A target date for launching a coordinated coalition attack on Soren's Menkara was set. Early in the morning on the twenty-first day, the invasion would begin.

Before dawn on the agreed upon day for launching the invasion, a joint communique would be issued stating that the armies of a three kingdom coalition were marching into Menkara to depose the tyrant Soren of Thorheim. At dawn the armies would cross into Menkara; Galatia from the west, Nesa from the north, and Mittani from the south. William would begin by traveling with the Galatian army and use his sorcery to facilitate the capture of the provincial capital in western Menkara. If necessary, he would then travel to the Nesan army on the northern front and then to the Mittani army on the southern front to help those armies capture their targeted provincial capitals. In less than three weeks, three provincial capitals would be occupied by the invading armies.

That three prong strategy would be used again in stage two, moving the invading armies deeper into the heart if Menkara, thereby tightening a noose around King Soren, bunkered in his palace in Zenkara, the capital of Menkara. The third and final stage of the war would be a three army attack on Zenkara, ending with the capture or slaying of Soren by William. William insisted on and won his demand that the honor of capturing or slaying Soren be his and his alone. If all went according to plan, the war would be over in less than three months.

After Soren learned from his spies that the kingdoms of Nesa and Mittani had agreed to join Galatia in the attack on Menkara, he called a war council meeting. The council consisted of Soren, General Danton, Ariadne, and Menjaro, lord of Altaria representing the rebel alliance. Lord Lucien had wanted to be on the council, but a majority in the rebel high command felt that Lucien's hatred of Soren would cloud his judgment and lead to bad decisions. Hence instead they picked Lord Menjaro, not much of a diplomat, but a very good military strategist, who was trusted and respected by all the leaders of the rebel alliance.

Soren opened the meeting by summarizing the history of the coming conflict. "How did we get to where we are today? The beginning was a coup attempt by provincial lords unhappy with my plans for modernizing Menkara. The coup failed to dethrone me, but split our homeland into two regions preparing for civil war. The traitor William took advantage of the ensuing turmoil to flee the country. He defected to Galatia and persuaded King Ramades to invade Menkara and depose me as king. Next, the Bezrielite sorceress Ariadne, who had thwarted William in the past, offered to help defeat the invasion if I and the rebel lords formed a united front to defend Menkara against the invasion. Both sides agreed to the united front. But as we became stronger, so did the enemy. Galatia persuaded Nesa and Mittani to join the attack on Menkara.

"We now know from reports from spies in the three hostile kingdoms, that they will attack soon, in about ten days. It will be a three pronged attack, Galatia invading from the west, Nesa from the north, and Mittani from the south. We meet here today to finalize our defense plans. Lord Menjaro, you are noted as a grand strategist. Would you begin the discussion?"

Ariadne was surprised by Soren's courteous words and manner. Fear has had a beneficial impact and made him more civil, she thought. Even so, a minute later she was amazed by Soren's lack of reaction to the opening words of Lord Menjaro, "Thank you, Lord Soren." The rebel lord had addressed Soren as Lord Soren rather than King Soren and Soren, unflustered had let it pass without comment. To Ariadne's amazement, this new Soren did not lose his temper, as the old Soren would have. Ariadne smiled because the notoriously proud king was allowing a rebel lord, now an ally, to address him as if they were social equals. What Ariadne did not know was that in return for the rebel lords accepting him as commander-in-chief for the duration of the war, Soren had accepted their demand that they not be required to formally acknowledge him as king of Menkara. Even Mentaxes had been impressed by how few points Soren had to concede to be recognized as commander in chief. The decisive argument in persuading the rebels had been Lord Menjaro's insistence that to fight efficiently an army must have one universally recognized head.

Menjaro, as requested, opened the discussion of strategy. "The war will soon begin with a three pronged attack on Menkara by superior numbers. The most obvious response is to divide our forces into three parts and strive to block the enemy on all three fronts. And that may well be the best choice. But we should at least consider alternatives. One alternative is to stoutly resist the advance of two of the armies while allowing the third to penetrate deep into Menkara, where we can try to isolate and destroy it. A second alternative is to send an invading force into one of the three hostile kingdoms, before they attack us. That invading force could be either small, a mere distraction to buy us time, or large, an attempt on our part to flip the situation."

"Very interesting, Lord Menjaro," said Soren. "General Danton, you seem anxious to comment."

"Yes your majesty, I have much to say. I have almost no experience with defensive warfare. Leading your armies in your long campaign to gain the throne and re-unite Menkara, I was almost always attacking rather than defending. Thus my spirit soars with enthusiasm to the aggressive alternatives suggested by Lord Menjaro. Why should we fight on Menkaran soil when we can be fighting on Galatian or Mittani or Nesan soil? They are not yet ready to attack, but we are. Your twenty years of campaigning has created an army that is always ready for combat. I suggest that we send an invading force into Galatia led by your elite Cerberus battalion and accompanied by the sorceress Ariadne."

Without waiting for recognition by Soren, Ariadne, was on her feet trembling. "No, general. Send an army into Galatia if you think that best, but I will not accompany it. I volunteered to help defend Menkara. I did not volunteer to attack Galatia, and I will not do it."

Soren did not rebuke Ariadne. Instead he addressed his general. "Danton, for more years than I care to remember, I have admired your aggressiveness, your courage. But we must adapt to the situation that confronts us. We will not win this war by being aggressive, at least not at the start. The attacking force always suffers higher casualties. To begin we are outnumbered and face the greatest military sorcerer in history. We must conserve our forces and seek for ways to reduce the imbalance, not recklessly increase it.

"But I, too like Lord Menjaro's suggestion of developing an unexpected strategy. Lord Menjaro would you elaborate your first alternative, luring one of the three enemy armies into the heart of Menkara where we can isolate and destroy it."

"The idea is simple. We are outnumbered. The strategy I suggest is to lure the enemy into situations where they are outnumbered. Whenever that happens we launch an all-out attack, both conventional and employing sorcery, to overwhelm an enemy that is far from home, suddenly cut off from their relief lines and hence demoralized. If we adopt this strategy we need to study probable entry points for the three enemy armies and determine where one of those armies one can most easily be led into a trap. The army that we try to trap must not be the one accompanied by William. Lord Soren, do you think your spies will be able to get that information about William?"

"No. We have no spy in their high council. But even without a spy, I know the answer to your question. King Radames of Galatia needs to impress King Cato of Mittani and King

Archon of Nesa. He will not be separated from William, his greatest military resource, at the start of the invasion. At the start of the invasion, William will accompany the Galatian army."

Strategy analysis went on and on for hours. Ariadne, who understood little of the technical issues being discussed almost fell asleep. Eventually Menjaro's suggestion of luring one of the three invading armies deep into Menkara, then isolating and attacking it was adopted and developed into a detailed plan. A major reason why it was adopted was that Soren, despite his words of rebuke to General Danton, congenitally shared the general's distaste for a passive strategy.

It was decided to lay a trap for the Nesan army that would be invading from the north. The northern front was chosen because the northern terrain was most favorable for springing a trap. Also because William would most likely begin on the western front with the Galatian army and hence be far from the action in the north when the trap was sprung. Another important reason for choosing the northern front was that discontent with the coming war was strongest in Nesa. A disaster for the Nesan army early in the war might possibly lead to Nesa's withdrawal from the campaign.

Soren was loath to close the meeting because he sensed an underlying pessimism in the room. His twenty years of campaigning had taught him that a prerequisite of victory is belief that victory is possible. He could see behind the brave façade of his military commanders, General Danton and Lord Menjaro, both of whom were ready to fight as hard as they could, lurked a pessimistic belief that defeat at the hands of William was inevitable. Soren tried to rekindle hope. "Let us address the big issue. 'Can William be defeated?' Clearly Galatia, Nesa, and Mittani think not. They would never dare attack Menkara if they had not come under William's mesmerizing spell and led to mistakenly believe in his invincibility.

"But I tell you no man is invincible. In my campaign to reunite Menkara, I fought a long sequence of successful provincial battles. True, as my sorcerer, William speeded up my victory in a series of successful small one-front campaigns. What was new with William was not victory, but speed of victory. In the coming war as he joins the attack on Menkara, he will not be engaged in a small one-front campaign, but rather in a three front war spread out over a very large terrain. He can only be on one front at a time. We can be victorious on the two fronts where he is absent. Meanwhile Ariadne and the sorcerers that William himself trained can hold him at bay on the third front. Sooner rather than later, the three kings will tire of their costly and fruitless endeavor and retreat across the border to their homelands."

Soren continued to speak for another ten minutes. He did not convince Danton, Menjaro, and Ariadne that they would win, but he did rekindle hope, hope that if they could make the cost of conquering Menkara high enough, the three kings might call off the invasion in order to quell discontent in their homelands with the high cost of the war.

CHAPTER 15

As planned, before dawn on the appointed day, a joint communique was issued by the kingdoms of Galatia, Nesa, and Mittani stating that their armies were crossing the border into Menkara for the sole purpose of ending the menace to all peace loving peoples posed by the warmonger and tyrant Soren. The communique was deliberately provocative and insulting to Soren, referring to him not as king of Menkara, but only as war-monger and tyrant. The three kingdoms did not declare war on Menkara. Rather they proclaimed that they were liberating Menkara from the tyrant Soren.

Wars have many names. The war that began that day is known to historians as *The War of the Four Kingdoms*. But its popular name, the name that I prefer, is *Ariadne's War*. It was fought on many geographic fronts, each involving conventional clashes of infantry and cavalry, intense use of military sorcery by both sides, and, last but not least, multi-level struggles by both sides to win the hearts and minds of the population.

Despite Bezriel's long history of pacifism, Bezrielite sorcerer's were the most powerful military weapon for both armies, William for the invaders, Ariadne for United Front resistance of King Soren and his rebellious lords. William and Ariadne were both Bezrielites, but Bezrielites with completely different understandings of what it meant to be Bezrielite and of the nature and importance of Bezrielite sorcery.

As the war unfolded, the struggle between the two sorcerers became broader in its implications. For me, a Bezrielite historian, the two sorcerers represented different understandings of what it means to be a Bezrielite sorcerer, human. Or, to put the conflict in a broader context, William and Ariadne represented different understandings of the implications of the growing human ability to control nature, whether by sorcery or by science. Sorcery for William was the ability of the strong to dominate and control nature and other men, the possibility of becoming like a god. Sorcery for Ariadne was the ability to minimize pain and suffering, the possibility of understanding and becoming an organic part of the unity that was creation. For me as a Bezrielite historian, the battles between William and Ariadne were struggles for the soul of Bezriel. For me as a human historian, the battles between William and Ariadne were struggles over what it means to be human.

At dawn on the that first day, three armies crossed into Menkara, Galatian troops from the west, Nesan troops from the north, and Mittani troops from the south. In the early days of *Ariadne's War*, it quickly became apparent that some uses of sorcery that had been effective in Soren's march to the throne no longer worked. This was because for the first time, both sides in a conflict had powerful sorcerers and because neither officers nor rank and file could again be easily panicked by mere displays of sorcery, for example deploying dead ancestors to terrorize the living. Forewarned against the deployment of ghosts, the troops on both sides in the new war could not be panicked by such scare tactics. Success retired new tactics, and throughout the war, new tactics were improvised.

To begin, William travelled with the Galatian army. If all went according to plan, in just two or three weeks, three Menkaran provincial capitals would be occupied by the invading armies, and a noose ready to be tightened would have been fastened around Soren's neck.

But all did not go according to plan. Spirited resistance was met on all three fronts as the battle experience of the Menkaran officers and troops compensated for their inferior numbers. Despite that spirited resistance, the leaders of the invasion were heartened by the fact that all three invading armies were steadily moving towards their goals, although two were advancing slower than anticipated. The fastest progress was on the northern front, where during the first week, the Nesan army secured most of the border province of Coranado, and on the eighth day moved into the prosperous province of Thorheim with the goal of capturing Spartaka, Thorheim's capital city. Control of Thorheim had great significance for morale on both sides, because Thorheim was Soren's native province, and Spartaka had been Soren's military command center during his twenty year campaign to become king of a reunited Menkara. Its capture would signal to the world the fall from power of Soren

The Menkaran troops in Thorheim put on a good show of stout resistance while retreating against superior numbers. In fact their steady retreat was part of the entrapment strategy adopted by Soren. On the tenth day, when the Nesan supply lines were long and stretched thin, Soren ordered a counter-offensive. The elite Menkaran battle brigade known as Cerberus, which had been secretly deployed to Spartaka before the invasion began, emerged from hiding. Fighting fiercely under the direct command of Soren, Cerberus drove the Nesan forces northwest into an ancient forest known as Mondrien.

Before the invasion began, Menkaran sorcerers under the direction of Ariadne had enchanted Mondrien, causing its vegetation to issue vapors that would weaken the bodies and confuse the minds of all humans who entered the forest. Soren's troops pursued the invaders to the edge of Mondrien, but under strict orders did not themselves enter the forest. Instead they spread out and surrounded the forest. Within the enchanted forest, the ended until Soren was crushed; defeated and helpless. The only hope of victory for the three kingdoms was unity, the best strategy was pressing on with the invasion. In the end, even Nesa agreed.

Soren was happy but not exultant after his victory at the Mondrien forest. He was happy because his strategic ploy had worked brilliantly, and because he knew that an early victory was essential for creating high morale among the Menkaran troops and populace in the face of a massive foreign invasion that threatened to devastate the land. But he did not exult because the strategy behind this success, large scale ambush, would not work twice. He did not exult because he knew, even if his troops and the populace did not, that the three kingdom invaders still had a considerable advantage in conventional military power. And if military sorcery were to decide this war, was there Soren wondered, any real chance that Ariadne could defeat William? Soren had guessed correctly that William would begin the invasion with the army of Galatia, not the army of Nesa. If that guess had been wrong, he would now be staring at disaster.

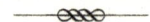

Five weeks into the war, Ariadne was soul-sick over the death and devastation she had witnessed, especially the death and devastation resulting from her sorcery in the Mondrien forest. Recognizing the long-term horror that would result if William conquered Menkara, she was determined to continue to fight. But she feared that she would not be able to be true to this resolve as casualties mounted, as her self-loathing mushroomed because of the devastation caused by her sorcery, and because it now seemed to her that the war would drag on and on endlessly. At Mondrian, the first major battle of the war, she had broken her sacred vow to never again seek victory by befogging the mind of the enemy. She had self-justified her actions by focusing on the fact that she was not again using telepathy to bewitch enemy soldiers and cause friend to slaughter friend. But she had used enchantment to drive Nesan troops half-crazy and then had had bewitched trees speak to scare the Nesan troops into running from the forest, straight into ambushes where many were killed or captured.

Once again to achieve her goals, she had accepted and acted on the hateful maxim, the ends justify the means. Stopping William, the all-powerful sorcerer for whom nothing was sacred, had to be achieved, no matter the personal cost. But Ariadne knew deep in her soul that she could not persevere much longer using tactics she abhorred. Sooner or later, she would be unable to continue.

Night after night Ariadne begged Esther to talk with her in a dream. Finally, Esther appeared. The setting for the dream sent a chill down Ariadne's spine, for it was a clearing in the Mondrien forest. But summoning her courage, she began by telling Esther "I can no longer continue using military sorcery."

Esther did not, as Ariadne feared she would, pass judgment. She simply stated facts and asked questions. "Ariadne, once you believed that violence was permissible to achieve good ends, believed that violence must be used to liberate Bezriel. Why have you changed your mind? Why do you now refuse to fight?"

"Why? My first-hand experience of the reality of war, the reality of killing! When Cerberus overran a Free Bezriel base and slaughtered my comrades. I went mad with grief and anger. In my madness, I cast a spell that caused the troops of Cerberus to slay their comrades. Afterwards, when I realized the horror that I, a Bezrielite healer committed to non-violence, had done, I vowed to never again use sorcery in military conflict. But I am weak. Again and again, I broke that vow and returned to battle. With Free Bezriel I was persuaded by family and comrades I love and trust to continue to use sorcery to protect Free Bezriel. Then responding to pleas and taunts, I abandoned my principles and agreed to a sorcerer's duel to the death with William in the vain hope that might lead to freedom for Bezriel. Instead that led to the destruction of Free Bezriel and to my arrest and imprisonment.

"Then much later, after it became known that the renegade William was about to lead an invasion of our homeland I persuaded myself that I must do my part in resisting that invasion. Almost immediately I once again became a war criminal, by enchanting the Mondrien forest in order to panic the soldiers of Nesa to flee the forest into an ambush. In many ways, this was my worst crime. Against Cerberus, I acted out of anger and grief. But this time, I carefully plotted the details of the deadly ambush of the peasants and workmen in the Nesan army. That is why I can no longer fight in this or any other war."

Esther did not relent in her effort to make Ariadne explain her decision.

. "I am hearing two explanations of your unwillingness to continue fighting. The first is that as a Bezrielite you have come to realize that you are a pacifist committed to non-violence. The second is that as a powerful sorceress you have come to distrust your ability to use restraint when fighting for a cause that you believe in. Trying to achieve your goals, you commit atrocities. Are both of these reasons why you are no longer willing to fight against William and the invasion?

There was a long silence, while Ariadne pondered her soul. "My self-knowledge is so weak, I cannot be sure. But I think both of those reasons are relevant. I was raised as a Bezrielite healer. While young I committed myself to walk the path of Bezriel as a path of peace and friendship. I wanted to help move Bezriel back to its true spiritual path. To walk that path requires freedom. To achieve that goal I became willing to do anything, including using violence against the enemies of Bezriel. But I now realize that what I had been taught as a child is true. The life of the spirit can only be reached using noble means. If freedom were achieved by ignoble means, that freedom could never lead to the life of the spirit, could never lead to Bezriel. In my heart, like my mother, I am a pacifist.

"Despite my pacifism, twice I volunteered to fight in a war for a cause I believed in. Both times, I was so focused on victory that I used my sorcery to cause abominations. So yes, even apart from pacifism, I am withdrawing because how I use my sorcery in wartime cannot be trusted."

Esther made no effort to change Ariadne's decision.

Recognizing that Soren and the others in the Menkaran high command needed to be told of her crippling self-doubt, the day after her dream conversation with Esther, Ariadne requested a meeting of the high command. Soren, sensing the urgency in her voice and demeanor granted the request and called the meeting.

King Soren, General Danton, Lord Menjaro, Chancellor Mentaxes, and high-priestess Grassic met with Ariadne at the high command council she had requested. Ariadne described her crisis of conscience and told of her crippling doubts about her ability to persevere in a long and bloody war. All in the high council, with the exception of Grassic, were surprised and outraged.

Soren, responded first, his voice cracking with suppressed rage. "Sorceress, are you no longer willing to defend your homeland?"

Controlling her anger, her fear, her self-disgust, Ariadne in a calm voice, replied. "There is nothing I want more than to help defeat the attack on all I hold dear by the renegade William, a sorcerer who recognizes no ethical restraints. I convinced myself that he must be stopped by any means necessary. I convinced myself that I could do whatever needed to be done to avoid conquest by a man who has passed beyond good and evil. Hence my enchantment of the Mondrien forest. But..."

"Precisely!" Soren's powerful voice rang out, cutting off Ariadne "Since any means may be used to stop William, there is no ethical dilemma. Simply do what needs to be done!"

Ariadne could no longer control her seething emotions. "I cannot! Mondrien taught me that I must ignore morality, ignore the spirit of Bezriel that is my soul, to try to win this war. I have struggled for weeks to accept that necessity. But I have discovered that I cannot."

Soren exploded, "This is war! What did you expect?"

"I was a fool. My mind knew that killing and ignoring the humanity of the enemy is the essence of war. I thought my soul could deal with that necessity in order to try to defeat William. I was wrong. I can no longer continue down a road that leads me away from Bezriel, that leads to hatred and enmity, that destroys love and community. I can no longer fight in this war. I can no longer fight in any war."

Soren was ready to strangle Ariadne on the spot. "Damn Bezriel! Damn your conscience! Your decision is not high ethics, not a noble act of conscience. It is a crime, the worst of all crimes; desertion in the face of the enemy. It is treason!"

Lord Menjaro then vented his anger. "You speak of conscience, girl. Yet you are now ready to break your solemn promise to the lords and people of Menkara. We rebel lords were planning to sit out the invasion. We joined Soren's war effort because of your plea for unity and the hope that unity plus your powers would lead to victory and a better future. If you withdraw now, we are left fighting a war we cannot win and facing an enemy whose retribution will be terrible."

Ariadne managed to hold back her tears. "I am sorry Lord Menjaro, I am so sorry. Everything you say is true. Everything I do leads to tragedy and disaster."

King Soren spoke again. This time out of despair rather than anger. Addressing his war council he spoke "This is pathetic. Disciplined and mighty warlords have become dependent on the will of the wisp mood swings of a child." He stopped, then turned his head and addressed Ariadne. "When you were with Free Bezriel, you sought to destroy me. I crushed Free Bezriel. But you have found a new way to destroy me. Your false promises lured me into a strategy dependent on your powers. Now when I have no other options, you betray me to my enemies."

Soren seethed as Ariadne made no reply to his charge of treason. Eventually the tense silence was broken by General Danton addressing Ariadne. "Sorceress, when you were with Free Bezriel, you created an invisibility shield that frustrated William. Can you do so again? Will you do so again?"

"Yes. I can create another invisibility shield, but not one big enough to protect an entire kingdom. The original shield protected a small encampment of less than seven hundred souls. To shield that small camp exhausted the limits of my power and endurance. Even with the aid of all the sorcerers working for Soren, there is no possible way that I could create a shield that would safeguard even the capital city from attack, let alone all of Menkara"

Danton persisted. "Can you at least create a shield around the king's command post?"

Before Ariadne could reply, Soren asserted his authority. "NO! A thousand times, no. For authority to be valid, leaders, especially royal leaders, must endure the same dangers as their men. I will not cower behind a magic shield. And neither will any of you!"

After another long silence, Lord Menjaro posed an important question to Ariadne. "How far does your pacifism go, sorceress? You tell us that you will not attack the enemy. But will you help defend us against enemy attacks?"

Staring off into space, Ariadne pondered her reply, thinking very carefully about what type of commitment she could make. When she reached a decision, addressing Soren and not Menjaro, she replied. "I am duty bound to use my powers to defend those who relied upon my empty promises against enemy attacks. But defense only. I will do nothing to injure or kill the attackers."

The king was not mollified. "How long, witch, before you break this new promise?" he asked. When Ariadne did not reply, Soren ended the meeting and ordered that they assemble again an hour after dawn the next day to decide on strategy in the new situation.

CHAPTER 16

King Soren opened the high council meeting the next morning by announcing that he had made a major decision. "I have accepted that Ariadne will no longer use her sorcery to attack the invaders. What follows from this? Will we surrender to the enemy? No! We will fight on. But we must change strategy." After a long pause, he asked his war council, "What must we do in this new situation to defeat the invasion?"

There followed a long discussion of general strategy for the defense of Menkara in the transformed situation. Everyone agreed that Ariadne's withdrawal from offensive military action should not be announced. Secrecy would buy them time. Eventually when her reduced battlefield presence was noticed, the invaders would be encouraged and the intensity of the hostile attacks would increase. Secrecy would not change the imbalance of power that favored the invaders, but it would buy time.

The longest debate was over defensive versus offensive strategy. Given the power of William and the size of the invading armies, a purely defensive strategy to buy time seemed the obvious choice. Mentaxes, supported by Grassic, held out hope for success of a defensive strategy of trying to wear out the invader's patience and resolve. They hoped that if the war dragged on long enough, the three kings might become open to a plea to end the bloodshed and restore peace to their kingdoms.

Soren argued strongly for the offensive strategy option. He emphasized a point admitted by Mentaxes, namely that a defensive strategy would succeed only if the invaders became demoralized by the long war and mounting casualties and called off the invasion. But he said there was very little chance of the three kings abandoning a costly war that they were all but certain of winning. And, he emphasized, there was no chance that William would ever tire and abandon his quest for revenge.

Soren made the case for a major counter-attack, invading one of the three kingdoms, preferably Galatia. Such an invasion might catch the enemy off guard and lead to an important battlefield victory for Menkara. That combined with the rout of Nesa in the Mondrien forest might be enough to break the resolve of the coalition against Menkara. Soren claimed that a strong counter-invasion, gave Menkara its best chance of victory, its best chance of survival. Lord Menjaro and General Danton, military men, aggressive by nature, strongly supported Soren's counter-invasion option.

Ariadne was heart-sick as she listened to the debate over strategy drag on hour after hour. Yesterday's meeting when everyone had denounced her had been less painful. Even without resorting to sorcery to read minds, she could sense the emotions of the others from their voices and body language. She perceived that behind the debate over which strategy to adopt, each of these proud leaders in his or her own way had given up. They were only debating the most honorable way to die. Spiritual Grassic and peace-loving Mentaxes preferred to die holding out an olive branch of peace. King Soren, Lord Menjaro, and General Danton, warriors all, wanted to die on the battlefield, leading a desperation counter-attack to try to cheat destiny. And it was all the fault of her damned inconstancy –first, volunteering to fight, and later, overcome with guilt, backing out.

Finally, Ariadne reached a decision. Rising to her feet, she swayed dizzily before gaining control of her body. Speaking not much above a whisper, she asked permission to speak. Grassic, without waiting for Soren to decide, broke protocol, and said "Speak, child. Soren glared at Grassic, then addressed Ariadne. "What now, sorceress?"

As she spoke, Ariadne's posture and voice grew in dignity. "My inconstancy created the nightmare scenario about to play itself out. I beg you to let me try to end the nightmare. I have looked into my soul and discovered I can no longer fight a war to try to save what I love, since war means the death of innocents. But I can fight a sorcerer's duel with William to decide the war. One of us will die, but neither of us is innocent. King Soren, if somehow you can get William and the kings of Galatia, Nesa, and Mittani to agree, I will fight a sorcerer's duel to the death with William to determine the outcome of the war."

Lord Menjaro, without waiting for King Soren to respond to the proposed duel, angrily addressed Ariadne. "Sorceress, this is neither the time nor the place to try to assuage your guilt by offering to fight a duel that the enemy will never agree to. With victory on the battlefield certain, why would the three kings allow William to gain all the glory and credit for victory by slaying you in a sorcerer's duel? I …"

Menjaro was cut off by Soren. "Lord Menjaro, you are over hasty in rejecting the sorceress' suggestion. The enemy is far from certain that they will win the war on the battlefield.

They have had major setbacks, most notably the Nesan disaster in the Mondrien forest. They do not know of Ariadne's desire to withdraw from offensive warfare. I think it is possible we could persuade them to agree to decide the war by a sorcerer's duel. But first we must decide, do we have a better chance of defeating the invasion on the battlefield or through a sorcerer's duel."

King Soren then turned and addressed Ariadne. "You are full of surprises sorceress. Before considering your offer, we must know.

Can you defeat William in one-one-one combat? Or are you offering to commit ritual suicide?"

Ariadne's reply was grave. "I am not volunteering to commit suicide. I want to live. I do not know if I can defeat William. William is much more powerful, thus logic says I cannot. But when I prepared for a duel with William when I was with Free Bezriel, my spiritual guide, the Seeker Esther, taught me that good sorcery always has a chance to defeat evil sorcery, no matter how strong. To answer your question, King Soren, I believe that with the help of the Seekers, there is a chance that I might be able to defeat William."

Soren had one more question. "Tell me sorceress, given your non-violent scruples, how can I have confidence that if a duel is arranged that you will not only fight the duel, but try to win even though winning would mean slaying William, a fellow Bezrielite?"

This question hit Ariadne where she was most vulnerable, knowledge of her own inconstancy. "How can I who at crucial moments have reneged on solemn promises to fight, both for Free Bezriel and for you, convince you that this time I will persevere? How can I even convince myself? The only evidence I can give is that I did go to the dueling site for the first duel and was prepared to fight. I would also remind you that both with Free Bezriel and with your army, I withdrew from offensive action to avoid harming innocents. William is no innocent."

Discussion of whether Ariadne would keep this promise dragged on another twenty minutes, but no new points were made until Grassic asked about inconsistency. "It is clear, Ariadne, that as a believer in non-violence, you hate the idea of fighting a sorcerer's duel to the death. Why then do you offer to do so?"

Without hesitation, Ariadne poured forth her answer. "Because I saw the horrors that William triumphant will cause in the world. Because I heard the despair in the hearts of all in this room, despair based on the belief that victory for William is now inevitable. I know that my inconstancy is the cause of that despair. My religious beliefs no longer allow me to fight in wars, even just wars. But

William must be stopped and, unfortunately, no one has a better chance to stop William than I. It is far better that I forego non-violence to fight this one battle, than that I sit passively on the sidelines and let William conquer and rule the world."

A few minutes later, Soren ordered that Ariadne be escorted from the conference room while the high command discussed whether to accept her offer.

Ariadne was unhappy that she had been ordered to leave. She understood that she could not be part of the group that decided whether or not to accept her proposal. But she did not want to be alone, did not want to agonizingly consider and reconsider whether her offer to fight a sorcerer's duel with William was a good decision or utter folly. She tried to talk to her two guards. But afraid of the anger of the king and leery of Free Bezriel sorceress, the only words they uttered were "wait here" when they ushered her into an empty room.

Ariadne then sat quietly and tried to meditate. That proved impossible, because she could not quiet the chaos in her mind. Strangely, when at last she gave up trying to meditate, stopped trying to control her mind, calmness came to her and she felt at peace. In the deepest recesses of her soul she understood that she was committed to non-violence, committed to not knowingly injure any sentient being. Her commitment to non-violence was essential to her walking the path of Bezriel. But she also understood that the path of Bezriel was not the easy path of passively walking away from the world and its problems. Rather the path of Bezriel was actively participating in the world and trying to help solve its problems.

The Bezrielite commitment to non-violence was not a mechanical rule to never raise one's hand in anger against another. For a Bezrielite, non-violence was commitment to spreading love and compassion and reducing hatred and greed in the world. Typically that meant not injuring others, but not always. William gaining power would devastate whole generations not only in Bezriel, but in all of Menkara and surrounding kingdoms. Morally, she had to be part of the effort to stop him. Fighting a duel with William, she told herself, would be an affirmation of Bezrielite non-violence not an abandonment of Bezriel and non-violence.

Unknowingly Ariadne had fallen into a meditative trance. More than two hours later, she came to with a start when the guard roused her to tell her that she was being recalled to the high command meeting room.

After Ariadne had been escorted from the room, Soren addressed the others. "To decide whether to agree to try to set up a sorcerer's duel between William and Ariadne, we need to answer many questions. The first set concern the character of the sorceress, Ariadne. Is her offer to fight a sorcerer's duel sincere? If sincere, will she remain constant and fight the duel if it can be arranged? Or will she once again change her mind and back out?

"The second set of questions concern the duel. Would it be wisdom or folly for us to stake everything on a duel between William and Ariadne? Ariadne is a very powerful sorceress with ties to powerful sorcerers from the distant past. But William is the most powerful sorcerer in recorded history. What chance, if any, does Ariadne have of winning a sorcerer's duel against William? Finally, if the duel is wisdom for us, how can we persuade William and the three kings to agree to a sorcerer's duel to decide the war?"

After a long silence, in which each leader pondered the difficulty and gravity of the issues they must decide, Soren spoke again. "Let us begin with my first question. Is Ariadne's offer to fight a sorcerer's duel with William sincere? Mentaxes, of the five of us, you know her best. What are your thoughts?"

Mentaxes weighed his words carefully and spoke slowly. "Ariadne, as we have learned to our sorrow, changes her mind and is inconstant. But I have never known her to lie. Since she has offered to fight, I am certain that she is now willing to fight a sorcerer's duel with William."

Based on knowledge of the history of Ariadne and observation of her demeanor that day, all five present believed that Ariadne's offer to fight a sorcerer's duel with William was sincere.

"Good," said Soren. "We are agreed that today her offer is sincere. But will she persevere or will she once again find an excuse to change her mind and back out? I am used to judging the characters of soldiers and politicians, not the character and likely behavior of ethical extremists and the religiously devout. High priestess Grassic, can you help us understand religious fanatics and ethical extremists? How do you understand Ariadne, the self-described daughter of Bezriel? Will she keep her pledge to fight a sorcerer's duel with William? Or will she find some last minute excuse to back out?"

"King Soren, I well understand those for whom religion and ethics are foremost in living their lives and making decisions. I understand for I am one such. But based on my lifetime of observations, I tell you that Ariadne is unique. She is in contact with and receives instructions from, not God, but the long dead founders of Bezrielite mysticism known as The Seekers. It was they who revealed to her the secret of the invisibility shield, a secret that one so young could never have discovered on her own.

"This mystical connection with the soul of her religion and her people explains why Ariadne, a believer in the mystical unity of all life, volunteered to fight in two wars, first for Free Bezriel against you and more recently for you against William and the invaders. It also explains why each time, after using her sorcery to commit what she considers atrocities while fighting for her cause, she withdrew from offensive military action.

"Will she then also back out of fighting a sorcerer's duel to the death with William? In my opinion, no, she will not back out. She will remain true to her word and fight the sorcerer's duel. Why do I believe this? Because by fighting and winning this duel, she would achieve what is most precious to her: Bezriel, her people and way of life would be preserved, the violence of this war would be ended, and the threat of a world controlled by William would be averted."

After much wrangling in which everyone had their say, but little of substance added to what Grassic said, Soren ended that discussion by declaring "Ariadne's withdrawals were precipitated by her remorse that she had secured victories by using her sorcery in ways that according to her extremist ethics reduced humans to mere objects to be manipulated. If nothing now triggers such remorse, she will keep her word and fight the duel against William."

After a brief pause, Soren pushed on. "We must now consider the sorcerer's duel. First, will it be wisdom or folly to stake everything on a sorcerer's duel between William and Ariadne? Our situation on the battlefield is desperate. Is a duel our best chance of snatching victory from defeat? Ariadne is a powerful sorceress, but her accomplishments pale compared to William's. Hence we must ask. Does Ariadne have any chance of winning a sorcerer's duel against William? One factor seems to offer hope. Ariadne is aided by ancient Bezrielite sorcerers known as the Searchers. Let us not forget that the invisibility shield they helped her create did stymie William. Who knows what other help they can provide Ariadne?"

Noticing the agitation of Lord Menjaro, Soren turned to him. "Lord Menjaro, you seem eager to be heard on this topic. Please share you views."

"Please forgive my rudeness, Lord Soren, but I must be blunt. There is no chance that Ariadne can defeat William in one-on-one combat. Her powers though great are several grades of magnitude weaker than William's. Furthermore, she has had no training and no experience of one-on-one combat. Her major victories, over Cerberus and, more recently, at Mondrien forest were based on confusing the minds of her opponents. Does anyone believe that Ariadne can befog the mind of William?

"Why do we even consider this absurd idea of staking our lives and futures on a duel that 'our champion' has no chance of winning? Is it not because we now believe that defeat is inevitable? If that be so then let us die fighting on the battlefield and not live as passive spectators hoping for a little girl to save our sorry hides."

Grassic spoke next and spoke movingly. "I am versed in neither warfare nor sorcery. But I do know that after centuries of decay the world is slowly regaining some of the knowledge and powers of the early golden age of mankind. Except for one small omission, Lord Menjaro makes a convincing case that Ariadne cannot defeat William in a sorcerer's duel. The omission is failing to take into account that Ariadne is guided and aided by the Seekers, the powerful ancient sorcerers that founded Bezriel. Perhaps it is foolish to place one's hopes for the future on aid from ancient mystics. But the alternative, as Lord Menjaro, so eloquently argued, is to give up and seek out an honorable death. I for one prefer taking the path where victory and life are at least possible."

As expected General Danton supported Lord Menjaro and Mentaxes supported Grassic. After all four had spoken, there was a long silence. Finally Soren delivered his verdict. "I am sorry that we are so divided on this decision on which our future rests. As I see it, with the help of the Seekers, Ariadne has a chance to defeat William. Like Lord Menjaro, in a hopeless situation, an honorable death on the battlefield is how I want to die. But our situation may not be hopeless; with the help of the Seekers, Ariadne may win. Thus I choose the sorcerer's duel. Let us consider how we can persuade William and the three kings to agree to a sorcerer's duel to decide the war."

Even with Ariadne's sorcery, the chances of Menkara defeating William and the armies of the three kingdoms had been slim. Without Ariadne, the chances of defeating William and the armies of the three kingdoms were non-existent. How then could they get William and the three kings to agree to a sorcerer's duel to decide the war? William they felt sure would jump at the chance to win the war all by himself and to avenge his earlier humiliation by

Ariadne's invisibility shield. The problem was how to get the three kings to accept a sorcerer's duel to decide the war.

Soren argued persuasively that his earlier proposal to launch a counter-invasion of one of the three kingdoms had the best chance. The three kings would agree to a duel only if they felt uncertain of winning the war or believed that the cost of winning was too high. Such pessimism could only be created by battlefield defeats. Adding a humiliating set back in their own territory to the Nesan disaster in the Mondrien forest might be enough.

Their future depended on two improbabilities. First, Soren must devise a counter-invasion plan that could lead to battlefield victory even with William on the other side? Second, Ariadne, with the aid of the Seekers, must find a way to defeat William in one-on-one combat.

Soren recalled Ariadne to the high command meeting room. He told her that her proposal of offering to decide the war by a sorcerer's duel had been accepted. He also outlined his plan of a counter-invasion to induce the panic that would hopefully persuade the three kings to agree to the duel.

Ariadne on hearing this felt as if she had been cast into an airless tomb from which there was no escape.

CHAPTER 17

The week following Ariadne's withdrawal from offensive warfare was organized chaos at Soren's headquarters. With the three pronged invasion slowly squeezing the air out of the lungs of the defenders, Soren's proposed counter-invasion must be launched soon. But Soren's troops could not move before strategy for the counter-invasion was developed. What should the target be? It had us to be a target against which the attack had both a reasonable chance of success and high propaganda value. Necessary conditions for success were that William be far from the target to be attacked and that his quick access to the battlefield be blocked.

Another important decision to be made was whether the quick strike counter-invasion should be led by King Soren, General Danton or Lord Menjaro. Those three met round the clock until a plan was finalized. The plan that emerged was to deliberately allow the Galatian army commanded by General Ptolemy to penetrate to the edge of Zenkara, the capital city of Menkara. Most likely, William would spearhead that advance. If not, he would certainly join that army as it neared the capital. King Soren would organize and command the defense of the capital. The only sorcerers aiding him would be Ariadne and Petrov. All other military sorcerers would be with Lord Menjaro or General Danton. As the invaders advanced on the capital, the Altarian troops of Lord Menjaro, seemingly rushing to help defend the capital, would change direction and speed towards Mittani. Moving as rapidly as possible, the Altarian troops would on the same day reach and cross the border into Mittani. Once in Mittani, they would destroy Mittani border outposts and then lay siege to Xenopolis, the second most populous city in Mittani. Simultaneously, loyal Menkaran troops under the command of General Danton would attack the besiegers of the capital from the rear with the goal of blocking any attempt by William to get to the action in Mittani.

King Soren and the other lords defending Menkara knew that this strategy would lead to heavy military loses for the loyalists and make prolonged defense of the homeland impossible. Such a high cost was acceptable, because the plan was no longer to defeat the invasion by forcing a prolonged and costly war. The new plan was to use the invasion of Mittani to create dismay and panic among the three kings in the invading coalition, thereby creating conditions under which the kings would either decide to abandon the invasion of Menkara as counterproductive or agree to King Soren's proposal of a sorcerer's duel between William and Ariadne to decide the war. To make invader acceptance of Soren's proposal more likely, a propaganda barrage would downplay Menkaran losses in the war and exaggerate public support for Soren. At this critical juncture, the high priestess Grassic would be sent as an emissary to the three invading kings to propose a sorcerer's duel to decide and end the war.

At that time, with considerable help from the military sorcery of William, the Galatian army, commanded by General Ptolemy and accompanied by King Radames, was slowly advancing on Soren's stronghold in Zenkara. Four days after the Menkaran high command had finalized their counter-invasion strategy, the Galatians broke through the defense perimeter around Zenkara.

The next day, General Ptolemy, with the consent of King Radames and William, ordered an all-out assault on Zenkara.

During those four days, Lord Menjaro had moved his Altarian troops to the staging area that had the shortest and militarily easiest route to Mittani. As soon as the Galatian attack on Zenkara began, Menjaro led his troops on a mad dash to the Mittani border. It was almost a full day later that King Radames and William learned of the counter-invasion. Responding to an appeal from Cato, king of Mittani, Radames ordered an elite regiment to escort William to the Mittani border to crush the counter-invasion. But they found their route blocked by a seemingly suicidal Cerberus brigade under the command of General Danton. Despite the ferocity of resistance by Cerberus, after four days of fierce fighting, the Galatian troops, aided by William's sorcery, forced their way through. But Soren's strategy had worked. William had been delayed long enough for Menjaro's troops to capture and sack two Mittani border towns, burned crops in the district, create near panic in Xenopolis, before returning to Menkara by a different route.

As expected, both Cerberus and Menjaro's Altarian troops suffered heavy losses. For an outnumbered army striving to wage prolonged guerrilla war, such losses would have been catastrophic. But the plan of the Menkaran high command was that those battles would be the last of the war. Soren's propaganda machine immediately released bulletins describing and exaggerating the success Lord Menjaro's military strike into Mittani. Those same bulletins promised that more attacks into the nations that had invaded Menkara would soon follow.

The unexpected and successful Menkaran raid into Mittani, led to bitter divisions within the invading coalition. The kings of Nesa and Mittani wanted to dissolve the coalition and end the war immediately. Radames argued that the Menkaran surprise attack was a desperate gamble by seriously weakened enemy. To quit when victory was in sight was foolhardy and shortsighted. The king of Mittani replied angrily "So, Galatia, you dare call me a fool. The war on Soren was your idea. You and your sorcerer assured Nesa and myself that achieving victory would be a stroll in the park. Perhaps for you this war against mighty Soren has been a pleasant stroll, but Nesa and Mittani have suffered grievous losses. And now when we want to limit our losses, you call us fools."

But the coalition did not fall apart so easily. Radames apologized profusely for his ill-chosen words. William once again pointed out that dissolution of the coalition would increase dangers for Mittani and Nesa as Soren sought revenge on those who had invaded Menkara. Two days later, Grassic arrived protected by a white diplomatic flag, and expressed a desire to speak with the kings and negotiate.

The group that meet with the unexpected visitor from the enemy high command was small: only Radames, king Of Galatia, Cato, king of Mittani, Archon king of Nesa, and the renegade Bezrielite sorcerer, William. The kings, not knowing why Grassic had come, nor what she would say, wanted no one else present. King Radames opened the meeting by addressing the visitor. "High-priestess, do you come here today on a private mission or as an emissary of Soren, usurper of the throne of Menkara."

Grassic replied in the magisterial voice that had inspired her people for decades. "It is true, King Radames, that Soren seized his throne on the battlefield. But that is also how your ancestors seized the throne of Galatia. And that is how the ancestors of Cato and Archon seized their thrones. But, enough! I did not come here to argue claims of legitimacy. The Menkaran high command has sent me as their emissary to negotiate with you, the enemy high command." She then presented to Radames a sealed letter signed by each member of the Menkaran high command appointing Grassic as their emissary.

After the three kings and William had examined the letter, Radames again addressed Grassic, courteously this time. "High priestess, what message do you bring us from the Menkaran high command?"

"My message is this: wars between mighty kingdoms devastate populations and economies. The current war has devastated four kingdoms. Losses for both sides are great and growing greater daily. Rewards for the victor will be small. This war must end! I bring to you a proposal from the Menkaran high command to end the war."

Grassic was interrupted by William, speaking in a haughty voice. "A proposal to end the war! Another duplicitous ploy by Soren. It will not work. In a matter of days, the armies of the three kings aided by my sorcery will march into Zenkara and capture Soren, dead or alive. We have no need for a negotiated peace!"

Grassic's reply was insulting and just as haughty. "Boastful word from the mighty sorcerer who could not make it to the battlefields in Mittani until after Lord Menjaro's victorious raiders had devastated the border region of Mittani and safely returned home."

Before William could reply to the insult, Grassic turned her head away from William and towards the three kings, whom she addressed. "William mistakes my purpose. I said the war must end. I did not say I come offering a peace treaty to end the war, leaving each side to go home unsatisfied, having gained nothing for their grievous losses. Rather than a peace treaty, I come with an offer from the Menkaran high command to end the war by a winner-take-all sorcerer's duel between William and Ariadne."

The first reaction of her audience was disbelief. It was William who broke the stunned silence. "The Menkaran offer, if sincere, is admission of defeat, since I can easily defeat Ariadne. But I doubt its sincerity. The treacherous Soren proposed a similar sorcerer's duel to end his war with the Free Bezriel guerrillas. Then like a coward, having lured the guerrillas into coming out from behind their invisibility shield, he arrested all the rebels, including the witch Ariadne, who trusting his lies, came. Doubtless, once again, Soren has an infernal trick up his sleeve."

Grassic began her reply with a surprising admission. "What you say of the past is true."

But then she made a distinction. "This time there is no deceit. The Menkaran high command, on which Soren is just one member, authorized the offer of a sorcerer's duel to decide the war. Such a duel is the only way to avoid four kingdoms self-destructing through a war that neither side can win. To guarantee no duplicity and no tricks, the terms of the duel and the conditions under which it will be fought must be agreed to in advance by both sides."

William began to reply, "You speak of a war, neither side can win! That is absurd…"

Before William could claim that this time, his side would soon win this war, he was cut off by King Radames. "William, stop. Before replying to this offer we must confer." Turning to Grassic, he continued. "High priestess, the three kings to whom you made the offer need time to think the offer over and confer. You will be escorted to a royal guest residence where you will wait. When we have reached a decision, you will be notified and escorted back here to hear our reply."

After Grassic left, King Radames sent messengers to find top generals currently at invasion headquarters. After the generals arrived and were told of the proposal of a sorcerer's duel to decide the war, deliberations began. Given the unlikelihood of Ariadne defeating William in a sorcerer's duel, the kings and their generals quickly agreed that Soren and the Menkaran high command must be desperate. But the kings of Nesa and Mittani argued that the desperation of the enemy did not mean that the enemy's offer of a sorcerer's duel to end the war should be rejected. Those two kings accepted and emphasized Grassic's point that deciding the wat via sorcerer's duel would put an end to casualties and the devastation to the economy created by the war. Therefore they were in favor of agreeing to the duel, unless Ariadne had a better chance of defeating William than Soren's armies and sorcerer's had of defeating the invasion.

In response to a question from King Archon of Nesa, William replied "I am absolutely certain that I can defeat Ariadne. My powers, my military experience, and my knowledge of sorcery are all far greater than hers."

King Cato of Mittani, who had developed a strong dislike of William, then asked a question with an insulting undertone… "How can you be so confident of victory over an opponent aided by ancient sorcerers that defeated you once before? How can you be certain that your powers, experience, and knowledge are greater than the powers, experience, and knowledge of the ancient sorcerer's who will be helping Ariadne?"

The phrasing of the question infuriated William, but he controlled his emotions to answer proudly but civilly. "I have researched the sorcery of the ancients, especially the Seekers, the ancient mystics that have pushed Ariadne forward. I have learned how to recognize and defeat what is different and unique in what little military sorcery they developed."

The interrogation of William lasted more than two hours. At last he convinced the three kings that if they accepted the challenge, he would defeat Ariadne. In the middle of that long interrogation, an interesting exchange occurred. King Cato remarked "If we agree to the duel and your confidence is unjustified, the three kingdoms will have lost much wealth and many brave warriors will have died in vain." To which William replied. "My confidence is justified. But if it were unjustified, it is I, not you, who would die."

Once the three kings were convinced that William would win the sorcerer's duel, they discussed whether they should continue with a full scale attack on Zenkara or accept Soren's offer of a sorcerer's duel to end the war. The kings of Nesa and Mittani were strongly in favor of agreeing to the duel because the duel would minimize, and hopefully put an end to the unexpectedly high economic and human cost of the war.

As the meeting wore on, William, who had initially been opposed to accepting, because he feared being duped by yet another duplicitous trick of Soren, changed his mind. In existing circumstances, there was no way any trick of Soren could succeed. William also recognized that if the duel was fought, their could be no denying that it was through his sorcery alone that war was won and Soren driven from the throne.

The only man with serious doubts about the wisdom of accepting was King Radames. He worried that after William won the duel, his power and influence in the region, especially in Menkara would be too great, and next to impossible to limit. But he did not voice those doubts because he knew that to do so would anger William, and the duel would still be accepted by a vote of three to one.

That evening, Grassic was recalled and informed that the Menkaran offer of a sorcerer's duel to end the war had been accepted. Grassic and the three kings agreed that precise terms for the duel would be worked in negotiations between the chancellors of the four kingdoms. But basic terms were preset. If Ariadne won, the invaders would recognize Soren as king of Menkara and recall their troops home. Reparations, however, would not be paid to Menkara for the economic devastation caused by the invasion. If William won, the Menkaran armies would surrender. There would be an interregnum in which Menkara was ruled by the three kingdom winning coalition. Soren would be arrested, but given a chance to defend himself at a fair trial.

CHAPTER 18

Grassic returned to Soren's battlefield headquarters with the news that William and the three kings had agreed to Soren's proposal for a sorcerer's duel to determine the outcome of the war. In her opinion the kings had accepted because heavy battlefield losses and the successful Menkaran raid into Mittani had made the war unpopular in the three kingdoms of the invading coalition. The duel opened up for them the possibility of ending losses while still winning the war. But William, she was sure had accepted out of vanity. He was sure that he would win the duel, and by winning he would become the sole provider of victory and the dominant power in the winning coalition.

Over the next week, the prime ministers of the four kingdoms developed the exact terms of the sorcerers duel. It would begin at dawn ten days after the signing of the agreement, and would not end until either William or Ariadne was dead, unless to save their sorcerer, Soren or the three kings conceded defeat. But all parties knew that Soren would not concede defeat to save Ariadne and that the kings of the alliance would not concede defeat to save William. Despite the non-lethal option, everyone knew it was a duel to the death.

Ariadne asked for and was granted permission to spend the ten days in virtual isolation, being instructed by Esther in her dreams at night. She would meditate and practice battlefield tactics with Marcus during her waking hours. Marcus was ill at ease with Ariadne's proposal to fight the duel, wondering why Ariadne has abandoned her reverence for life in agreeing to a duel to the death with William. Fearing that she had agreed because of a wish to die, he did not have the courage to ask her to explain herself. But Ariadne sensing the fear behind his unease raised the issue herself.

"Do not fear, Marcus. I have no desire to hasten my death. But I cannot live with myself as long as this senseless slaughter that we call war continues. I helped bring the hatred and violence on. I must do what I can to end it. I could see no way to end the war other than the sorcerer's duel with William."

"Thank you, Ariadne. Your words have given peace to my soul. But if in proposing a duel with William, you are not choosing suicide, does that mean that you think you can defeat William?"

"No. I cannot defeat William. Or rather, alone I cannot defeat William. But perhaps with the aid of the Seekers, I can be the tool by which Bezriel defeats William. But whether I win, or more likely lose, fighting the duel is the right choice. If I lose, I will die young, die never having giving birth to new life. My parents will mourn, you will mourn. But there will be no reason to mourn. My death will not be in vain. The war will end. Peace will return to the four kingdoms. Peace will return to Bezriel."

Marcus was shocked by Ariadne's claim that who won the duel, who won the war, was less important than the fact that the war would end.

"No, Ariadne, winning does matter. If William wins, the peace that follows for Bezriel will be the daily grind of the exploited slave. If William wins, the peace that follows will merely be a short interlude before his next war. You must try to win!"

The words of Marcus struck like a knife at the soul of Ariadne. Before, her emotions cooled, she replied. "Marcus, I know all too well the horrors that will befall Bezriel if William triumphs, the horrors that will befall all of Menkara if William triumphs. Yet even in those conditions, the spirit of Bezriel can and will survive. But the spirit of Bezriel cannot survive a prolonged civil war, cannot survive for long if Bezriel becomes a nation of butchers and slaughtered sheep. I will try to win this cursed sorcerer's duel to the death. But if I lose, at least there will be peace, and that peace might be the fertile soil in which the spirit of Bezriel may once again flourish."

Marcus understood then that in proposing the sorcerer's duel, dying was not the motivation of Ariadne. But while dying was not her motivation, she believed and willingly accepted that she would die in the duel, willingly because the war would end. "Ariadne, if you die in this duel, your death will not be in vain not because it was the price of peace, but because

your life and death will become for Bezriel, a symbol of defiance, of a willingness to live and die for freedom, to live and die for Bezriel. Your life and death will serve as a rallying point in the struggle for Bezriel to become free."

"Are you telling me, Marcus, that in dying to end this war, I am turning myself into a symbol that will inspire future wars! I can only hope that you are wrong."

Ariadne was saddened by her conversation with Marcus. Fortunately, when Esther appeared to Ariadne on the first of the ten nights, her joy at seeing Esther made her forget her sadness. Esther made a promise. "I will come to you every night to help you prepare for your duel with William. I will help you prepare in terms of learning and mastering sorcerer's skills that will improve your chances of winning. And I will help you prepare spiritually for the awful ordeal of a duel to the death on which the fate of many depend."

Bowing in reverence, Ariadne simply replied, "Thank you, Seeker."

"Tell me, Ariadne, chosen defender of Bezriel, in the duel to come, which is more important, sorcerer's skill or spiritual awareness?"

"Spiritual awareness. Without awareness, skill can accomplish little."

"True. But in your duel with William, awareness of what?"

Ariadne opened her mouth to answer "awareness of Bezriel", but realizing how glib that answer was, she hesitated. After a long silence, she finally replied, "I do not know. I await your instruction."

"Modesty does not become you, Ariadne. I cannot teach you what you already know. To find the answer, look not to me! Look within yourself! What must occupy your soul when you are the champion of Bezriel in a duel to the death?"

This harsh reply made Ariadne wince. She thought long and hard on Esther's question. She considered many possible answers – that to be champion of Bezriel one must first purify one's soul; that one must act for the greater good and not for one's own glory. Finally, Esther interrupted the young girl's struggles. "Relax, daughter of Bezriel. Think with you heart, not with your brain."

Ariadne tried to relax. She let her mind go blank. She tried to hear the heartbeat of Bezriel. After listening with all her soul, she gave her answer. "All life forms a unity. I must try to win, but in striving to win, I must never forget that Bezriel lives as much in my opponent as it does in me. I must never forget the humanity of he who I am trying to kill."

"What you are saying, Ariadne. You speak in paradoxes. William is the antithesis of the spirit of Bezriel. If Bezriel dwells within him and you see that, why do you intend to try to kill him?"

Ariadne recognized the paradoxes and had no answer. Finally Esther spoke again. "In a good society, different visions of the world are resolved by debate and by examples that inspire repetition. But where is the good society, today? In the corrupt world of modern times, civilized compromises are rare. Either William's lust for power and dominion over everything will triumph or he will be defeated and the age old world of compromises will be restored. Can you now answer my question: how can a champion of Bezriel try to kill William, even while recognizing the holiness within him?"

"No, I cannot answer. I am more confused than ever. I thought you agreed that I must see William as a son of Bezriel. But you paint a portrait of William as evil. In what sense does Bezriel live within a man who does evil?"

"I did not say that William was evil. That was your interpretation of what I said. I said he has a vision, a vision of the way things ought to be, a dream of the future that is the opposite of your dream of the future. There can be no compromise between the two dreams. But William's dream emanates from the same life force that gave birth to your dream."

"Forgive me Esther, but now it is you who speak in paradoxes. If William's vision of the good and my vision of the good contradict each other, how can they emanate from the same life force? How can they both be manifestations of Bezriel? Is Bezriel self-contradictory?"

"Ariadne, are you prepared to hear me speak scandal? The answer to both your question is "yes". I do believe that Bezriel is self-contradictory!"

Ariadne was numb with shock. "You are my guide Esther. I trust that you speak truth. But what you say makes no sense to me. I do not see how it can be possible that William and his quest to control everything and everyone and my Bezriel that teaches the organic unity of all things manifest the same life source."

"I am pleased that you trust me, Ariadne, even when my words make no sense to you. But I am also displeased that you trust me when you think I speak nonsense. Be vigilant! I try to always speak the truth. But I do not always succeed. Remember that basic point! All humans, all sentient beings, are limited and finite. We see and understand only a small part of what is. To truly live is to fight for what you believe to be right. But to remain part of Bezriel, you must recognize that this is also true of your enemies, also true of those who fight against you."

"Your message is not easy for me to grasp, Esther. I need to meditate on it. "

That is all that I ask. Sleep now, daughter. Tomorrow we will begin to refine your skills for your sorcerer's duel with William."

The next morning the perplexed Ariadne talked over with Marcus her dream discussion with Esther on spiritual preparation for her sorcerer's duel with William. After many requests for repetition and explication, Marcus made a comment that proved useful to Ariadne." It seems to be that Esther is emphasizing one of the hardest passages in the Bezrielite sacred canon, the injunction to love thy enemy."

Ariadne grew excited. "Yes. Marcus, yes, yes. I was thinking in the abstract about the ideal of Bezriel as the unity of all life. But you point to the practical meaning of Bezriel: the command to love all things, including the hardest command of all, the command to love your enemy." After a brief pause, she continued "But more than that. I think Esther is asking me to not only love my enemy but to reflect on why Bezriel tells its children to love their enemies. To reflect on why Bezriel tells me to love William. It is not enough for me to accept the paradox, and love the man I hate. I must also understand why it is vital for me to love the man I hate."

Now Marcus was puzzled. "Are you saying that understanding and following the Bezrielite injunction to love your enemy is the key to winning your duel with William? Does that mean it is not enough for you to win, but that you must win not as a great sorceress but as a true Bezrielite?"

"What I am saying has nothing to do with winning the duel and everything to do with truly being a Bezrielite," she replied. Ariadne and Marcus made no further progress that first day in understanding the words of Esther.

Throughout the next three nights Esther taught Ariadne how to defend against attacks by William's powerful sorcery, attacks that had created his reputation as the most powerful sorcerer in modern times. She also taught Ariadne how to counter-attack against these probable thrusts of William. During the days following those nights, Ariadne practiced with Marcus the moves and tactics that she had been taught.

Then for two nights Esther taught Ariadne how to be prepared for the various ways in which William might try to trick her into letting down her guard. On the days following those nights, Ariadne discussed and practiced deceptive techniques with Marcus. Together they tried to think of deceptive tactics, both how to use them and how to be prepared to defend against them

On the seventh night, Esther began to discuss with Ariadne how she might defeat William and win the duel. "I know Ariadne that you do not believe that victory over William is possible. It is true that William is a more powerful sorcerer than you. He is also more experienced and much more ruthless. Knowing this you have convinced yourself that you cannot defeat William. But victory over William is possible. Our basic source of hope is that William has character flaws that if properly exploited can lead him to make mistakes that will give you a chance for victory."

Esther paused for questions. Instead of a question, Ariadne offered a reproach. "Seeker, please do not offer me false hope."

"Child, there is no guarantee, but there is hope. Are you prepared to listen?"

"Forgive my insolence, teacher. I will listen."

"A basic character flaw of William, that can become a battle flaw, is his supreme confidence in his own power and superiority. The invisibility shield that you created frustrated him and for a short time caused him to doubt his pre-eminence. But he has long since explained away his failure to penetrate the invisibility shield as simply being unprepared for confronting a sorceress aided by the Seekers. But he has long since regained total self-assurance. That overweening confidence is the flaw you can exploit."

`After a lengthy pause, during which Ariadne asked no questions, Esther moved on from character analysis of William to advice for the sorcerer's duel now just three days away. "Listen well, Ariadne. You must carefully create a crisis situation where William believes he has overpowered your defenses and weakened you. When he moves in for what he expects to be the kill, he will be overconfident and not think you capable of the strong and sudden counter-attack that you will launch. You will create an earthquake around him. Caught unprepared he will not be able to stop or divert the earthquake, nor have time to flee to safer grounds. I will teach you the earthquake spell. With this strategy and spell you may prevail."

Esther and Ariadne assumed that at the beginning of the duel, William would be cautious, fearing new stratagems and curses that Ariadne might have been taught by the Seeker Esther. In the beginning Ariadne would use optimal tactics and power. She would eventually unleash a yet to be decided upon ancient curse that William was familiar with and would defeat. Ariadne's second major attack would employ the once popular but for centuries rarely used reverse crescendo, a strategy that lulled one's opponent into complacency by attacking with steadily decreasing power.

Then when an opponent is least expecting it, you unleash your strongest curse. Esther knew that William was familiar with the reverse crescendo and would probably defeat it, unscathed. The point of these early tactics would be to encourage and strengthen William's supreme confidence in his own superiority in sorcery. Eventually believing he had defeated Ariadne's strongest attacks, William would move in for the kill. In preparation for her decisive blow, Ariadne would watch for an overconfident slip in William's preparations and maneuvers. When she found it, she would cast the earthquake spell, the most powerful ancient attack that Esther had taught her. Hopefully William would be caught off guard and be unable to adequately defend himself.

For the remainder of the seventh and all of the eighth night, Esther and Ariadne discussed possible scenarios to induce William's moment of overconfidence leading to Ariadne's triggering a localized earthquake where he was standing.

Other scenarios were developed and analyzed for presenting opportunities for successful surprise counter-attacks by Ariadne. If William attempted to use mind control, Esther and Ariadne developed a strategy of response that they hoped would lead William to disastrous overconfidence. Ariadne would try to deceive William into believing that he had achieved greater control of her mind than was in fact the case. Scenarios were developed in which that false belief would lead William to make a fatal mistake. But, Esther warned, such mind games were very dangerous, for in trying to trick William into overconfidence, Ariadne might fall deeper under William's mind control than she realized.

Another aspect of the strategy developed by Seeker and student stemmed from the fact that William's superiority in sorcery was so extreme, his battles had been short. He had never had to learn endurance, how to fight when mentally and physically fatigued. If Ariadne could stretch out the battle long enough, William might tire and become more likely to make a mistake.

As dawn of the eighth night approached, Esther told Ariadne that her military training for her sorcerer's duel with William was complete. During the final two nights, they would return to spiritual preparation.

Late the following day after hours of rigorously prepping for counterattacking after inducing false optimism, Ariadne and Marcus once again discussed the paradox of opposite visions of the good arising from the same source, Bezriel. Each of the solutions they considered left them unsatisfied. But they refused to accept the idea that it was a mystery that human understanding could not resolve.

As dusk approached, Ariadne rejected the paradox. "I can understand that based on very different experiences different well-intentioned people may develop very different conceptions of right and wrong actions, of good and bad social mores and structures. But surely there is a difference between those like my parents who want a world in which everyone has access to strong education, good health care, and meaningful work, and those like

William who want to dominate and exploit others and are willing to commit violence to get what they want. Even if different visions of good may be valid, surely there is an unbridgeable difference between actions based on love and compassion and actions based on greed and selfishness."

Ariadne did not believe that her training for the sorcerer's duel was complete. But she trusted Esther's judgment that the little remaining time should be spent on spiritual preparation. Esther sensed both the doubt about military preparedness and the pupil's trust in her teacher's judgment and was pleased by both. She thought it wise to address Ariadne's doubts.

"Daughter of Bezriel, you are correct that more can be done to increase your military skills for the duel. But we have only two nights. On our very first night of preparing for the duel, looking within your own heart, you told me that in your duel with William, spiritual awareness was more important than sorcerer's skill. If you still believe that spiritual preparation is paramount, we will spend our remaining time on spiritual matter."

After a minute, Ariadne replied. "Over the days of preparing militarily for the duel, I forgot the importance of spiritual preparation. Thus when you said, we were finished with military preparation, while I outwardly accepted your words, my soul was tormented by fear that we would be wasting the few precious hours that remain to us. But now, my fears have been quieted. Let us proceed."

The next forty minutes were spent in yogic exercise to calm the mind and bring the senses to maximum attentiveness. Then Esther spoke. "In all complex athletic activities, the key to success is training so that the complex physical response to any situation is automatic once the situation is recognized. Your mind has been trained to differentiate situations and your body has been trained to respond appropriately. The level of efficiency of both your mind and body will reflect the degree of harmony your soul has reached with Bezriel. That is why most of what we will do on these last two nights is practice the ancient calming meditation by which the ancients of Bezriel prepared for battle. Once the battle begins, your actions will be ninety percent conditioned response and only ten percent conscious adaptation. The ancient yoga of Bezriel is designed to increase your efficiency at both."

In the rest breaks from practicing the ancient yoga, Esther took advantage of the deep calm in Ariadne's mind to discuss the paradox of an adherent of Bezriel fighting a duel to the death and to elaborate on her paradoxical advice that Ariadne should accept the ethical validity of William's position.

Ariadne accepted the first which is why she had not been tempted to back out of her sorcerer's duel with William. But she could not accept that there was any ethical validity in William's desire to control and dominate others. With respect to hard commandment to love thine enemy, although Ariadne recognized that she must love, not hate, William, her soul could not make that leap.

The day before the sorcerer's duel, Ariadne practiced meditation techniques with Marcus who made several helpful suggestions. They returned to the discussion of whether it was conceivable that there was some sense in which both Ariadne's and William's conception of the good might both be valid. They thought not and questioned whether Esther was serious in suggesting both were valid.

On the tenth night, Esther said "Since the duel is tomorrow, it is essential that that you have a night of calming yogic sleep so that you are well-rested and fully alert when the duel begins. But it is essential that we first discuss the essence of Bezriel. Does Bezriel teach that the essence of each creature that lives is good?"

"Yes."

"Even though their essence is good, do men and women sometimes do evil things?"

"I wish the answer was no, but I know the answer is yes. I myself have done evil."

"What brought you back from evil to good?"

"The love and forgiveness of my parents and comrades."

"Without that love and compassion, would you have found your way back to the good? Back to Bezriel?"

"Possibly, but I doubt it. And even if I could have made that journey on my own, it would have been far more painful and taken far longer?"

"Daughter of Bezriel, you who have been saved by the love and compassion of family and friends, should you not show similar love and compassion to those you meet that have done evil? Should you not show the same love and compassion to William?"

"Revered Seeker, I have tried to accept your teaching that I should. But I have not been able to."

"It is hard, but you must keeping try. Will you?"

"The duel is tomorrow!"

"Yes, the duel is tomorrow. But it is not too late."

Ariadne said nothing.

Esther spoke one final time. "I will help you to sleep well and deeply tonight, Ariadne. Tomorrow you face your day of reckoning, the test for which you were born."

CHAPTER 19

William's preparation for the duel reflected both a life-long arrogance and a newly emergent cruelty. The arrogance sprang from his belief that the power of his sorcery was unmatched. The cruelty was fueled by resentment, resentment of Bezriel for casting him out and resentment of the nobility in both Menkara and Galatia who regarded him as little more than a useful servant.

William assumed that the power of his sorcery was so great that the only way Ariadne could defeat him would be if the Seekers taught her some long forgotten enchantment that would catch him unprepared. Thus, William, like Ariadne, spent much of the preparation time for the duel talking to ancient sorcerers. But whereas Ariadne humbly sought instruction from the Seeker Esther who freely gave what her pupil sought. William obtained secrets from ancient sorcerers by using threats of harm to their living descendants if they held back any information. These brutal tactics paid a large dividend when on the third day, a powerful mage from the early days of Bezriel, terrified of what William could do to his living descendants, revealed details of the ancient and forbidden earthquake spell. That earthquake spell was, in fact, being taught by Esther to Ariadne. If unprepared, William might have been defeated by it, but thanks to his cruelty, he had time to devise a defense against it. If Ariadne was strong enough to cast the spell, he now knew how to reverse the tremors so that they would destroy the ground and terrain from which the spell had been cast and thereby kill Ariadne. William thanked the unfortunate spirit who had given him the vital information by ravaging his mind so that he could tell no one what he had told William.

Only after William became convinced that there were no longer any powerful ancient sorcery assaults he did not know how to use and how to defeat, did he relax. Only then, supremely confident of victory, did he indulge in the luxury of plotting what he would do after his victory in the duel. Even with Ariadne dead, Soren was unlikely to surrender. That pleased William, for the alliance kings had promised him that if Soren refused to surrender, he could slay the tyrant himself.

William gloried in the fact that after he had defeated and sent to Hades both Ariadne and Soren, his power and influence in the four kingdoms would know virtually no limits. He could if he desired become king of Menkara. But he decided that becoming king would be a strategic mistake since it would unite the nobility of the region against him. Much better to be the behind the scenes power on the subcontinent on which the recognized kings and nobles depended for their safety than to be an upstart ruler they would do anything to be rid of.

As the sorcerers prepared for the duel, the kings, nobility, and commoners on both sides were gnawed by anxiety.

Soren finally admitted to himself that his dream of empire was dead. If Ariadne won, he would remain king of Menkara but would have to make endless concessions to nobles and to organized ethnic and religious groups. But, if, as was far more likely, William won, he, the mighty warrior who had reunited Menkara would be ingloriously defeated, and ignominiously executed. He had agreed to the duel based on the belief that Ariadne had a better chance to defeat William, than his exhausted, depleted, and outnumbered armies had of defeating the invading armies of the three kingdoms backed by William. He hoped against hope that Ariadne had a chance to win and hence that he had a chance to survive. But in pondering how he had been reduced to this sorry state, Soren never once considered his own vaunting ambition as the core reason.

Most of the Menkaran lords aligned with Soren believed that William would win and were hoping that the kings would retain enough control of the three kingdom alliance to enable their cousins, the Menkara nobility, to negotiate favorable terms of surrender. But these lords aligned with Soren feared their fate if surrender terms were imposed by the wrathful William.

Bezrielites, distrustful of Soren, had been thrilled and made hopeful by the attempted coup d'état that had liberated large many parts of Menkara, including Bezriel, from Soren's control. But then the three kingdom invasion of Menkara had changed everything. Once again Bezriel was trapped in the middle of a war between great powers. But this time, Bezriel was not an irrelevancy, for in this war sorcery was the key to victory and the most powerful sorcerer on each side was a Bezrielite. Opinion in Bezriel was divided, but most Bezrielites strongly trusted Ariadne and feared William, despite the fact that Ariadne was aligned with Soren, a lord Bezrielites had learned to their sorrow they could not trust, whereas William was aligned with powers, little known to Bezriel, powers whose proclaimed goal was unseating the tyrant Soren.

After the sorcerers duel between William and Ariadne was announced, the people of Bezriel were stunned by the prospect that the fate of four kingdoms now hung on the outcome of a sorcerers duel between two Bezrielites. Accustomed by centuries of living far from the realms of power and influence, most Bezrielites did not rejoice in their new prominence. To the contrary, most were terrified by the spotlight now shining on Bezrielite sorcery.

The three allied kings were not euphoric at their expected triumph. Losses in the war had been far greater than William had led them to expect. Even worse their military dependence on William had become much greater than even the doomsayers had forecast. After William won the duel, they saw no way short of assassination to check his power. But could such a powerful sorcerer be taken unawares and assassinated?

However, Diamant, chancellor of Galatia, was exultant. He assumed that as William's most loyal ally, his power and influence after the war would be greater than that of King Radames. He did not realize that to William, he was a mere political tool whose usefulness had been exhausted.

When Ariadne awoke before dawn on the day appointed for her sorcerer's duel to the death with William, she was simultaneously, relieved, exultant and terrified. Relieved, because her long wait, her dark night of the soul, was now over. Both exultant and terrified, because today was the day foretold in her mother's prophetic dream; the day that the child her mother bore would lead her people either to freedom or servitude; either the freedom to walk the path of Bezriel or the servitude of an exploited people, valued only for the military sorcerers that could be stolen from its protective arms. Today was the day the prophecy would be fulfilled. But in what way, opening the road to freedom or the road to servitude, she did not know. She knew she was not worthy to perform such a fateful duty, but she now accepted that it was her duty.

Despite her acceptance that fighting this duel to the death was her sacred duty, Ariadne felt guilty, because by fighting this duel, she would be deliberately breaking her solemn vow to never again use sorcery to try to kill. A vow she had taken because of her remorse that in anger she had once used mind control sorcery to cause the enemy soldiers who had slain her mentor Gwydian to slaughter each other.

On this day she would probably be slain by William, thus damning Bezriel to another epoch of domination and exploitation by cruel masters. It would be much worse this time because the tyranny would be the result of a Bezrielite misusing the sacred gift of Bezrielite sorcery. In this new epoch, Bezrielite sorcery, rather than being suppressed, would be perverted into a state engine of conquest and exploitation.

Ariadne desperately hoped that what she had told Marcus was true, that once again the soul of Bezriel would survive another era of exploitation. That is what she hoped, but in her heart and soul she was unsure.

The other possibility, a very unlikely possibility, was that she would defeat William, thereby saving Bezriel, but damning her own soul by violating her sacred vow to never again use sorcery to kill. But in the pre-dawn darkness as Ariadne waited for the rising sun to signal that the sorcerer's duel had begun, both the confidence and peace of mind she had with great difficulty achieved over the last ten days began to evaporate.

Once again the sorcerer's duel between William and Ariadne was to be fought on the fields surrounding the Bezrielite Temple of Origins. This time, there would be only eight observers, three from each side to guarantee that both sorcerers obeyed the agreed upon rules and one sorcerer from each camp to communicate with the combatants, if necessary: Marcus from the Menkaran side and a non-Bezrielite, Zachariah, representing the three kingdoms. Both were accomplished at communication of minds at a distance. Despite close proximity to the deadly sorcery of the duel, the eight would be safe because their bunker was protected by a magic shield and well outside the line of fire between the two sorcerers. But the main reason they were safe was because the four kings and two sorcerers had agreed that injuring those in the observers' bunker was grounds for disqualification.

As on the day of the aborted duel when Ariadne was betrayed and arrested, the weather for this duel was cold, damp, and dreary. I recalled the words of my father that fateful day. To those like me, his young son, who sought portents in nature, foolishly believing that the weather was the gods' way of telling us the results of the duel, my father said "There is a bond between humanity and nature.

That bond is what we call Bezriel. Nature does not care who wins when we fight, but weeps that we still settle our disputes through violence. Who will win today is uncertain. What is certain is that on this day one child of Bezriel will kill another child of Bezriel. If you seek a portent, it is this: the skies weep because we are tryingh to build the foundation for the future of Bezriel on fratricide." I saw the wisdom of my father's words, but could not accept them. What other option did Ariadne have? What other option did Bezriel have?

Each of the eight observers later wrote of what happened that day. These eyewitness reports along with interviews with many others, and not just my childhood memories, are the basis of my narrative of the sorcerer's duel between William and Ariadne. There are discrepancies between the reports, but enough consensus to reconstruct with a high degree of probability what happened that day. My interpretations of why what happened happened and of the historical significance of the duel are of course more problematic.

To the surprise of the observers, both sorcerers were reluctant to take the initiative and attack first. Each seemed to prefer counterattack to initiating hostilities. During the first hour neither combatant made a serious attempt to injure the other. It was as if they were shadow boxing.

Ariadne was the first to lose patience with the waiting game. She launched a very old mesmerizing spell, not known by many modern sorcerers. It is a spell that if unnoticed reduces the alertness and slows the reflexes of those it envelops. But William, who was familiar with the spell, effortlessly pulverized the hypnotic aura that Ariadne had cast and scattered its fragments. William then took the offensive, causing stones objects near Ariadne to explode. Rather than encase herself within an impenetrable shield which would inhibit her ability to counterattack, Ariadne calmly and effectively deflected the debris flying in her direction. Attacks like these, easily defeated by master sorcerers such as the two combatants exhausted the second hour of the duel.

In the third hour, Ariadne implemented her strategy of launching powerful ancient spells and curses. She expected that William would defeat these early assaults, but hoped that defeating them would not only strain and tire his reflexes and powers of concentration but also lull him into overconfidence. She began this phase of the duel with the reverse crescendo, a series of attacks of diminishing strength on William's sorcerer's armor. After a strong initial thrust, she would gradually diminish the power off her attacks, for example 7-6-5-4. The goal of gradually diminishing the power of her attacks was to lull William into a false sense of security. Then hoping to catch William off guard, Ariadne suddenly reversed to a super strong 10 level attack. Her 10 move was deceptive in two ways; first, because of the sudden reversal of trend, but also because in an innovative wrinkle introduced by Ariadne, it was a very strong blow delivered in a deceptively mild way.

Many ancient battles had been won by the reverse crescendo. Ariadne used it hoping but not expecting that the diminuendo and mild delivery would lull William into overconfidence and unpreparedness for the surprise 10. It did not. William effortlessly blocked Ariadne's surprise haymaker. In his memoirs on the duel, Marcus writes that he was discouraged by the ease with which William defeated the reverse crescendo and had tried to console himself with the hope that such an easy victory over a classic maneuver would itself lead William into overconfidence.

Mere minutes after defeating the reverse crescendo, William unleashed a powerful curse causing the spirits of the hills in which Ariadne stood to scream very loudly in blood curling voices unnerving to any human. The curse worked for a few minutes until Ariadne was able to focus enough to counter with a binding command to the hills to be silent. What ensued next was a fierce struggle between William and Ariadne for command of the hill spirits. After ten minutes that strained the stamina of both sorcerers, William ceased his attack, satisfied that the pitched battle had tired Ariadne more than it had tired him.

Shortly thereafter, Ariadne launched her second ancient attack. Just as William had tried to unnerve her through prolonged bloodcurdling screams from hill spirits, she now tried to unnerve William, by besieging him with a phalanx of long dead Bezrielite sorcerers, led by two of the Seekers, who damned William for perverting the spirit of Bezriel through his lust for personal power and glory. Being cursed by long-dead revered Bezrielites would have rattled Ariadne, but had no effect on William, who had long since abandoned traditional Bezrielite morality.

Nonetheless, one dead mega-sorcerer, Ezekiel, made a strong impression on William. Four centuries earlier, Ezekiel had used his great powers to grow rich and become a feared and powerful agent of the king of Menkara. William of course knew that Ezekiel had been despised as a traitor by his own people and had never been trusted by his royal masters, but he had not known of the torments of Ezekiel in the land of the dead until on this day, Ezekiel described his torments after death. But rather than motivating William to abandon his quest for ultimate power, Ezekiel's miserable fate only made William more resolute in his quest to discover the secret of the philosopher's stone, the elixir of life that would make him immortal.

Defeating Ariadne's army of the dead did not make William overconfident, but being lectured by Ezekiel did make him angry. In his fury, he tried to end the duel with one blow, a lightning strike aimed at the heart of Ariadne. The bolt was so strong and so sudden, that the onlookers were amazed that Ariadne managed to deflect it. She was not killed, but she was rattled, her self-confidence shaken.

Ariadne then unleashed the earthquake curse, the strongest spells of the ancients that Esther had taught her. She created a localized earthquake in the sector of The Temple of Origins occupied by William. The sorcerer's power needed to cause an earthquake is enormous. An earthquake had not been started by a sorcerer since before the age in which the Seekers had opened the path of Bezriel. Centuries ago at an assembly of all Bezrielites, living and dead, an assembly called by the Seekers, the earthquake summoning spell had been banned as a sacrilege against nature. It was declared a mortal offense to use it or to teach it.

But, at a secret meeting of the Seekers called by Esther shortly before the sorcerers duel between William and Ariadne, permission was given for Esther to teach the spell to Ariadne and for Ariadne to cast the spell. The justification that the Seekers gave was that William represented a mortal danger to Bezriel, hence employing the sacrilegious earthquake spell to defeat him was justified. Because of respect for holy mother Earth, the Seekers had not allowed Ariadne to fully execute the earthquake spell while preparing for the duel. But Ariadne had mastered all the steps and components of the spell.

The Seekers did not request permission from the community of all Bezrielites living or dead to authorize such a sacrilege because they knew if they did so, William would learn of it. They did not anticipate that one of their friends would be tortured into disclosing the spell to William. But shortly before the duel, Esther learned that a friend had had his mind destroyed. She immediately suspected William and feared that he had learned the secrets of ancient spells including the earthquake spell. She informed Ariadne. They decided that Ariadne should still cast the earthquake spell, although they knew that if William had learned of it, he would have devised a defense.

The defense and counterattack to the earthquake spell used by William was to reverse the tremors started by Ariadne and send them rippling back to the area where she was standing. When Ariadne felt the tremors begin to reverse, she struggled against it. Pushed from both ends, the tremors traveled sideways and destroyed the Temple of Origins. Ariadne was horrified. But William, exultant that he had defeated his foe's strongest curse, immediately launched his own attack, using sorcery to hurl weighty chunks of the pillars of the destroyed temple at the distracted and distraught Ariadne, who was barely able to summon enough energy to alter their trajectory at the last second.

Ariadne's execution of the earthquake spell had succeeded in boosting William's confidence in his superiority. But it was not overconfidence, because Ariadne was exhausted by the effort of repelling first the reversed tremors and very soon thereafter the rapidly incoming pillar fragments. Ariadne was also spiritually rattled at having destroyed the sacred Temple of Origins. Physically and emotionally drained, she lacked the strength to effectively launch a counter-attack. Most of the eight onlookers believed that she would be unable to survive William's next attack.

But then remembering what was at stake, Ariadne employed a mystical technique, taught to her years ago by Esther, to regain her energy and composure. Her whole being vibrated to the thought that to preserve all that she loved, she had to find a way to stop William.

At that moment, a voice began to speak in Ariadne's heart. "Remember Bezriel," were the first words of the voice. The voice Ariadne heard was not the voice of Esther. It was the voice of her mother, Sarah, an herbalist healer; a peacemaker, not a warrior. Her mother's voice continued. "Bezriel is the harmony of all life. It cannot be saved by a son of Bezriel rising to power. Nor can it be saved by a daughter of Bezriel slaying a son of Bezriel. Ariadne, remember what it is to be Bezriel before it is too late."

Visions began flashing in front of Ariadne, First was the vision of the desolation and corruption of Bezriel if William won the war for the three invading kingdoms. Bezriel would be reduced to a supply source of powerful wizards of war. With sorcery firmly established as the key to military superiority, Bezriel would be a closely guarded prize. Hope for a free and independent Bezriel would be bleak.

Next was a vision of Bezriel if it became free through her slaying of a fellow Bezrielite. Kaitlin and her Free Bezriel supporters would find in her victory confirmation of their belief that only through military might could Bezriel ever be free. The government of the newly independent Bezriel would recognize the military importance of the powerful sorcerers that Bezriel produced. Independent Bezriel, just like King Soren and just like King Radames, would train young Bezrielite sorcerers to become military sorcerers. That would provoke a reaction among the religious traditionalists in Bezriel who would struggle to recreate Bezriel along traditional lines. If the traditionalists won, Ariadne feared a Bezrielite version of the intolerance that defined Baron Frederick's cruel reign of intolerance over Bezriel when she was a child. The same intolerance that had led to the arrest of her mother and William, the arrests that had begun the era of troubles and bitter wars, that had divided family against family. In none of these futures, did Bezriel resemble the Bezriel that Ariadne loved.

In that moment, Ariadne became convinced of the contradiction of trying to open up a spiritual path to enlightenment by fighting a duel to the death. She saw that the violent means she must use would eventually poison the fruit that grew from the trees on that path.

It was in that moment of despair that Ariadne made the fateful decision that destroyed the visions of the future of all the contending parties. Seeing both victory and defeat leading to unacceptable futures, Ariadne created a different future. With every ounce of strength in her tortured soul, she created a massive earthquake that destroyed the entire Temple of Origins battlefield. Both William and Ariadne were badly injured and rendered unconscious. They survived the quake, only to die from their wounds days later.

CHAPTER 20

After the tremors from the earthquake subsided, troops from both armies and many Bezrielites who lived in the vicinity rushed to the Temple of Origins. They were shocked by the devastation that lay before them. No one was sure if they were looking at a natural catastrophe or the result of the sorcerer's duel. Then the eight observer's came out from their observation platform, which had not been destroyed by the earthquake. They told the crowd that Ariadne had created the devastation. The confinement of the quake to the field of the sorcerer's duel made their claim plausible, no matter how hard it was to believe that any sorcerer had such awesome power.

The kings were informed. Word came back that the armistice was still in force and that troops from both armies should search the staging area to find the bodies of the sorcerers. It was assumed that both were dead. To everyone's surprise, both were found alive; their mangled bodies crushed under debris. Five days later, just hours apart, first Ariadne, then William, died.

It had been assumed that the sorcerer's duel would end the war. If William won, Menkara would become a vassal state of the invading powers. If Ariadne won, Menkara would remain an independent nation with Soren as king. But neither had won.

There was no provision in the signed agreement of what happened in that case. That difficulty was soon resolved. With William out of the picture, the kings of the three invading nations had no appetite for continuing a war that had proved much more costly in terms of casualties, destruction of property and financing than William had led them to expect. The kings' dreams of empire had died with the sorcerer who had incited them to war. Two days after William's death, the three kings proposed ending the war. The invading armies would withdraw. No reparations would be paid to Menkara.

Soren and the rebel lords allied with him were tempted to reject the offer. With William dead, they could certainly repel the invasion and might even be able to launch a successful counterattack on their belligerent neighbors. But losses of men and destruction of resources and food supplies on the Menkaran side had been very severe. King Soren and the Menkaran lords knew that rejecting the invader's offer to end the war would be extremely unpopular with the Menkaran peoples and might lead to mass desertions and insurrections. Popular support for the war had been support to defeat the invasion. But now that the enemy had offered to end the war and withdraw, there would be little or no popular support for continuing the war. Thus the end-the-war proposal of the three kings who had invaded Menkara was accepted both by King Soren and the Menkaran lords.

The invasion had driven King Soren and his rebellious nobility from the precipice of incipient civil war into an uneasy alliance to repel the invaders. But with the invaders withdrawing would civil war re-erupt? Visions of the future for Menkara were still divergent enough and animosities still raw enough that resumption of civil war remained a real possibility. However, both Soren and the rebel lords realized that even if personally they could stomach the fraternal violence of renewed civil war, the peasants, artisans and merchants of Menkara could not. That gave the peacemakers led by Prime Minister Mentaxes and the high priestess Grassic of the Vesparians, the opening they needed to successfully broker an agreement between king and nobility that while preserving

Menkara as a unified kingdom with Soren as king, also gave the provinces and their regional lords a large measure of autonomy in local affairs and created a parliament through which the regional lords had a voice in national affairs. That compromise which many, myself included, feared would not survive even one year, still structures Menkara seventy years later.

Bezriel remained part of Menkara. It was split off from the province of Zandor and recognized as an independent province to be governed by its council of elders rather than by a regional lord. The council of elders was restructured to give a voices to all groups and factions within Bezriel; traditionalists who wanted to maintain age old customs, rebel leaders such as Kaitlin and Joshua who had led the Free Bezriel insurrection and wanted to modernize Bezriel, and moderates such as Daniel, Ariadne's father, who favored tradition on some issues and modernization on others. Freedom of conscience on all religious issues was the very first decree of the new council of elders. Having been persecuted for their beliefs under Baron Frederick, many traditionalists abandoned the radical preservationists in their party who wanted to make Bezriel the state religion.

After his broken body was found in the debris from the earthquake, William was brought to the invader's battlefield hospital. The doctors who were with William in the five days before his death reported that after he regained consciousness on the second day, he alternated between feverish incoherence and semi-rational speech. After an unconscious William was brought in, King Radames had ordered that if and when the sorcerer awoke and showed signs of coherence, he should immediately be notified. Radames met with William two days before the sorcerer died. I find the king's account of that meeting unconvincing.

After the death of William, King Radames put full blame for the invasion of Menkara on William, claiming that the sorcerer had misled the three kings into believing that as soon as the invading armies crossed into Menkara, announcing their aim of dethroning the tyrant Soren, the Menkaran people would rise up to aid the invaders. The king claimed that on his death bed, William confessed he had deliberately misled the three kings because he wanted revenge on Soren. William, he claimed, begged for forgiveness. Serious doubt about the veracity of King Radames account of the death bed repentance of William has always been prevalent.

A more believable account of William's last hours exists in the secret journals of Diamant, Chancellor of Galatia. His journals were published fifteen years after the death of William and two years after the death of King Radames. Kept hidden by Diamant because of its unflattering portrait of Radames, the journals were published after the throne had passed to Tiberius, an ambitious nephew of Radames who wanted to discredit his predecessor.

Diamant had been the closest ally of William in the three kingdoms. His journal depicts the venality and greed of King Radames and his allies in the other two kingdoms. According to Diamant, King Radames was not deceived by William. Radames when ordering the invasion had been solely motivated by greed and lust for the wealth and power that he expected William to win for him.

Diamant claimed that William was unrepentant. He did not accept that he was dying. He insisted that since Ariadne had used the forbidden earthquake spell, he was the rightful winner of the duel. In his feverish mind, he was now the rightful sovereign of Menkara. His last words before falling into a coma and dying hours later was that Ariadne and Soren were traitors and ordered their execution.

Can either Radames or Diamant be believed? I doubt it. But as to William repenting, Diamant's account of William's delirium-infused lust for vengeance against Soren and Ariadne is much more believable than Radames portrait of a repentant William begging forgiveness.

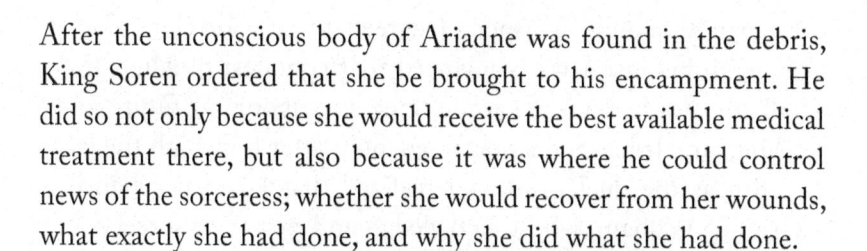

After the unconscious body of Ariadne was found in the debris, King Soren ordered that she be brought to his encampment. He did so not only because she would receive the best available medical treatment there, but also because it was where he could control news of the sorceress; whether she would recover from her wounds, what exactly she had done, and why she did what she had done.

Ariadne was feverish and in intense pain the entire time between the earthquake and her death, five days later. Fearing what Ariadne might say, King Soren ordered that only medical personnel, both modern and traditional be allowed to see Ariadne. He demanded that she tell him why she had done what she did. At the insistence of the rebel lords who did not trust Soren, the Vesparian high priestess Grassic, and Lord Lucien of Caxtonia accompanied the king to hear what Ariadne had to say.

Ariadne knew that she was dying and desperately wanted to explain why she had triggered the earthquake. But even more she wanted to spend her last days with those she loved. She told Soren she would explain her actions to him only if afterwards she would be left alone to spend her final hours with those she most loved: her family, Abigail, and Marcus.

Four prominent figures in the history I have recounted later wrote accounts of their time with Ariadne as she lay dying: Soren, Grassic, Marcus, and Ariadne's mother, Sarah. In reading the various accounts we must bear in mind their author's relationship to Ariadne and the author's goals in writing his or her memoirs.

I quote first from the tribute chapter to the national heroine Ariadne in King Soren's official "autobiography". For Soren, Ariadne was his greatest military weapon, but a weapon with a mind of its own, and values very different than his, hence a constant challenge and pain in the neck. Soren's goal was to complete the unification of Menkara by promoting in its people love of Menkara as their homeland.

Wracked by fever, chills and coughing, Ariadne spoke to me in a barely audible whisper. "I agreed to the sorcerer's duel to the death because I was convinced that conquest of Menkara by William and the invading armies meant an agonizing future for all of Menkara. It had to be prevented, no matter how high the cost.

"But as the duel wore on I realized that I had no chance of defeating William, whose knowledge and power of sorcery were far greater than mine. The sorcerer's duel to which I had challenged William to decide the outcome of the war was leading inevitably to disaster. But then in the depths of despair, I saw the answer. William had defeated my earthquake spell by redirecting the tremors. I would try to create an earthquake so powerful that the tremors would envelope and kill William before he could redirect them, I knew that a quake so powerful would also kill me, but that mattered little, since I felt sure that with William dead the invading kings would call off the war. I did not want to die that day, but we all have to die eventually and saving Menkara my homeland was the best death I could imagine.

Not only do the memoirs of Ariadne of Grassic, Marcus, and Sarah about her last days contradict Soren's official version, but they also contradict each other. Grassic never spent enough time with Ariadne to become close friends, but deeply respected her values and courage. She saw Ariadne as a great ally in rallying the people towards a more ethical and religious approach to life. When Ariadne died young, Grassic mourned the loss of a great soul with so much to offer the world. Her account of Ariadne in her memoirs, including the account of Ariadne's death was meant to offer a portrait of a virtuous and heroic soul for inspiration of the young. The quote that follows is from the long suppressed, but eventually released memoirs of the high priestess Grassic.

Ariadne died young, too young, but she accomplished much in her short life. She was a passionate warrior for justice. Her greatest passion was to free her people Bezriel, free it from a long history of oppression. By the ultimate self-sacrifice she succeeded. Today she is honored far beyond Bezriel because her self-sacrifice which freed Bezriel also ended a senseless and bloody war which was leading four great kingdoms down the road to ruin.

But if many honor her, many despise her. They say she won her sorcerer's duel by casting a forbidden spell to slay her opponent. They say her death was not self-sacrifice, but a miscalculation. They say the earthquake she caused, meaning to kill William, was too strong and also killed her.

Ariadne's defenders, I among them, reply that the Seekers, who centuries earlier had initiated the ban on the earthquake spell gave her permission to use it in order to end the menace that the renegade sorcerer William posed not only to Bezriel but to the entire region. Ariadne had agreed to the sorcerers duel because of fear of what would happen if William and the invading armies won the war, and out of a desperate hope that she could prevent that tragedy. I believe that Ariadne cast the devastating earthquake spell that killed both William and herself because she was convinced that it was her only hope of preventing the conquest of Menkara by William and the invading armies which would mean an agonizing future for all of Menkara, but especially for Bezriel as William took his revenge on those who had opposed him and because the victorious kings would transform Bezriel into an unholy breeding ground for military sorcerers. Making the ultimate self-sacrifice, Ariadne chose to die to prevent a reign of terror by William.

There are two moving accounts of Ariadne's final days, the time she spent with her family and dearest friends after Soren, Grassic and Lucien left. One account is by her comrade Marcus, the other from her mother, Sarah. Soren promoted idolization of Ariadne as the warrior/savior of Menkara and prevented contradictory accounts from being published. But after his death, the political climate in Menkara changed enough for differing remembrances of Ariadne to be legally published. Among the first published were tributes by Marcus.

Marcus met Ariadne in the Free Bezriel guerrilla movement. He grew to love her and had hoped to eventually marry her. Ariadne, by triggering the quake, saved Bezriel, and fulfilled Marcus's dreams for his people. But it shattered his hopes for his own future. After Ariadne's death his memory of her became less realistic and more idealistic. His portrait of Ariadne, especially of her duel with William, was the portrait of a self-immolating savior of her people who at the end tragically came to believe that there was no place in Bezriel for military sorcerers such as William and herself. This is what Marcus wrote.

Ariadne offered to fight a sorcerer's duel with William in order to end the war that had caused so much death and suffering and in order to create the best opportunity to win freedom for Bezriel. After the duel, on her deathbed, she told us that while fighting a duel to the death was abhorrent to her, totally contradicting her values as a Bezrielite, it was much better that only two forsake their humanity for the barbarism of a kill-or-be-killed confrontation in a duel, than that entire populations do so in a war. She added that since she and William were responsible for so much of the war's devastation, it was only fitting that they fight the duel, that either he or she be the last casualty.

Many believe that she triggered the earthquake that killed both William and herself because she would rather die than let William win and corrupt Bezriel for generations. Based on my conversations with Ariadne on her deathbed, I know that the truth is more complex. Tragically Ariadne had come to believe that she too must die. Just as she created a quake that did not destroy the eight observers in the observation area, she could have created a safe zone for herself. She did not do so, because she believed that both sorcerer's had to die, that military sorcery was an abomination that must be ended. She hoped that her immolation of William and herself would be the first step to that desired end. She died a true hero, destroying her own life in order to create a better world for her people.

The last memoir of those who were with Ariadne during her last days is that of her mother. Sarah wrote it thirty-one years after the death of her daughter, when she knew that she herself would die soon. There are two reasons to doubt the truth of what Sarah wrote. First is the doubt that any mother can be objective about the premature death of her child. Second is the reasonable doubt of the accuracy of an old woman's memory of events more than thirty years in the past. Yet, to me at least, her words have the ring of truth. I believe that she had a deep understanding of the complex soul of her daughter.

At times I reproached myself for telling Ariadne of the prophecy that she would be the instrument of either Bezriel's freedom or Bezriel's destruction. Knowledge of the prophecy destroyed her youth, made her reject what would have been a happy marriage with Marcus, and ultimately led to her suicidal sorcerer's duel with William. But on her death bed, she thanked me for allowing her to live with knowledge of who she really was. She confessed to me that that knowledge had frequently led to bad decisions borne out of her feelings of inadequacy to honorably bear the burden placed on her young shoulders. But, she also said, that knowledge of her foretold destiny made her ponder in her mind and in her soul, the deep issues of what it meant to truly be a Bezrielite and to walk the path of Bezriel. She said it prepared her to confront with courage her sorcerer's duel with William.

In her short life, she was exposed to many ideas of what it meant to be Bezrielite. First was the spiritual tradition she was raised in, the tradition which teaches that to walk the path of Bezriel is to seek harmony with all people, with all life, with all of creation. Next was the secular belief she learned from the prevailing tenor of modern times conveyed to her by friends her own age, the belief that you can best help your people by becoming a success in the world. The belief that if enough Bezrielites became successful doctors, lawyers, artisans and politicians, that Bezriel would become a term of praise rather than opprobrium. Third was the proud belief she learned from Free Bezriel that Bezriel must be free to determine its own fate, that the way out of the political and economic exploitation of Bezriel was for true Bezrielites to take up arms to fight for the freedom and independence of Bezriel. Finally, she learned from William just how great the powers of sorcery that had been given to Bezriel were. William enabled her to see that sorcery could be used to achieve power in the world. His career taught her the dreadful effects on both the sorcerer and on Bezriel of using sorcery to gain power over people and events.

Ariadne abhorred violence, both for the injury it did to others and for its corruption of the souls of those who were violent. But so deep was her abhorrence of the persecution and exploitation of Bezriel under Baron Friedrich, that she volunteered to use her sorcery in the armed rebellion of Free Bezriel. The comradeship she experienced with Free Bezriel transformed her from a child into a mature adult. But when uncontrolled anger over the slaughter of her comrades including her spiritual mentor Gwydian led her to bewitch the mind of enemy soldiers to kill each other, she came to distrust her instincts and to despise herself. She eventually decided to stay with Free Bezriel, but to only use her military sorcery to defend her comrades, and never again to initiate an attack. But twice, once when fighting for Free Bezriel against Soren, and once when fighting with Soren against the three kingdom invasion, she agreed to fight a sorcerer's duel with William. In each case the duel was to end the fighting and by winning or losing decide the fate of Bezriel.

If Ariadne was a pacifist, why did she twice agree to fight a sorcerer's duel to the death? The only way she could win would be to violate her deepest beliefs and knowingly kill William. The explanation she gave was that it was better that she be damned and only one die rather an immoral war in which many were maimed and slaughtered and had their souls brutalized continue. That I believe, the most basic reason why she agreed to the duels with William.

But it does not explain why she triggered the earthquake that killed both William and herself. On her deathbed she confessed to me that she knew that for the sake not only of Bezriel, but all of Menkara, William had to be stopped. Unfortunately the only way to stop William was to kill him. It was then, that her pacifist nature reasserted itself, telling her that if freedom for Bezriel was won by one Bezrielite deliberately killing another Bezrielite, that freedom would be polluted and the spiritual soul of Bezriel would begin to wither and die. The only way out she could see was for both William and herself to die, hence her decision to trigger such a massive earthquake.

Was the earthquake a good decision by Ariadne or an evil decision? I, Bartholomew, do not know. What I do know is that it avoided disaster, not only for Bezriel, but for all four kingdoms fighting the war. A dark age would have resulted if William had won the duel thereby enormously increasing his power in the four kingdoms. Worst of all would have been his power over his own people Bezriel, his own heritage that he had come to hate.

Ariadne had come to believe that if the duel ended with the death of both sorcerers the war would soon end. But she also knew that the peaceable kingdom of everyone walking the path of Bezriel would not be established. I believe she had come to accept that such a kingdom can never be established on earth. The best we can do is establish societies in which space for life of the spirit exists. I believe that Ariadne's self-sacrifice accomplished that for Bezriel.

CPSIA information can be obtained
at www.ICGtesting.com
Printed in the USA
BVOW03s0342310317
479947BV00001B/1/P

The Big Farm
in Old Sodus

© 2012 Michael Leonard Jewell

All rights reserved. No part of this publication may be reproduced, stored in a retrieval system, or transmitted in any form or by any means, electronic, mechanical, photocopying, recording, or otherwise, without the prior written permission of the publisher. The only exception is brief quotations in printed reviews.

ISBN: 978-0-9829756-2-6

Published by:
First School Press
P.O. Box 115
Sodus, Michigan 49126

Edited by Rachel Starr Thomson
Cover Design by Jay Cookingham

Printed in the United States of America